TIP TOP

Recent Titles by David Craig writing as Bill James from Severn House

DOUBLE JEOPARDY
FORGET IT
KING'S FRIENDS
THE LAST ENEMY
HEAR ME TALKING TO YOU

TIP TOP

David Craig

severn
House

This first world edition published in Great Britain 2005 by
SEVERN HOUSE PUBLISHERS LTD of
9–15 High Street, Sutton, Surrey SM1 1DF.
This first world edition published in the USA 2006 by
SEVERN HOUSE PUBLISHERS INC of
595 Madison Avenue, New York, N.Y. 10022.

British Library Cataloguing in Publication Data

Craig, David, 1929-
    Tip top
    1.   Women detectives - Fiction
    2.   Informers - Fiction
    3.   Police corruption - Fiction
    4.   Detective and mystery stories
    I.   Title   II. James, Bill, 1929-
    823.9'14 [F]

    ISBN-10 : 0-7278-6320-7

Typeset by Palimpsest Book Production Ltd.,
Polmont, Stirlingshire, Scotland.
Printed and bound in Great Britain by
MPG Books Ltd., Bodmin, Cornwall.

One

E sther said: 'Locks?'
'The doors and cabinets, all lockable,' he answered.
'Yes, I expect so,' Esther said.
'I'll let you have keys at once.'
'No, it can't be like that, not at all like that, can it, Mr
Yates?'

He had given Esther and Sally a tour of the headquarters
building, and now they'd reached the office suite set aside
for them. He was polite enough, even affable now and then,
and daddy to a fetching smile. But Sally Bithron saw he
detested them, chiefly detested Esther, as main woman, but
detested herself a bit, too, and detested what brought them
here. She could understand. Of course. Hadn't Sally felt the
same about purity teams herself when she and her colleagues
were on the other end?

To her the two rooms looked fine: big enough, three
almost state-of-the-art computers, two new filing cabinets,
four phones, fax, a drinking-water machine, à l'américaine.
Esther offered *him* a smile now, a lingering, kindly smile,
as to a slow child or crippled pet, and returned to the tricky
topic. 'No, it can't *really* be like that, can it, Mr Yates? I
need all locks changed, and changed while I or Detective
Constable Bithron is present. It should be handled by an
outside civilian firm dealing direct with me, and supplying
keys only to me and my party, each key to be signed for,
and a list of holders kept by me. The holders will be only
me and mine.'

Maybe Yates thought, *Me, me, me, and more me*, but he
didn't say it. 'I expect that can be arranged, ma'am.'

'You bet it can,' Esther replied. 'And then a full anti-bug

1

sweep of the room daily, again by outside specialists, vetted by us and reporting only to me or DC Bithron.'

Yates said: 'Oh, do you really think that's—?'

'Enough? You're right. Perhaps twice daily if I get uneasy,' Esther said. She crossed the room and pulled the water dispenser away from the wall for a look at its back. She spread one hand to prop herself against the wall, took off a shoe and heartily rapped the machine with the heel a few times. 'Am I hurting listen-in, can-covered eardrums some-where? Ever see that Gene Hackman film about hidden mikes, *The Conversation*, Mr Yates?' She replaced her shoe but not the water dispenser. 'At least two phones are outside lines, no switchboard?' She picked up a receiver to check. 'Good, good. That's basic, isn't it, Inspector?'

'I'm really happy to say I'll be your permanent liaison,' Yates replied in a tremendously warm voice. 'The only aim being to make everything conducive. Yes, conducive. Whatever at all you want, please let me know. For instance, clerical help.'

Esther giggled a while. 'Oh, sure. I'm going to put all our papers out for public view, aren't I? We bring our own desk folk. Arriving in a couple of days.'

She and Sally had been handed that most unlovely, unloved and unlovable of all police jobs – investigation of another force for . . . for allegedly unkempt behaviour. Or call it corruption? No matter how you ran this kind of audit, a hate harvest came by the wagonload – wagonloads. From the start, they'd be spied on by those they were due to spy on – snooping as art form, snooping squared, an infinity of snooping. Non-cooperation by the people under scrutiny, and by all colleagues of the people under scrutiny, would thrive and flower into polished, magnificently systematized, unflinchingly thorough hindrance.

Yet, although Sally knew the time ahead could only be rough, possibly *too* rough, and frustrating, she welcomed the role, and somehow sensed Esther Davidson might, too. Didn't it take them away for a while from home? They were different homes, of course, and different home lives, but Sally thought their reasons for delight in the flit, even to a duty like this, had a basic sameness. This job a long way off might be a sort of escape. Which sort? Call it emotional. Call it marital in Esther's case. Call it partnerly in Sally's. The escape could be only short-term, but was acceptable to Sally Bithron, just the same. She had the idea Esther might also feel this, though obviously it could not be spoken about. Not yet, at any rate.

'Shall I get you a list of reliable local locksmiths and counter-surveillance people?' the inspector asked.

'Reliable how?' Esther asked.

'Well, people we've used ourselves and can vouch for.'

'Thanks, no. I'll pick from *Yellow Pages*.'

Yates must have been on a Patience and Diplomacy course: 'I know the chief is keen to cooperate to the utmost, and has instructed the whole force to give every help during your visit, ma'am. This is possibly not typical. Sometimes, I gather, investigating officers descending on a force from outside run into crude, all-out hostility. Incredible, perhaps, yet certainly so. But the chief has said that, if you meet any obstruction, or *feel* you have met an obstruction, he wishes to be notified immediately in his individual capacity, via myself, with a view, obviously, to clearing such obstruction, or imagined obstruction, at once.'

'That's great,' Esther said. 'Isn't it, Sally?'

'Great,' Sally replied.

'In his individual capacity?' Esther said.

'Exactly,' Yates said.

'Via you?' Esther asked.

'Right.'

'In *your* individual capacity?'

'Yes.'

'In the chief's individual capacity via Inspector Yates in *his* individual capacity, Sally,' Esther said.

'Great,' Sally replied. They were cops scrutinizing cops they did not know and were absolutely required not to know. Standard practice. When major Home Office figures detected a stink in one police domain – and especially the stink of death – they told officers from a different outfit to get along there, move in for as long as it took, and uncover the rot. Remember Manchester's John Stalker, sent to discover whether security patrols had a 'shoot to kill' policy in Northern Ireland? That kind of highly awkward thing. Remember Sir John Stevens, then head of the London Metropolitan Police, sent to prove murderous collusion between the security services in Northern Ireland and Protestant hit men – his office arsonized to destroy records and offer general discouragement? That kind of highly awkward thing. The force Esther and Sally had been told to look at lay two hundred miles north of their own, a comfy interspace. Assistant Chief Constable Esther Davidson led. Detective Constable Sally Bithron travelled as aide.

The geographical distance mattered. It helped produce cultural distance. Their duty was to bring gifts from afar, like the three kings. These gifts were: wholly independent eyes, tough brains and blazing righteousness. The incursors must be uncorrupted by local knowledge, local influence, local loyalties – the last above all. They had no loyalties – not here. They wanted to break through and dismember local loyalties. The job could not be done otherwise. They claimed they wanted truth. This disregard for force loyalties – this suspicion and contempt for homeground loyalties – such attitudes explained why they were loathed, why all police prying into police were loathed. Didn't they want to smash the established police Brotherhood, and Sisterhood, here?

And the Brotherhood and Sisterhood could reasonably be seen as precious. It might be argued they kept the country from chaos. It *was* argued they kept the country from chaos, especially argued by those who were in the particular Brotherhood and Sisterhood under hard and possibly dangerous examination. *What do these two fucking women want, barging in here with their special powers, their rampant nosiness and insolence?* Sally could read the reactions as well as she could read a poster. Not a happy workplace. Unconducive.

Still, at this time – and maybe *only* at this time – she felt content to be somewhere off her own patch, and temporarily not upset by her life's tangled intimacies there. And she thought the same went for the ACC. But, yes, guesswork. There had been only one fragment of conversation with Esther

4

Davidson, so far, that Sally would regard as even marginally personal. She could not decide whether it gave comfort. Esther had spoken the words in the car park just after they arrived, and before chaperon Yates took them in charge. It seemed reasonable to suppose a car park unbugged. 'Sally, the Home Office will be pleased to have you and me handling this. They'll reckon that, no matter how scared of us the people here are, and no matter what we unearth, and how high we trace the taint and rot, it's unlikely that, to protect their future, any British police officers would kill other British police officers when those other police officers are ladies.'

Kill? Christ, a joke? The genteel word 'ladies' for 'women' suggested playfulness, didn't it? Didn't it? Esther's face had shown no humour, but perhaps the knack of gorgeous deadpan came with big rank, like budget skills, hate for council police authorities, and flair at dodging blame. Did it stand up, Esther's analysis? First, would that in fact be Home Office thinking? And second, and much more vital, if this did amount to Home Office thinking, might Home Office thinking have it right? The doubt stopped Sally drawing total reassurance, or even ten per cent reassurance, from what Esther said then in the car park about managing to keep in one piece because they were 'ladies'. By now, Sally could sense a lot of gifted, well-researched detestation around them here – and not just from Inspector Yates. Also, some very intelligently based panic. These factors made a harsh and dangerous mix.

Still better than being home? Oh, yes, Sally had relationship troubles back there. To walk away for a spell might turn out medicinal. And Esther? It could only be speculation about her. She did not discuss such private things, not with Sally. Naturally. Esther had a big and possibly growing status to look after – assistant chief now, chief constable next year? Women could reach that, and reached it more and more often in the new climate. Some rumour hung to Esther, though, helping Sally's guesswork and intuitions. After all, rumour didn't care about status. Or rumour actually *did* care about status, *adored* status, worked even harder on and around those who had it because . . . because, weren't they more worth maligning and dragging down and fucking up than nobodies?

5

Ask the tabloids. Not loudly, but often, gossip reported a drift away from her husband by Esther.

Yates left them to settle in. Esther said: 'We are truly blessed in that man, Sally. I feel integrity there, and wholesome respect for our mission. You'll ask me why – how. Oh, don't protest. I know you will. And I cannot answer. But – and this surely is the point – *but* I *feel* it. That must be enough. If one had *cojones*, it is in the *cojones* that this impression would be centred. Again, I sense an objection from you, but invalid, invalid, invalid! I have learned to trust my instincts beyond even the dictates of reason and evidence. I can envisage Yates's fine and stable family life – marvellously supportive wife, honourable children, tropical fish – water regularly changed – rubbish sorted weekly for recycling.'

Sally tried to cope with this barmy speech. Who was it meant for? Really for her? *What* was it meant for? Esther had already shown she thought the suite might be wired and, if so, had informed those at the end of the wire she knew about them. As a result, they would expect no secrets. They'd realize that what Esther said in this florid, breathless language had nothing to do with her real thoughts. Welcome to an Esther-type game, though Sally could not understand what kind. She wanted to take part and would probably be expected by Esther to take part. But for now Sally didn't see how. God, did she seem stupid? Would Esther regret bringing her as sidekick? Sally knew she must have a go.

The ACC said: 'You, Sally, in your chancer's style, will probably wish to wager on which of us gets to fuck Yates first.' She held up a hand. Perhaps Esther wondered about a camera bug, as well. 'No, no, I've told you I will not listen to protests. One can't tolerate false primness. Myself, I don't by any means view the issue as cut and dried. All right, *you* have the under-thirty bit, and a certain basic allure and arse-pertness when seen from the right angles, I suppose. And I'm ready to believe you're clean. Yet, *I* have the rank. You'd be surprised how many men are turned on by clout and yearn to woo it.'

'I imagine you've run into that pretty often and have

learned how to, well, *accommodate* it, ma'am,' Sally replied.

'I felt him lighting up to me. Rapport. Even empathy. Did you spot that, I wonder. The empathy. Would you recognize it – empathy?'

'As a matter of fact, I felt him lighting up to *me*,' Sally replied, 'and "rapport" – the very term *I'd* use, as a matter of fact – progressing to empathy.' She thought she saw Esther's purpose now. If they had secret listeners, this mocked them, would amaze them, catastrophically disorientate them, destroy all expectations of how an investigating ACC might behave and talk – a *woman* investigating ACC. Or lady, even. And she meant the eavesdroppers to relay this confusion on and up to those who'd instructed them to eavesdrop, probably as far as to the sweetly cooperative chief himself. The management would not be able to make sense of Esther. Sally couldn't, so how could they, for God's sake?

Two

*M*s *Angela Leach QC*: 'My Lord, my learned friend has no objection if I occasionally lead this witness. Mr Staple, you were at what was then known as the Knoll Public Amenity Site early on the morning of the twenty-fourth of June, were you not?'

Mr Stanley Basil Staple: 'Yes.'

Q: 'The amenity site was, I believe, a municipal refuse tip then. It is now being turfed and turned into a park.'

A: 'Yes.'

Q: 'Would you tell us how early you were on the tip?'

A: 'Just after five a.m.'

Q: 'Why were you there at that time?'

A: 'I needed to be away before work started for them others for the day – like dumping and that.'

Q: 'Why did you have to be, as you term it, away?'

A: 'I wanted to recover some items. If I could.'

Q: 'Particular items?'

A: 'You never know what you'll find on a tip. A tip's a bit random, like meals from a pissed cook – oh, excuse me, I mean a drunk cook.'

Q: 'You were hoping to recover any dumped items that might be useful or valuable?'

A: 'People throw away all sorts, you see, in that regard – stuff they're tired of, or surplus because they've bought new, such as garments and considerably pitted dartboards, especially around the double twenty, which all players have to hit before they can score.'

Q: 'You sift discarded material to find things of value you can sell. It is how you make your living?'

Judge: 'It's called "totting", Ms Leach.'

Leach: 'Thank you, My Lord.'

Judge: 'Totting. With two *t*s.'

Leach: 'Thank you, My Lord.'

Staple: 'Totting, yes. Or some say salvaging.'

Q: 'And you went to the site early because once tipping began for the day your activities would be stopped. Is that so?'

A: 'They don't like it.'

Q: 'Don't like? Strictly, it's illegal, Mr Staple, isn't it? Theft. But nobody wants to make anything of that now, I assure you. After all, isn't there a long British tradition of such careers?'

A: 'The totting career? Well, I don't know about—'

Q: 'We instantly think, don't we, of the man in Charles Dickens' novel *Our Mutual Friend*, who made his fortune from material recovered in dirt mounds?'

A: 'Well, yes, now you mention it, of course, I expect we do think of him. Oh, yes, *instantly*. All the time.'

Judge: 'Does this come into things, Ms Leach?'

Leach: 'My Lord?'

Judge: 'Charles Dickens.'

Leach: 'Merely an illustration, My Lord – to put the practice of totting into an, as it were, historical context.'

Judge: 'Ah.'

Q: 'Let me come to the point, then, Mr Staple.'

Judge: 'Ah.'

Q: 'I would like you to tell My Lord and the jury what you found at the amenity site on the morning of June twenty-fourth. I mean, in addition to the kind of discarded items you might also have found.'

A: 'A body. The body of a man.'

Q: 'This must have been a shock.'

A: 'Well, yes, a shock. I never seen anything like that before on Knoll. I mean, to my knowledge, nor spoke about by colleagues.'

Q: 'Quite. Could you describe for us the condition of the body?'

A: 'Well, condition – that's just the word.'

9

Q: 'What exactly did you see?'

A: 'I said to myself right away, like after the first shock, I said, this was a body that must of had bad treatment prior.'

Q: 'Prior to death?'

A: 'Yes, prior.'

Q: 'What kind of bad treatment?'

A: 'Wounds.'

Q: 'What kind of wounds?'

A: 'Yes, wounds. Cuts. A knife. Or more than one.'

Q: 'Knife wounds on the body? Which part of the body?'

A: 'All. Nearly all.'

Q: 'How could you tell this?'

A: 'I told you. This was wounds, big wounds, deep wounds. I could see, couldn't I? By that time, in June, it's light.'

Q: 'Quite so. That's not what I meant. How could you—?'

A: 'Cuts to the neck and face, and then his clothes soaked with blood from other wounds.'

Sally reread – or re-re-reread – this slice of court transcript. Naturally, for their investigation here she had studied pretty well everything about the pitiless death of Justin Maidment Tully – transcripts, newspaper reports and pictures, unused witness statements. It was routine groundwork for Esther and her to do before arrival, and, as assistant, Sally had brought all the documents. Eventually she might file them in one of those lockable cabinets. For now, though, she wanted what she regarded as the vital ones close, and carried them in a duffle bag. The rest remained at the hotel.

In a sense, of course, the Tully case was closed. There had been arrests, a trial, and two men went down for the torture and murder. But then the questions started. Above all, the press and a clutch of politicians asked and went on asking how Justin Maidment Tully, a long-time and valuable police informant, had found himself suddenly exposed to the hellish dangers preceding his death. On their own ground in

South Wales, Sally had dealt with grass killings before, which might be one reason Esther had chosen her as clerk, adjutant and junior mate now. There would be a lot of very tough and – with luck – very factual nosing to be done here.

Sally left her car and walked up a gravelled path to where Tully's body had lain, or as near to it as she could guess. Knoll had reached capacity as a tip not long after Tully's murder and was then greened and landscaped to emerge as a country park, splendidly environmental. Perhaps this awful death had made the council accelerate plans for the trans-formation – a kind of exorcism. Now, a warden in a rural-style hut supervised the park. On the Tully spot, a children's adventure playground had been made, with wooden benches for their supervising parents. Sally took a seat and looked back down the slope, the duffle bag on her lap. Transcripts said a wooden fence used to encircle the tip's base, with a wide, double gateway to allow entrance for loaded lorries. The gates were closed once work finished, but easily climb-able by Stanley Basil Staple in the early morning, even when carrying recovered items such as garments and considerably pitted dartboards, especially around the double twenty. It would also have been climbable by the men who brought Tully up here at night, and climbable by Tully himself when forced, probably prompted by the first knife jabs.

Sally stood and descended the path a little way, then turned and came back, trying to think herself into Tully's mind as they manhandled him, stumbling over the rubbish, pleading with the two of them occasionally and sobbing non-stop – so said Barry Jolliffe, one of the convicted pair, in his trial evidence. Despite her wish to re-enact the sequence, she did not imitate these sad noises now. Children played on the swings and rope bridge and she mustn't scare them, or their watching parents.

Did she have any real chance of thinking herself into Tully's mind? What would it be doing, the mind of a disastrously rumbled police pigeon? Would he feel he deserved whatever came, because he'd committed the unforgivable sin, God knew how many times, and finked? Or would he consider himself entitled only to praise and salvation as a noble freelance agent of law and order, who helped guard the public from crime, though possibly not from his own, the totting – obviously a different matter. Could even a gifted professional actor get a hold on such complexity? Sally wavered.

Tully had fallen a couple of times but they made him get up and go higher on the tip. Regardless of what Jolliffe said in court, she couldn't understand why they kept climbing. It was dark then and the tip as deserted at one spot as another. She sat down again, took the trial transcript from her bag and did a fast forward. Jolliffe had been turned somehow and became a prosecution witness. Well, no 'somehow' about it. A deal. Esther and Sally must dig into the details of that. The prosecution lawyer could lead this witness also, although he was implicated.

Ms Angela Leach QC: 'By means of stabbings, other physical violence and threats, you made Tully get over the wire mesh gates and then the three of you began to ascend the tip, is that correct?'

Barry Jolliffe: 'Yes.'

Q: 'In what condition was Tully then?'

A: 'Weak and panicky.'

Q: 'This was understandable, wasn't it? He'd already been beaten in the van, hadn't he? And he had lost a lot of blood.'

A: 'Some blood, yes.'

Q: 'What do you mean when you say he was "panicky"?'

A: 'Gasping and sobbing and weeping, but trying to talk to us all the time as well. Plus staggering.'

Q: ' "Trying to talk". What was he saying?'

A: 'Hard to understand.'

Q: 'Because of the sobbing and weeping?'

A: 'The sobbing and weeping. And blood in his mouth.'

Q: 'The blood in his mouth would be because of the beating in the van, would it?'

A: 'Gordon hit him in the face as well as lower.'

Q: 'But despite the troubles with his mouth, were you able to distinguish some of what he said?'

A: 'He wanted us to let him go. Of course. He said he had money and promised to see us all right. He had piled up grassing money. That was one word he kept on with, "promise, promise, promise", like a kid saying he'd never be naughty again. He told us this grassing money was a real lump. Yes, a real lump. So, he coughed to grassing because he knew he had to because we knew. It was not just because Gordon beat it out of him in the van – sort of interrogation. And Justin said he had never grassed anything about Gordon or me – not us, person-ally – and he never would. He said we were still like mates, the three of us, regardless. Another word he kept on with – "mates". If we let him go, he would not tell his handler in the CID about anything on the tip or in the parked van, he would forget it. Plus he would give each of us a grand, at least a grand – that's a thousand pounds – and he would tell the CID always to be nice to us, not just about the beating and that, but about all our work from now on. What's called blind-eyeing. Well known in police matters, blind-eyeing, also known as you-scratch-my-back-and-I'll-scratch-yours. He kept on about that, like when he said the "promise, promise, promise" and "mate". That was how I could understand it, because of the way he repeated some of it.'

Q: 'You said he staggered. Did he fall?'

A: 'Twice. On a tip – all the stuff there, big stuff, some of it, it's not easy to walk. Like old TVs and wooden ladders, rotted. And dark.'

Q: 'Especially for someone panicking, who has lost blood, would you agree?'

A: 'I swear I didn't realize it would be like this. Just to give him a scare and a slap – that's all, I thought. I thought, just a warning, to stop him as a grass. We knew about the grassing from a source, and how he got stuff to his handler and was paid.'

Q: 'When he fell, why did you make him get up and climb further? Why not stab and kill him where he was?

If his legs were bad, this was bound to take much more time, wasn't it?'

A: 'Gordon said he wanted him higher up, on a part of the tip already filled in and where they were not dumping any longer. He had been watching this tip and the lorries.'

Q: 'Did he say why he wanted that?'

A: 'He thought the body might not be found straight away and it would be a plus.'

Q: 'Because you'd have a better chance to find an alibi for yourselves and get rid of stained clothes and shoes?'

A: 'Like that, yes.'

Q: 'So, this was a well-prepared killing, wasn't it? It was thoroughly premeditated?'

A: 'Gordon always looks ahead. Famed for it. People say that when they talk about him – "Gordon looks ahead."'

Q: 'You say he had watched operations on the tip, in order to pick out the most suitable place?'

A: 'He's been in the army. There's an army saying – "time spent on reconnaissance is never wasted". Gordon told me that.'

Q: 'And when you eventually reached this suitable spot, Tully was first tortured with stab wounds not meant to kill at once – seventeen wounds – and finally executed by one devastating blow to the heart, is that right?'

A: 'I never knew it would be like this. Gordon never told me it would be like this. I could not really believe it when I watched him work on Justin with the knife like that.'

Q: 'How long did he torture Justin Maidment Tully before the blow to the heart?'

A: 'Well, it's hard to know that. I mean, exactly.'

Q: 'Try. Ten minutes? Half an hour? An hour? Longer?'

A: 'Not longer than an hour.'

Q: 'An hour?'

A: 'Perhaps an hour. It was beginning to get light.'
Q: 'And was Tully conscious for most of that time?'
A: 'For most of it.'
Q: 'Did he continue to plead with you?'
A: 'He was pleading with Gordon nearly all the time, except when he was crying out.'
Q: 'Crying out because of pain?'
A: 'Yes, pain. Of course, pain.'

Also of course, this was Jolliffe trying to put himself all right and stick everything on to Gordon Ralph Chamberlain. Or, at least, to put himself as near all right as feasible. The cross-examination when it came tried to expose the deal. Just the same, Jolliffe's performance worked and Chamberlain went down for life, with the judge's recommendation of a minimum twenty-five years. Jolliffe got four, which meant less than two if he behaved himself and kept his remorse rosy.

Sally could not tell how much of Jolliffe's evidence in chief, as brought out by the prosecution QC, was true. It aimed to show that Tully's butchery and death had not been the result of sudden, uncontrolled rage at discovering a supposed friend had grassed, but the culmination of skilled, thoughtful, vicious planning. So, the twenty-five years. Probably Jolliffe had been given some deft help ahead of the trial, with what he should say, to make sure no member of the jury experienced even a fragment of sympathy for Gordon Chamberlain. Juries did sometimes let their contempt for grasses show, by favouring the villain informed on. Sally had come across it in other cases. Juries were a marvellous institution and deserved to be saved from their own stupidity.

And there'd have been a second intent. Jolliffe must be made to look a powerless sidekick, pulled into murder by his dominant, ruthless pal. Jolliffe said it was at Chamberlain's command they went high up the tip. No, Sally did not see the point of this. One aim in brutalizing and killing an informant was that the punishment should get known, to frighten and deter others. Chamberlain, and those using Chamberlain, would want the body found, and quite possibly

15

found soon after Tully had been exposed as a grass, so the connection and the lesson shone brilliantly, unmistakably.

A very young, blonde mother sat on a swing, holding its chain with one hand while she steadied the baby on her lap with the other. They rocked back and forth gently. The child stared up at the woman, grinning. Sally looked a little beyond them and saw Tully on the then lumpy, stinking ground, clothes blood-drenched, and Chamberlain bent over him digging, playfully at this stage, with the knife, also grinning. In her concocted picture, Barry Jolliffe shifted about. Sometimes he also was bent over Tully and stabbing down. In other versions, Jolliffe stood back, not part of the attack, and horrified. No knives had ever been found, and forensics said the wounds could have been caused by one or more than one, if they were the same size and pattern. Jolliffe maintained in court he did nothing with a knife except jab Tully mildly in the calf to make him climb the gate – this at a time when, so Jolliffe claimed, he thought the only object was to continue the interrogation begun in the van by Chamberlain.

Sally left the bench, walked past the swings and briefly lay on the grass in what could be the Tully spot, as if taking a little sun. She shut her eyes and tried to persuade her mind to give a sense of how he felt. But she got nothing. She realized her fantasizing abilities, acting abilities, were not up to it. Or perhaps the mind could apply its own tact and refused to simulate those horrors, trivialize them in a stretch of shoddy, vulgar make-believe. She stood.

Of course, Sally's job – well, *Esther's* job, with Sally as dogsbody – their job was not about who did what to Justin Maidment Tully. This had already been decided by the trial. Chamberlain carried out the murder, with Jolliffe an accessory and partner in the abduction and beating. Chamberlain and Chamberlain's lawyer had said differently, but were disbelieved and the appeal upheld the convictions and sentences. Although the arguments might continue, they did not interest Esther and Sally. These two must unravel – or try to – the twisted mysteries of Tully's life as a long-serving grass. If they succeeded with that, they might discover who put the finger on him. And why. Exactly how many knew enough to betray him? His handler knew, obviously. And so would the handler's controller, plus the registrar of all the force's official informants. Esther and Sally must talk to handler and controller. At least those. Hierarchy: perhaps one of those rotten ladders Staple spoke of.

But were others also in the know? They should not have been. Leaks did leak, though, and grasses got grassed. How could Tully finish unprotected on Knoll dump after all the public interest help he'd provided? Bought public interest help, yes, but still help. Sally found such basic questions nudged hard at her while she sat reading and re-reading, so this reverie in the little playground was not totally a waste. Some of the questions had been hinted at in a round-up newspaper article published after the verdicts, under the headline, 'Doubts Persist On Police Tactics in Tully Death.' She found this clipping now. It showed head-and-shoulders photographs of Jolliffe and Tully and a full-length one of Chamberlain in army sergeant's uniform.

It would be time to move on from the country park, ex-amenity site soon, but she wanted to glance at part of the article first, starting about halfway down.

'Despite yesterday's verdicts, some aspects of this case remain unclear. During the trial it emerged that Tully had for many years been a very successful, paid police informer. It was never established how his cover was suddenly blown, leaving him fatally exposed. Police witnesses confirmed he had been an informant but could not tell the court how this became known outside the handful of detectives officially aware of his role.

'The case gave vivid insights into how the relationship between an informant and his police "handler" operates. Tully was apparently unwilling to trust the telephone and always insisted on meeting his detective at constantly switched rendezvous points – the Coronet cinema car park, one of three laundrettes, the beach at Moonmain, a second-hand car sale yard in Stayley Road. The money was, of course, passed in cash and recorded by his handler in a special account against a code name, to hide the real identity from auditors. Questions were asked in court about the amount and monitoring of these funds. It was alleged by Chamberlain's defence, though not confirmed, that hundreds of thousands of pounds were involved.

'On the night of his death, Tully was picked up at Moonmain beach before being taken to Knoll tip by Chamberlain and Jolliffe in Chamberlain's van. He was apparently alone on the beach and police witnesses said no rendezvous had been arranged with Tully on that date. It was not established why Tully should have gone there by himself on the evening of a wet, unsummery day.'

Sally went down the path and drove to Moonmain. It was more a stretch of foreshore than a beach, mainly pebbles, with mudflats at low tide. Few sunbathers and swimmers used this stretch of coast, which might be why Tully or his detective handler chose it. She walked on the stones towards Cardle headland and tried to divine what might have brought Tully here – tried also to get herself a glimpse of what he must have thought, what he must have realized, when he saw Chamberlain and Jolliffe approach. The secret contact spot suddenly no secret. Apparently, Tully did not attempt to run. After all those years of accomplished duplicity, he might believe he could bluff his way out of anything. The terrifying shock of finding, soon afterwards, that he could not perhaps explained why he disintegrated and turned to pleas and weeping and panic. Sally almost wept herself, visualizing that collapse. Had he been set up somehow? Wouldn't all those years of accomplished duplicity also have sharpened his alertness to such danger? Didn't the elaborately careful list of meeting locations suggest this? Had he felt as safe as ever strolling here? Why couldn't he sense that all the rigmarole of caution had finally turned out dud? Sally, in her theatricals, knew she couldn't simulate all Tully's thinking, but believed she sensed his Moonmain smugness, then sudden alarm and dread. It was imagination, but imagination nicely, feasibly, built on her familiarity with what would come next.

Imagination, imagination. She realized she had started to do a lot of it. Too much? In part, she blamed Esther and that far-far-out performance she had given for the supposed listeners-in after Inspector Yates left them. Sally had eventually tried to contribute to the show herself. She'd enjoyed it. She approved of Esther and her nonsense game. It was fine, and more than fine – by which Sally meant fine and more than fine for *her*. The officers here might not be so happy. *Christ, a mad assistant chief let loose on us, and with tits.* But Sally had decided she could take a kind of licence from Esther's grand whimsy and tomfooling – a permission. Couldn't she, Sally Bithron, also offer a slice of extravaganza, if that's how Esther wanted things played? And so the Tully scenarios at the tip, now a park, and at this beach.

Sometimes Sally did like to apply a bit of theatricals. That could help, even on a case like the present one – so bloody and dark and terrifying. Obviously, such make-believe might turn out risky. Imagination had great possibilities, but go easy. Imagination? Imagination! Who was she, the thinker-poet Coleridge? Theatricals? Who was she, Meryl Streep?

However, the ACC's frolicsome episode did provide . . . provide what? Perhaps a little unusual scope and promise? They were away from base. Adapt? Adapt. Things might be different here – or *made* different. She could imagine – yes, imagine, *imagine* – she could imagine they occupied a capsule, self-sealing and special, for as long as their inquiry lasted.

No question, Esther was as professional and hard and precise as anyone – and even as any ACC – about how the operation would run. About locks and bugs and personnel and admin. But, as a bonus, perhaps she'd slip again into one of those spasmodic, riotous mind-romps and skittishly dark burlesques. Sally loved all that and felt liberated.

She had to imagine these events as if occurring now. Re-run his death. That would be the trick, the illumination. Sally must *feel* the moment, moments. Esther and she came as strangers to this ground, and Sally would try to fantasize and flashback her way into core knowledge of it, and so to a degree of power over it, power through insight.

But, oh God, was this bullshit? Did she imagine – imagine – she'd become Sherlock Holmes? Could she get power through insight, near-mystic insight? Planchette-land? No, it could not be *all* imagination for her. Tully's murder was fact, the method undisputed. And the traditional pre-death torture of a grass was also fact, the method undisputed. Official papers and press clippings told things right . . . No, not true of the newspapers. To make reports bearable for readers, some descriptions had been softened.

Obviously, Esther also realized how much they were strangers and enemies here, but brought a different style of response from Sally's. Esther would make herself unscannable, undefinable, titanically obstreperous, seemingly chaotic. Her reactions and Sally's were individual, the aim identical – to crack apart this alien police realm and find what went on in the run-up to Tully's death and in its aftermath. A minor start might be to smash the sweet, deputed prying of Yates. Neutralize the nanny. Esther had spotted it straight off – probably the kind of flair that brought big rank.

She had made a work roster, with staggered spells of time off for each of them. In unfamiliar land, these leisure spells could be hard to fill, and on some free half days, or full days, for something to do, Sally went out often to the inquiry's key locations. She had already seen them with Esther as first moves, but later made these solo visits. Sally used a police pool Ford and – as she had done today – would sit in the car for a while and flip through the documents in the duffle bag in any old order and decide like that where she wanted to go. She had highlighted sections in the transcripts, clippings and extra witness statements, and cruised among them randomly until an extract grabbed her, set her off. Some of them set her off more than once. Sally did not want method or system. Imagination. Let it bounce about, like a kid in a party-time inflatable fort. Imagination had to be imaginative. Didn't she recall from sixth-form Eng. Lit. that after a hell of a lot of big thought, Coleridge deduced this and wrote it up as his philosophy? Yes, imagination had to be imaginative.

She returned to the car and looked out her favourite newspaper clipping so far. It made her feel mighty and clean:

'The Home Office has ordered an inquiry into police handling of the Justin Maidment Tully murder in 2004 and circumstances leading up to it. The inquiry has been called following public uneasiness about some matters revealed during the trial, in which Gordon Ralph Chamberlain was convicted of the killing and another man of lesser offences. The court heard that Tully had been a much prized police informer. In the intervening months, doubts about the circumstances of his death have persisted. Several M.P.s have asked questions in the Commons about the implications of Tully's relationship with certain detectives, and civil liberties organizations have also expressed concern.

'A Home Office spokeswoman said yesterday: "Some unresolved questions remained at the end of the trial and the Home Secretary will ask officers from another Force to carry out a thorough and wholly independent investigation into all contentious aspects of the case and report to her."

'The inquiry is expected to last at least six months. Its findings could have widespread effects on the use of informants by British police. Although it is generally recognized that insider tip-offs from "grasses" are indispensable in the battle against organized crime, there is recurrent anxiety about the influence a major informant may be able to exert over the officers supposedly "running" him, or her. Special treatment available to secret "sources" can involve condoning their own crimes for the sake of crucial pieces of intelligence, as well as systematic police persecution of an informant's criminal enemies as a reward component. Also, it is sometimes alleged that an informant who has lost usefulness or has offended his police contacts may be abandoned by detectives and even betrayed, for the sake of switching to a new, more approved insider "voice".'

Three

Then Tully's woman.

But this was crude, cruel: Tully's *woman* – the kind of slur some police would stick on any low-life's steady partner, just one up from 'Tully's slag'. Sally had to escape such professional smear language, for a while, part of that general escape from home-patch conditions, and from home. For a while. Permanent escape? Just not on. Just not on.

She drove over to the house Tully and his partner had shared, and parked at a good distance, but close enough to observe any movement. Of course, Sally knew it to be a useless ploy by the standards of any real police surveillance – uncontinuous, only off-and-on. In fact, at some stage and soon, she would probably have to come here with Esther and make an official call, not hang back like a burglar casing for serial busts in a rich neighbourhood. Sally even realized she would possibly mess up the proper inquiry, because Pamela Lorraine Felicity Grange might spot her despite precautions, and have more time to get her guard up. Perhaps she'd thought everything was closed once the trial finished and people jailed.

Just the same, Sally needed the contact, if it amounted to that. She wanted sight of Pamela, and something beyond the sight offered by those staring, snatched newspaper pictures. This hanging about in the car was part of Sally's inspired theatricals – inspired? Oh, yeah? – part of her special insight programme. She recognized that 'special' meant half-daft, unprofessional, woolly. But also irresistible. That is, irresistible until Esther found out about it, if she ever did, and *ordered* her to resist and stop, or sent her home. Unless, of course, Esther understood. She might. After all, what Sally wanted to do simply matched, in an amateur way, what those criminal psychologists brought in by police to help on cases did. There'd been a television series about one of them, hadn't there – *Cracker*? They attempted to define the villain's personality from what he/she had done, and so direct the chase. This was not hocus-pocus. Sometimes it worked. Sally wanted to try more or less the same, though not necessarily with villains. Possibly Esther would sympathize. Esther's mind did not seem to operate like the minds of other staff-rank police. Esther was Esther, and unknowable.

Sally longed to *know* Pamela, though, know her as she had tried to know Justin Maidment Tully in hindsight, on the tip and on the beach. She aimed to *become* her for a while, through guesswork, intuition, imagination and – maybe – pretentious, impossible magic. She'd go for the whole osmosis game – let Pam's personality seep into hers. So much about this fine-featured, tall woman could fascinate Sally. Like, how was life for the established live-in of a grass? Did she and Tully discuss his work, as people talked about their day when home from the factory or office and before TV took over the night? *So I said to him – I stayed firm, Pam, really firm – I said to him, Harvey, it's all very well for you, with a regular salary, accelerated promotion prospects, plus eventual two-thirds fuzz pension – besides which, as handler, you can siphon off for yourself from the informant fund – but as to me, personally, I'm sure you'll understand, I have to think of very hefty dabs in the palm at bloody once, to compensate for the perils and untenured nature of* my *career. At bloody once, yes.*

This looked the perfect street for someone with Tully's heavy, dubious incomes. It had modern, detached, big houses, though less than palatial. And here, now, appeared Pamela Lorraine Felicity Grange, emerging through the stout front door of number twenty-nine with her and Tully's young son, and settling into the BMW on the drive, as of right. Sally loved this. It gave the kind of insight she craved. Probably the smaller Corsa standing alongside had been bought as Pamela's car, but – to put it brutally – no his and hers applied now, there being no he. She knew how to change when things changed, did she? All right, she had been someone's woman, but was not a woman who would fold and wither just because her earning, grassing someone got taken on to a tip and left like that for Staple or a dawn totting colleague to find. This woman could build a new settled ordinariness for herself and the child. Style – she seemed full of it, BMW style, high-cheekbones style, in-my-own-right style.

The street had trees, not trees preserved from the original green-field development site, but trees thoughtfully planted afterwards, beautifully spaced, and probably inside wooden cages for their first year, to keep vandals off. Householders in such a district would be continuously on neighbourhood watch for vandals, anyway, and ready to repel them. Owners were galvanized by love of nature, plus, of course – of course – the need to win a 'leafy' label for this area and bump up values. The street was actually an *Avenue*. Trees helped with that. Milton Avenue would have conferred on Tully a surface of decent, on-the-up bourgeois status. Surfaces mattered, and not just to geometry. Surface offered social OK-ness, until the surface cracked, *was* cracked. Did Chamberlain and Jolliffe take Tully to the tip as a reminder that he still rated only as contemptible rubbish – a parable on that 'know thyself' theme Sally also recalled from school?

And yet, because the properties were not farcically large and bulbous, just large, Tully had possibly hoped to avoid making underworld mates wonder too long and dangerously how he afforded the address and all the accessories. Perhaps he failed at this. *Go have a look where the fucker lives. I mean, just* look *at it. Suddenly the fucker's Mr Three En Suites and a genuine wood front door – I mean, wood wood, not wood-style wood, such as oak veneer, sawdust innards – this is fucking wood, I tell you, with fucking iron iron studs in, like to keep out the Moors in* El Cid *on the Movie Channel. How'd he get there? Yes, how?* That sort of curiosity and question was deadly. That sort of curiosity and question could lead to Knoll in a van.

All right, all right, Tully might, *might*, have managed the full, on-the-nail price just by piling up solid business profits over a period. Certainly there would be very good gains from what Sally thought of as the straight side of Tully's crooked-

24

ness, his own considerable drugs firm. She tried to remember whether the transcripts said anything about the quality of clothes Chamberlain and Jolliffe slashed on Knoll. A Home Office report out a while ago – and perhaps a serious underpricing by now – reckoned that Dutch ecstasy tablets, bought at fifty pence each and shipped to Britain in loads of 100,000 or 200,000, could be sold for up to fifteen pounds a shot on the street, and more in clubs. No wonder dealers hit on this name. Amphetamines originated at two pounds a gram and retailed eventually at ten times that. Or think of cocaine. Yes, do. The report suggested a run-of-the-mill dealer offering it at £1000 an ounce should be able to make over £150,000 a kilo. Even novice traders could soon have profits of £10,000 a week. A place like Tully's would probably cost around £350,000, so if he knew how to squirrel, he might have stocked up enough money fairly fast.

Sally adored the way that, when Pamela came out of twenty-nine with the boy, she gazed about the avenue, as any resident here might gaze about, frankly and proprietorially, taking in the happy trees and other pillared porches, the brilliant absence of old bangers and footway dog turds. And why not – this easiness? There'd be no debt on the property, and, by will or palimony, it would go to Pam. House purchase for people like Tully had to be through-and-through cash. Mortgage companies and banks would not lend to him, even if he could have told them his earnings and where they came from – which he wouldn't, couldn't. *'Oh, in the occupation section of the application form just put, "Police informant and importer of illegal substances by the tonne," Mr Tully, please.'* This residence in this avenue with these tasteful pavement trees told of a very gorgeous, once-and-for-all cheque, or more likely a big suitcase crammed with twenties for the estate agent. Yes, around £350,000 to £400,000, despite the houses being not exactly mansions, only executive style. Prices in the north had begun to move up fast lately.

Tully would have known he must do everything to forestall, neutralize, throttle, any rumour that fees from the CID grassing fund fattened his business income and set him up for the higher suburbia. Also, he would not have wanted it to appear that his firm did so nicely because, as extra kickback for his useful whispers to them, police blind-eyed his trade activities and messed his competitors around through heavy surveillance, breath tests, tyre checks, exhaust checks and small-hours, indelicate house searches. Therefore, he'd gone in only for a smart urban niche, not a modernized abbey with acres and half a mile of salmon river. Similarly, he'd picked the BMW and Corsa , not a Rolls and Mercedes. They'd probably had no live-in servants, and definitely no butler. No genuine Michelangelo statuary in the pillared front porch.

This modest, tactful show had worked for nearly a decade, until Stanley Basil Staple found him at dawn on a dump, looking worse than the double twenty on an old dart board. So, why had Tully's tactfulness stopped keeping him safe? The major question for ACC Esther Davidson and Sally. Well, perhaps some folk came to see the tactfulness as only that, a wise understatement of Tully's actual loot, so he and his could continue untroubled, and, of course, acquire more actual loot. After all, Tully worked with very suspicious, very non-naïve folk, and *against* very suspicious, very non-naïve folk.

Or perhaps the pretence collapsed for a different reason. Maybe too much information about Tully and his various earnings, and especially his informant earnings, suddenly became perilously public. This possibility interested someone mighty in the Home Office, and now brought Esther and Sally here. Had Tully lost his hidden, police-headquarters right to protection? Who talked about him and why? Did someone decide he should be sacrificed? Did a treacherous word go to those who knew how grasses should be punished and annihilated? But, shop one's own grass – abuse that sanctified relationship between informant and detective? Sometimes it did happen: for instance, if the detective began to fear his/her informant had come to know too much about his/her activities in grey areas. Such activities sometimes involved dirty personal gain. Obviously, no detective would want stuff like that blurted.

Sally could detect nothing furtive or scared about Pamela's behaviour now, as she helped her son fix his seat belt, although, of course, she might be scared, and perhaps ought to be. Some people would be wondering how much Tully had talked to Pam about his careers as dealer and informant. Sally herself wondered. Did Pam know as much as he had known? Perhaps there was still information she could raise money on, via Tully's police handler, Detective Sergeant Harvey Moss. It would be fairly old information by now, but some of it could still count. Plus, there might be old associates of Tully whose uncomplex hate philosophy would be, *Loathe a grass and loathe his woman and kids, for* being *his woman and kids. Harsh, you say? Of course. But, come on, come on – only standard business thinking, surely.* Even months after the trial, such detestations could linger, could erupt.

How much of the Tully gains did Pamela still own? The house and cars were obvious, but might she also have inherited notable cash – business cash, grassing cash? Possibly some felt that treasure on such a scale should be redistributed, not far-flung redistributed, as in pure, old-time Socialism, but redistributed to *them*. And, for instance, jewellery. Rings? She had some on, though Sally was too far away to make out their quality. The glint looked good. If she wore prestige stuff now, former associates might wonder what use turning Tully into rubbish on a dump if his bird continued to flash grand rocks. Former associates would operate a fairly basic kind of logic.

All these thoughts could make Pamela a target. She did not act like one, though. Instead, she performed as someone entitled to the avenue and all its gentle graces, confident in the goodwill of neighbours and always ready to offer similar goodwill in return. Style, yes, but also strength, strength that reached a kind of dignity. Her clothes were extremely non-bimbo, even anti-bimbo, but non-dreary, too. The day seemed a throwback to winter and she had on a long, wide-skirted black or navy greatcoat – like a nineteenth-century admiral's, Sally thought. Yes, some madly lucky, brave and risk-taking admiral, possibly Nelson himself, but Pam still with both arms and eyes and probably taller. She topped this billowing garment with a silver and scarlet striped scarf, naturally worn slung once around the neck, ends dauntlessly loose. It would be a treat for Sally to inveigle and percolate her way into this girl's being, if she could.

Sally had fantasized that slice of talk between Tully and Pamela about the handler detective, Harvey Moss, but did anything like it actually take place? No, surely. This dream exchange had been one of her jokes. She found she wanted to believe Pam might never have really understood what it was Tully did to get the money for the house and the cars and her fine topcoat and possible jewellery. She seemed too . . . too good for all that. Yes, good – the spot-on word. But could someone as intelligent-looking as Pam have failed to understand, or at least failed to ask the necessary questions?

'Dear Justin, we're doing remarkably well aren't we?'

'Remarkably well, dear.'

'I mean, the house, the cars, the holidays.'

'Right.'

'But where exactly does it . . . well come from?'

'What, Pam?'

'You're so successful, so fortunate, so industrious . . . but what exactly is it that—?'

'Buying and selling.'

'Ah.'

'Oh, yes, buying and selling, Pam. This is how many a business operates, buying and selling. ICI, Microsoft, BP. Ask the heads of such concerns how they thrive– they will all reply, Buying and selling. In that order.'

'Yes?'

'Certainly.'

'I'm so glad you've told me. It's the kind of thing I'd wonder about.'

'Entirely natural, Pam.'

'Without being, I hope, nosy.'

'Not in the least. An intelligent, perfectly justified interest.'

'Thanks for taking it like that, Justin.'

And could Sally kid herself such educational conversations ever happened, and that a woman with Pamela's obvious grandeur and vim and three first names would be content to stay ignorant? This dialogue sounded no more authentic than Tully's supposed recitation of his talk with Sergeant Moss. Sally recognized that sometimes imagination might become wishful and addled – hers, anyway. She'd been captivated

28

by Pamela's elegance and vitality, and longed to believe her untainted by Tully's dirty trades. Crazy to believe it? Probably.

Imagination occupied only short interludes, anyway. Sally couldn't live on it. No, she was not the thinker and poet, Coleridge, but a DC, and actuality would always force its tough, nobbly way back. A few days after her loiter in the avenue, actuality in fact struck. An official, early-evening visit to number twenty-nine took place, but this time inside with Esther. Now came a chance for Sally to lay her dream material alongside events. Esther said: 'Unquestionably, even so long after the event, there ought to be a guard on you and the child, Pam – may I? – but when it comes to guards, we have obvious problems.'

Her son opened the door of the sitting room and came a few steps in. From her Tully dossier, Sally had his name as Walter. He was nine, very slight, dark-haired, like his mother, with large, brilliantly unfriendly eyes. Or perhaps the eyes were only brilliantly suspicious, brilliantly wary, wisely afraid. That would be natural enough if your dad ended up slaughtered on a tip and you afterwards heard from TV news, or from other kids, the sort of life he'd had. The boy asked if he could go and play computer games at a school friend's house in the avenue. Pamela said all right, but told him to be back by seven.

'That's nice – to have a pal nearby,' Esther said.

'Yes,' Pam replied. Or nearer to, *Yes?* – as if asking Esther if she really thought it so strange her son should have friends.

'You're well settled here,' Esther said.

'Why not?' Pam said.

'Private school? I don't imagine many children from the avenue go state,' Esther replied.

'Yes, private. But you'd know that from your records.'

'Yes,' Esther said. Sally couldn't work out what the tone of this interview was, and would be. Considerate and tactful? Harsh and destructive? That might be Esther's method – the uncertainty. She did soft and hard cop in one. Her voice could soothe, her voice could stab.

'A police guard?' Pamela said. 'What problems with that?'

'Absolutely.' Esther struck the arm of her blue upholstered chair lightly twice with her fist, as if to signal pleasure at Pam's quickness. 'Yes, you've hit it exactly, damn formidable problems. Wouldn't you agree, Sally?'

'*I* didn't say problems. *You* did,' Pamela replied.

But Esther had no aim to make sense or follow a normal sequence. She wanted confusion. 'Yes, so true – problems,' Esther said.

'You don't trust the possible guards – or the officers who'd place them?' Pamela asked.

Esther said: 'Think of it like this, Pam. The prison people give Barry Jolliffe extra protection on a specially secure landing, but he's still been attacked three times for his evidence, twice nigh unto death. We have to ask, where was the special protection?'

'Where *was* it?' Pamela said.

'Yes, indeed,' Esther replied.

'I heard about Barry, but it's nothing to me, is it?' Pamela said.

'I'd like to think it's not – oh, I'd really like to – only it does show the situation's still active and perilous a long time after the trial. You might be part of it,' Esther replied. Sympathy. Sympathy? 'And if someone can't be kept safe in jail, what chance for folk more exposed, going about, as you do, in recognizable vehicles and on predictable runs to school, to Wal's music teacher, Asda and the hairdresser? You're not love-connected with anyone else yet, are you?'

'Love-connected?'

'It's a while since Justin's death. You're looking wonderful. You'd be entitled. But that could lead to other chartable, dangerous journeys, obviously, if you're using his premises sometimes.'

Sally saw that the sympathy had its sharp purpose, too. Esther would try to unnerve Pamela so she might be more ready to talk when the rough questions came. Well, of course the sympathy had its purpose, for God's sake. This was Esther, and Esther had made it to assistant chief. A woman didn't get there through grief counselling.

'Is it going to help – you two around the patch, stirring

things? Re-stirring things,' Pamela said. 'The case is the past. Why can't it be let lie? We're trying to resume ordinary life.'

'Help? Oh, we're not here to *help*, for heaven's sake!' Esther cried, chuckling deeply, warmly, with kindness, at Pamela's error. 'We're here to fuck people up good, but we need it to be more or less the right people we fuck up good.'

'Which people?' Pamela asked.

'Yes, people,' Esther said. 'We're not sure which people yet, obviously. We're sniffing around, Sally and I, aren't we, Sally?'

'But when you say "people", you mean police?' Pam asked. 'You, as police, stalk other police? Is that your job?'

'It happens. Lads like your Justin can occasionally find themselves sacrificed,' Esther said. 'The order comes from somewhere, and possibly somewhere very high, to get rid. Time's up for him. What we have to discover, Sally and I, is why. With any luck, that takes us on to who gave the word.'

Pamela said: ' "Somewhere very high"? But surely the—'

'Think of Abraham and Isaac,' Esther replied. 'It was Jehovah in person who said, "Do him." All right, Isaac got away with it, but the knife's not always stayed, is it? No.'

Tone? Had Sally wondered about the tone of this meeting? She realized now there'd be no tone – no single tone. Esther meant to disorientate Pamela, swinging about between the true business of the inquiry and mad byways like Abraham and Isaac. Yes, this was Esther.

'As it happens, I'd like the memory of Justin left . . . left, well . . . undisturbed now,' Pamela replied.

'Of course you would,' Esther said.

'I've come to see the true tenderness of the phrase Rest in Peace,' Pamela said. 'Justin deserves that, I think.'

'I love a phrase now and then myself, as a matter of fact,' Esther replied with a good gush of comradeliness. 'Fortunately, there are still plenty around. You valued Justin despite the kind of man he . . . Sally and I would be among the first to understand that. But, look, Pam – aftermath. Consider aftermath. That's our area, Sally's and mine. It's big and baggy. And then procedure, also. We're interested in the procedure, aren't we, Sally?'

'What procedure?' Pamela said. Sally could see her struggling to keep some sort of hold on Esther's apparently stampeding mind. Apparently.

'It sounds bleakly formal, but chosen procedures can be very valuable indicators,' Esther said.

'What procedures?'

'Money procedures,' Esther replied.

'What money?'

'Grassing money,' Esther said. 'You knew he was an informant, of course? Of course. I think Sally would like to believe you remained innocent of all Justin's darker roles. I sense it. Isn't that so, Sally? There's a real sweetness to Sally. That's not necessarily an encumbrance in a police career, but keep it limited. I know this is delicate, Pam, but how did the money actually come? In what form? Delicate in the sense that people don't like to elaborate on – give the details of – how they or their loved one, were . . . well . . . purchased. Can we accept that unpleasant word? Dwelling on the method, the *procedure*, as I've called it – this might seem to bring a degree of grubbiness, even though these fees came for helping the police, and therefore the community. But, look, the note denominations Justin got – fives, tens, twenties, fifties? Used? New? Would he say how much? Better, did you actually count it all each time? Important for us to know the amounts. We have to check whether the money he collected and brought home matches that charged to the informant account.'

Pamela said: 'I don't think—'

'And then, *when*?' Esther replied. 'I mean, did the cash come like a salary, something regular – monthly, quarterly? Or more *ad hoc* – a payment each time he supplied fine information, so comparatively irregular, even random, like, say, Shirley Bassey doing a gig one week and getting paid, but nothing the week after? Give us the scene, do.'

Pamela said: 'I can't see what—'

'It's along these lines, is it?' Esther replied. 'Justin arrives home padded with cash after meeting his handler – whom we'll be talking to, naturally, when suitable – Justin arrives, not showy or bombastic, yet quietly aglow, and then what's the . . . yes . . . *procedure*? Sincerely, this could give us a

32

lead back to where things started to change, and to whoever changed them. Yes, that's our job.'

'But why should I want to—'

'Why should you want to help us like that?' Esther said. 'Because we assume you'd like to know who set Justin up for Chamberlain and Jolliffe. They acted on contract, of course.'

'All right, you could call it a procedure,' Pam replied. She spoke slowly, staring up towards the ceiling, as if holding the term "procedure" in the air for a good inspection before taking it. She was aware of her own great profile. So she should be.

'You miss it, do you, the procedure?' Esther said.

'I'd rather say, "I miss Justin,"' Pam answered.

'He and the very he-ness of him are certainly factors. Nobody's suggesting this is *only* a matter of loot,' Esther said.

'Oh?' Pam replied. 'That so?'

'We're sure Justin had real qualities – additional to the increasingly successful drugs-running villainy. Sally and I both know this. We've read it all up in the transcripts and press. Even without these, we'd have realized he must have had smatterings of true worth to attract and continue to attract a woman of your . . . Isn't that so, Sally?' Esther's eyes did a room tour. 'The decor of this house and some of the rugs show quite decent taste for an out-and-out career crook like Justin.'

'What qualities exactly do you think of as his?' Pam asked. 'I still need to hear him praised.'

'Beside *Homes and Gardens* taste? All we're saying, Sally and I, is that Justin's arrival from time to time with cash wads was bound to be well . . . a *feature* of your relationship – a workaday, not especially spiritual feature – but a feature, you see, Pam? All right, to put it on to a more personal, even emotional, plain, tell us how he looked at these times, his manner, his body language.' She struck the chair again. ' "Body language!" Jesus, sorry, I'm into bargain-bin psychology today. Would there be a grand smile as he proudly pitched excellent, rubber-banded packages on to your handsome, circular rosewood table there, accompanied, most probably I should think, knowing Justin's constructive nature,

33

with sincere promises of how exactly such gains could be spent on the lad, or your own wardrobe, and/or on yet further enhancements of this worthwhile residence? We have the hunter home from the hill, the sailor back from the sea, with family wherewithal and gifts. *Your* man.'

Sally heard real savagery here. Esther must have decided Pamela might not come across. The squeeze had begun, the mockery, the trowelled sarcasm: 'You know, Pam, Sally, I see a lovely picture. I see an intensely meaningful picture, and with funds. Just before he actually turned up so triumphantly, you, you individually, Pam, you're waiting in this terrific lounge – you call it a lounge, I expect – in this lounge, relaxed possibly, with a nice volume by Wittgenstein or a Gran Canaria holiday brochure. You hear the BMW approach along the avenue, its beautiful engine sound varying up and down as it eddies around the designer trees, until Justin pulls into the commodious drive and you stand joyously from that chair and go out to wait between the gorgeous little pillars with your beaming and deserved welcome. This would be a welcome to Justin as Justin, to the essence of Justin, not to Justin merely as bearer of a refresher fee, I know that, and so, probably, does Sally, but the fee would be a further plus, as it were. We wondered, Sally and I, whether, at these times of charming reunion, Justin occasionally spoke of the admirable source of his bung, fast-track Detective Sergeant Harvey Moss, or perhaps someone higher? That's crucial – the possibility of someone higher. Did you ever meet Harvey?'

Sally could get a good look at Pamela's jewellery now. She had a triple diamond on her engagement finger, no wedding band, and on her right hand a large single emerald with diamond surround, and an amethyst, also with diamond surround. Sally knew a bit about stones and thought these three rings together would add up to at least forty thousand. Pam's earrings looked Victorian, gold and enamel with a central pearl.

'The point is, I can't worry about Barry Jolliffe, whatever happens to him in jail,' Pamela replied. 'All right, he turned mouth in the box and made sure that fucker Chamberlain went down for plenty, but Barry was up there on Knoll, knife at work, whatever he says, whatever deal he did.'

'And then, sequence,' Esther said. 'Sally and I are very curious to know about sequence, aren't we, Sally? I know you're into phraseology, Pam. Well, a case like this has what is known among labellers as "a narrative", you see.'

'Sequence?' Pam said. 'Narrative?'

So, the attack continued. Esther obviously still believed Pamela could help more if she wanted to and still had to be roughed up; hilarious to hear Esther ask for sequence. She said genially: 'He comes home and there are sweet moments of togetherness and acclaim. I think of the dad osprey flying into the nest with something you can all get a bite of. Perhaps the boy is shown the jolly earnings so he can learn of the rewards for industry and intelligence – yes, intelligence, secret intelligence. Perhaps a counting out of the notes on the table to help Walter with his arithmetic. Can you recall figures? This would be such a help. But let me tell you what I'm getting at when I say sequence and/or narrative. After one of these cheerful days when Justin arrived home with a wad, did you actually notice via local press and media reports some particular, probably large-scale police operation? I mean, a raid, major arrests? It would be important for Sally and me to link some of these pay days for Justin with specific results, you see. If Justin earned for fingering some villain or gang, we'd like to know who. As a starting place, we need to see the pattern, don't we, Sally?'

Sally never had a chance to reply to such questions, with their suggestion that Esther and she acted together in pressurizing Pamela. An Esther ploy. She would know her behaviour was brutal and wished to share out the blame, that's all. 'Sally and I are not in the least saying you'd have a gloat, Pam, if you saw on TV news some heavy cop power squashing a big-time rogue and business enemy following one of Justin's grand homecomings here with informant cash. But we have to find a . . . yes, a sequence, you see. We need to track that. Call us narrow and mechanical but we have to line up effect with cause – the essence of narrative.'

Esther was in the blue easy chair, and Pamela in another opposite, across an Afghan carpet. Sally sat on a large white settee with a side view of both. Now, maybe in retaliation,

Pamela seemed to take up Esther's technique of apparently rambling, drifting talk. Sally found it hard to stay with either mind. Pamela said: 'Barry Jolliffe – someone who could have been regarded as a friend of Justin – yes, a friend – and yet he's there in the van and on Knoll.'

'Did you personally have contact with Jolliffe, or Chamberlain, during Justin's trading days?' Esther asked.

'How do you mean, contact?'

'Contact,' Esther said.

'What sort of contact?' Pam said.

'You seem especially upset to mention Barry,' Esther replied. 'Was there a betrayal by him beyond the obvious betrayal of Justin? A betrayal of *you*? Sally and I – we know how these things will go, especially Sally. Don't, please, tell us that love – sex – can always be neatly confined in a one-to-one relationship, even if Justin had set you up so well.'

'Or even, especially Assistant Chief Davidson,' Sally said.

'And yet, obviously, you wouldn't want Justin hurt and killed, whatever you and Barry had going,' Esther said.

'And if they came and offered me a police guard, have I a right to refuse it?' Pam replied.

'Of course, of course you've got the right, oh, yes. An inalienable right, talking of phrases,' Esther said.

'But would they take any notice?' Pam said.

'Ah, true. I think you're extremely wise to feel doubtful about any police guard drawn from the local force,' Esther said.

'But I didn't feel doubtful until you—'

'They'd need to live in, you see. Necessary closeness for full, continuous protection – that's what they'd argue. Of course they would, the devious sods. Or possibly a Portakabin as guardroom in the garden. You have the kind of garden that would take a Portakabin front or back. This is no pitiful little house straight on to the pavement. Very hard to imagine what kind of survival ploys you could use in those circumstances if these people, or the people who sent them, thought you knew dangerous stuff from Justin. That's the essence of it. They might decide only half the task's finished by his removal. Think of those grail quests in old stories – one obstacle overcome, but then comes another. Oh, you'll say, but this is well after the events and they haven't done anything against you. True. This inquiry, though – Sally's and mine – this inquiry might suddenly increase their anxieties. They'll know what a gifted detective Sally is. It could scare them.'

'Who – who exactly – are we talking about?' Pamela asked.

'Sally would want to come up and see things are all right for you, I know – those kindly, hormonal, fantasizing eyes – but she's going to be involved with other aspects of the inquiry,' Esther replied. 'Were accounts kept?'

'Accounts?'

'Cash accounts. Of what came in,' Esther said.

'You can't mean actually written down,' Pam replied. 'You *can't*.'

'What would he call it, this money?' Esther said. 'Did he keep it distinct – income from the drugs dealership and income from the grassing? As, for instance, some political paladins would distinguish between their Commons pay and what they leech every week from landlording. Did Justin have, like, a royalties chart, to establish which source gave more to his cash flow? When he talked about the informant fees, did he refer to them as, say, "Harvey money", "Moss money"? Or some other name, maybe? "Albert Chave money" – that's Chief Inspector Chave, Moss's controller? Oh, look, may I tell you how the informant system works, in case Justin didn't? There's a handler for each grass – that is, a detective constable or sergeant who deals direct with the tipster. And then, above the handler, we have a senior officer supervising. He's the controller. Did you ever hear Justin query whether he was getting all he was supposed to get from the informant account? That's why I'm keen to hear about figures, you see. We've been highlighting interesting phrases during our chat here, and I'd like to mention a few more such as "skimming off the top", "kickback", "some for you, some for me". Did he ever mention one of these, in an accusing, angry way? I mean, perhaps an officer took money that should have been his. Yours. Walter's. Sally, I know, has been wondering if Justin might occasionally have used such terms, not in a favourable tone, and conceivably with reference to Harvey or someone above Harvey. Sally's "been around", as another phrase goes, and "knows the score". I rely greatly on her instincts – instincts, but *honed* instincts. Oh, she's kindly, yes, but not to a fault.'

'Now and then, of course, someone he knew, or more than one, would be taken in by the police and charged, but I've never seen Justin get all triumphant, as if he had helped with it,' Pam said. 'Not his nature. He felt concerned about folk, even those who tried to destroy his business so there'd be more for them. I've often heard him say, "Live and let live."'

'That's certainly yet another grand phrase,' Esther said. 'As you'll know, in full it's, "Live and let live, as long as letting the fucker live never for a moment fucks things up for me." Pam, if you could tie an incident when someone was charged like that – tie this to a more or less simultaneous grassing payment, it might give us a direction. It would show who might have been aggrieved at him, you see. Or whose relatives and friends might have been. That's why I wanted to find out if you knew which of his careers the money came from, when he returned home bearing funds. We don't close our minds to the possibility that this was entirely a villain-on-villain enterprise, no police involvement at all – as, of course, it had been designed to look. On the face of it, this could rate as an underworld spat, nothing else. The trial treated it so. That would be a very convenient way of dealing with it for some. The thing is, both of his enterprises were in cash, weren't they – drugs profits and the grassing fees? You could be confused as to which of his business sectors the earnings came from. It's not like someone working as a university vice-chancellor or hotel doorman, where there'd be one, clear, electronic salary transfer monthly.'

'Do you mean people might think I still have cash hidden around the house?' Pam said.

'And when he went out to meet Moss, would you know about it?' Esther replied. 'I mean, would he announce, "Pamela, just off to give Harvey some unique and precious murmur," and name the rendezvous point, in case things turned out bad and he didn't get back? Maybe you heard arrangements made by phone. Would he call Moss and say he had something? "Harv, I'm ready with a gem and bring something nice in cash." But, no, he wouldn't need to say "in cash", would he? The rule. Who pays informant perks by cheque?'

'What could I do if things turned out bad?' Pam said. 'They *did* once, didn't they, on the tip? Do you think something like . . . well, in that category might happen to me or Walter?'

But questions here did not necessarily qualify for an answer. Esther had her own route to pick, and her own questions. 'Would he use Harvey's name on the phone? Or perhaps someone else's?' Esther said. 'Chave's? Those meetings – you know, Pam, I don't like to think of Justin setting off heartily to one of them and nobody aware of it, except himself and the other party. Or him *thinking* nobody was aware of it except himself and the other party. What happens if there's a leak, accidental, deliberate? But we know, don't we? What happens is Moonmain beach.'

'Yet there was no rendezvous that day at Moonmain,' Pam said. 'This came out in court.'

'That's what I mean,' Esther replied.

'What do you mean, that's what you mean?' Pam asked.

'That's what I mean,' Esther said. 'It did "come out in court", but do we believe everything that comes out in court?'

'This was stated by the police – no rendezvous,' Pam said.

'Do we believe everything stated in court?' Esther replied.

'But you just told me there might be no police involvement. Now you say police evidence was possibly wrong,' Pamela replied.

'There *might* be no police involvement,' Esther said. 'We're feeling about, Sally and I. We're only at the start.'

'Are you telling me I shouldn't drive Walter to school or his bassoon lessons?' Pam said.

'As a matter of fact, I know someone who plays the bassoon rather giftedly,' Esther replied. 'Oh, yes.'

Pamela seemed to get suddenly fed up with Esther's dodging about. Pam said: 'All right, so you know someone who—'

'When I mention accounts, it's because an account would, of course, be kept at the police end, showing how much from the informant fund supposedly went to Justin, under his grassing code name,' Esther replied. 'It's a secret account, naturally – and very properly so. But *someone* has to check.

Now, if Justin and you also kept track of the amounts, and the figures don't tally, then, obviously, we have a situation that can be inquired into. It would show Justin didn't get full whack, because an officer, or more than one, was – were – taking a percentage. "Some for you, some for me" – this is exactly where such a phrase, as recently mentioned, would come into play. I'd need to know about that.'

Pam said: 'When they're picking police to do this kind of utterly filthy job on their own lot, how do they—?'

'Filthy?' Esther replied, sweetly.

'Underhand,' Pam said.

'We're trying to discover who really had your man killed and why,' Esther said. 'That's filthy? That's underhand? Don't you want to fucking well know? You'd like them to get away with it?'

Pamela said: 'He's dead. Does it matter now who—?'

'Sally thinks so. Once she gets set on something, she's more or less unstoppable, aren't you, Sally?'

Pamela said: 'I'm not sure I want—'

'Nice Renoir and Gauguin prints on your walls, Pam,' Esther replied, gazing at them. 'But *prints*. When Sally, with her startlingly tough, perhaps unduly frank mind – I say, when Sally looks at those items, she's bound to wonder whether the full grassing reward ever reached poor Justin. Now, I'm not saying Sally would expect you to own *real* Renoirs and Gaugins from grassing.' Esther smiled a while without pity. The 'filthy' and 'underhand' accusations had obviously enraged her. Yet she still wanted to pass off the cruel comments on the art as Sally's. God, but Esther would take some managing. She said: 'No police force can dish out millions, we all know that. But Sally, in her ruthlessly logical way, would argue that if Justin were earning to his true worth from grassing, he'd at least have genuine art, by someone fairly negligible but OK, and on genuine canvas, not prints on paper. That's Sally! "Insightful" is one of the qualities they attribute to her, Pam. Am I going to dispute it?'

Pamela said: 'Are some police . . . like . . . like specialists, going around to other Forces, trying to destroy officers and – you, you're an expert at that, are you?'

'You see, Pam, one of the likelihoods we have to think about, Sally and I, is Justin could have grown resentful and angry about his plundered earnings, resentful, angry and stroppy. Perhaps he threatened to make an awkward noise – a noise that could get an officer, officers, locked up for misuse of the informant fund. Courts are tough on that kind of police finagling. Rightly, of course. And so, someone grows tired of him, wants him removed, and carefully lets a careless word slip among people who listen carefully for careless words and can call on folk who know about knives and the higher areas of Knoll tip.'

Pam sat quiet for a while, staring at the Renoir print of *The Judgement of Paris*. 'All right, it's naff to hang prints, but we both liked them. What's wrong with that? We had something good going, Justin and I.'

'Of course you did,' Esther said.

'And, yes, I cared for him, still care for him, still feel crippled by sadness sometimes, despite the cool show I put on.'

'Of course you do,' Esther said. Something like real understanding touched her voice. She wasn't baiting Pamela. Or, at least, Sally *thought* she heard real understanding, and *thought* Esther had abated the baiting.

'We both wandered a bit,' Pam said. 'Sexually, that is.'

'People do,' Esther said. 'Ask Sally.'

'Ask Assistant Chief Davidson,' Sally said.

'You knew we both wandered a bit, did you?' Pamela replied. 'Research.'

'It's always a reasonable assumption,' Esther said.

'I guessed that's why you questioned one-to-one relationships,' Pamela said. 'Is it?'

'People can get restless,' Esther said. 'Ask Sally.'

'Ask Assistant Chief Davidson,' Sally replied.

'But we always cared for each other,' Pamela said.

'So you surely want to know who killed him, had him killed,' Esther said.

'I'm too afraid to help you,' Pamela replied.

'We have to find who Chamberlain and Jolliffe worked for,' Esther said. 'These were not themselves major people. Even through transcripts, they smell of nobodyism – merely people on the end of orders. One of their orders said, Get Justin at Moonmain and give him a slow finale in the van and on Knoll. Where did the instructions come from, though? This is the question Sally wants to put, I'm certain of that. She's been through all the court papers and press coverage but finds nothing explicit on who ran Chamberlain and Jolliffe, nothing to tell us definitely who decided against Tully after years of sweet safety, and for what. This never featured in the trial. What Sally would like to ask, I know, is this – if Justin Tully had been feeding the CID such prime material, why were Chamberlain and Jolliffe still around, not locked up? Shouldn't they have been fingered long before? These people did not suddenly turn villain when they got Justin into the van and on to Knoll. Career crud. There's a place for folk like that – behind a steel door.'

'I think I'll stay on in the house,' Pam said. 'I'm not sure what Justin would say, but I won't be asking the Ouija board.'

'Someone who wanted Justin gone probably conned him into the trip to Moonmain and mentioned to a contact that he'd be there and available for snatching. Is this how you see it?' Esther asked.

'I expect I'll sell one of the cars, though this is a property which actually *demands* multi-vehicle presence, because of driveway width,' Pamela replied.

Esther said: 'You're afraid to answer our questions, or even to recognize they exist, in case people come to think you've taken over Justin's grassing. You can't rely on being safe yourself, or your son being safe. That's it?'

'So right,' Pamela said. 'And don't talk to me about not answering questions. Of course, fear can occasionally turn into a kind of strength – make someone do a preventive hit on the cause of the fear. Like Mr Bush and Mr Blair.'

'A hit?' Esther said.

'Absolutely,' Pam said, and struck the arm of her chair. 'That's just the word *I* would have picked.'

'Where do you see the danger coming from – towards you and Walter?' Esther replied.

'Where do *you*?' Pamela said.

'So true,' Esther replied.

42

Four

Esther wanted to know how Justin Tully used to work – the drugs firms he ran, plus his role as informant. How were they linked? She asked Sally to do some quiet history on Tully's whole operation – operations. Esther required a comprehensive, graphic chart. This would list all local drugs firms by size and apparent success around the time of his death. She'd be especially interested in firms – Tully's or any others – that appeared consistently profitable over a period of months, even a year or more. Did it look as if some outfits – again, Tully's or any others – had protection, police protection? The signs would be: few arrests of its people; prime dealing locations tolerated by detectives; possibly blind-eyed openness of pushing in some venues.

Then, which drugs squad detectives monitored which firm or firms? How did the monitoring work? Did the informant, or informants, system run according to proper national instructions? If not, what departures? Were all informants officially registered? 'Of course, this is an impossible one,' Esther said. 'If some are *not* registered, how do you know they're not? They're unregistered because they and the handler want secrecy. But any time you sense you're not getting the full scene, Sally, this doubt should be entered on our chart – like "Here be dragons" on old maps when an area hadn't been explored.' Esther said unknowns could be as significant as knowns.

Sally thought Esther would be a specialist on the significance of unknowns, being one herself. Sally had encountered strangeness in the other assistant chief back home – Raging Bullfinch, as he was called – but his strangeness couldn't get close to Esther's.

She wanted it established whether informants received money, or had other forms of reward been used, such as cars, private health subscriptions, private school fees, university fees, jewellery, colonic irrigation vouchers, psychiatry fees, holidays, tarts/studs, clothes, mortgage deposits, house improvements, wigs, dentistry, drink, aromatherapy, eatery season tickets? This digging might not be a proper part of the inquiry, but boundaries were vague, and Esther probably liked that, would see chances.

She told Sally that one advantage of strange ground was you wouldn't be recognized around the streets as a detective and could try minor infiltration. Esther said she had done this herself at Sally's rank, when part of similar police-on-police probes. Now, though, Esther might be a bit too old and regal to go unnoticed in a club or youth pub. Besides, assistant chiefs didn't do undercover, not even assistant chiefs like Esther. 'As a matter of fact, Sally, I almost turned you down for this job because you're too memorable – face and body.'

'Thanks. But I find I'm very easily forgotten,' Sally said. 'I can leave a room with only a few people in it and nobody notices.'

'Well, yes. I just thought I should say something kindly. Now and then I feel like that.' Smelling of 'Red' perfume, but with restraint, Esther briefed Sally in their bug-swept, lock-changed room, totally Inspector Yatesless for now. No bug had been found, not in the water dispenser or anywhere else, but Esther required checks kept up.

She gave Sally advice on penetrating the trade: yes, easier than at home, but still perilous, so move slowly. You went to the kind of place where stuff would be on offer and did a little discreet asking and watching. When you located a pusher, the ACC said, you sidled, kow-towed, really fucking laid on the fucking respect, made a purchase, of course, then mentioned you were a stranger – apologized for being a stranger – and declared you would like regular looking after. Did he/she always use this spot, you asked. Good. '*So I'll be back, believe me!*'

You turned up a couple more times and bought again before

44

trying some chat, while still shovelling on the respect, oh, respect, respect. Keep things oblique at first. Esther thought that, in the present case, chat should go like this – you loved the stuff he/she sold, really loved it, the price was fine, but, *'Look, can you help me on this – I've heard a bit of a whisper – not more, a bit of a whisper – I heard a bit of a whisper that the substance picture is . . . well, a little fucking dangerous here, police dangerous, and also dealer-on-dealer dangerous. All right, it's still dangerous everywhere, despite the relaxations, but here, as I hear it, there's danger plus. Maybe too much. "Here, as I hear it" – wow, what a language we've got!'* Esther, said – yes, get a quip or two in, to promote relaxation. Then, though, *'For instance, wasn't a quite big trader found dead and cut about somewhere not all that long ago? Well, to be exact – again, as I heard it, that is – on a tip?'*

Esther did a fine wheedling, though occasionally jokey, voice for this chat-up. Respect, oh, respect, respect, billowed out of it all round, like fumes from a censer. In fact, respect of this amount and variety, Sally didn't think she had ever come across before. Esther went on with the script. 'Tell him/her you're uneasy – not long ago you found yourself too near something diabolical, down in Moss Side, Manchester, by accident – just through being an ordinary salt-of-the-earth user, no supplying, you got star spot in some crossfire and you don't want that kind of hit-the-deck, face-in-the-dirt hazard again, thanks. You're thinking – reluctantly thinking – you're thinking, perhaps you should drive elsewhere for your gear. You're sure he/she'll sympathize – bow, scrape, forelock tug, may I wash your feet?'

So, on the local club scene, where the music sounded to Sally like brilliant, non-governable Jim O'Rourke, probably post-*Eureka* – Jim O'Rourke, for God's sake, in a four-pound-entry, laser and plasterboard place like this – yes, in a four-pound-entry, laser and plasterboard place like this, and, soothed by the fierce, amicable guitar, Sally offered her intimate story to a dealer she'd spotted and done the sidle and kow-tow to then bought coke from a few times. He had a spot right over near a fire door in the corner, where for most of the time the sound system was just less than blank-out, though some shouting could be useful now and then. 'Manchester? Moss Side? Guns? You mean yardies?' he asked.

'The same.'

'Christ, they're not coming after you? You owe them?' He looked suddenly very non-interventionist. 'None of them in this town. Yet.'

'All right, but—'

'Poor kid.'

'Thanks, but—'

'Bar-fucking-baric they can be – a fact, I don't deny. Yes, truly, my sympathy. That's not this scene, though. Here, a sweet regime. We're OK, luckily.'

'No, not coming after me. We're all right. But, look, the guy on the tip,' Sally said.

'Tip?'

'Carved. Dead.'

'On a tip?'

'Knoll.'

'Knoll's a park.'

'*Was* a tip. There's a name. Like Holly? Curry? Tully.'

'Oh, Tully. Heard of that. Justin. He went out of line, that's all.'

'Like?'

'What whisper?' he replied.

'What?' Sally replied.

'You heard a whisper. You said you heard a bit of a whisper. Where? Who?'

'Just a bit of a whisper. You know – a pub crowd. The talk went that way a while. You know how it can be.'

'What pub?'

'Plus, in the papers back a bit, anyway, they said –' Sally replied – 'in the papers and on TV news, because of court . . . Two people sent down, one turned evidence.'

'Look, you want the fucking stuff or not?'

'Oh, don't get—'

'You don't want it – fuck off. What's with the talk? Have I got time to talk?'

'Just some worries. No need to—'

46

'You got worries, they're yours, so fuck off with them. Sympathy for previous episodes, sure, but if you're buying now, buy or else fuck off.'

'I want, yes. Sure, I want. Just uneasy.'

'So, you make *me* uneasy,' he said. Tall, fattish, with a porky round face and heavy-rimmed spectacles, he did not look made to be uneasy, he looked made to be hearty and/or a political lobbyist, but Sally saw she'd really turned him uneasy, all the same. Perhaps she'd been clumsy and unlavish with the respect Esther declared vital. Sally bought and shut up.

Twice when she went back to the Inclination club he was not there. Possibly she'd scared him. That damn film, *Serpico*, given a TV rebirth now and then, with Al Pacino playing an undercover cop, dressed like a derelict – that movie could mean the more you looked part of the milieu, the more they recognized you as law. But Esther said he would return. Keep going. Pushers couldn't move off their beat for long, because they'd permanently lose clientele. People with a habit had a habit of needing things habitually. And if he put himself on someone else's turf, he'd get his head blown off, yardies or no. 'Yes, but suppose he's sniffed me?' Sally asked.

'I don't believe it. You reek of authenticity, Sal,' Esther replied. 'You're authentic junkiedom. It's a gift.'

'Thanks.'

Esther said next time he came get hard with him. Do the *it's a buyer's market* patter. 'Tell him, as to uneasiness, he's so fucking uneasy he makes you even more uneasy than when you *started* getting uneasy about the trade here, so you've been driving and buying elsewhere. Reluctantly – the mileage drag of it. Settle on a couple of words for your themes – give him 'uneasy', obviously, and 'elsewhere', and keep giving them. They make you sound basic – brain crack-slowed, but still cagey. Don't – *don't* – get articulate. Say the stuff from the opposition is oomphier, richer, than you had from him. Say you've been over to elsewhere quite a bit for yourself and, also, buying some for new friends – these friends being even more uneasy and scared to come to places like Inclination if the deal is with someone uneasy.

47

Say you'll be on your way to elsewhere later but you just looked in because you personally like Inclination, regardless, but you can't persuade your friends. Tell him it's a big order for elsewhere. Here. Flash some of this somehow.' She gave Sally a wad of twenties.

'How?'

'Rolled in a denim outer pocket. He'll read the bulge. A job skill, like midwives can guess birth date from a baby bump. He'll spot to within forty what you've got. These are talented people.'

Sally didn't ask where the money came from, nor where the coke she'd bought and handed over went.

On the third night after the break, he appeared again at his position by the fire door, wearing a navy suit with magnificently heavy pinstripe, like a duke or owner of many pinball machines. This time when she arrived, the music might have been Candidate, which would do, but then slipped away to bluegrass that Sally did not recognize or want to. This club tried to appeal to all tastes. After midnight, when he had a slow spell, Sally sidled over and gave him the yarn as updated by Esther, and praise for Inclination and most of its crazily mixed soundtrack. 'What fucking elsewhere?' he said.

'Elsewhere.'

'What friends? I thought you was a stranger.'

'I said *new* friends.'

'They'll all buy?'

'If I'll do it for them. They don't want exposure. They're uneasy. This is for parties, socializing. Some are in big jobs. They'd hate bother and publicity.'

'They chipped in? You're fucking mad with cash on show like that.'

'How do you mean, on show? It's not on show,' Sally said.

'On show. Your pocket. Christ, three hundred, three fifty, how many friends?'

'Just friends.'

The music grew too loud for a while. She wondered if it was a giveaway that she didn't dance. But, no, originally she'd come here to buy, hadn't she, and would still look like that – serious activity, not just jig and sweat? Probably most of his customers came here as customers only. She wouldn't stand out. As a matter of fact, she wouldn't have minded some dancing, but thought she'd better concentrate. Long time since she danced. Pete didn't fancy it too much.

'I do quantity discount,' he said. 'I'd beat elsewhere.'

'Not to disrespect you, but I'd be too uneasy buying from you now. You sound scared. Yes, I pick up uneasiness. Like there's someone behind you?' That was a friendly move, making a statement into a question when you said something dark – a smarmy ploy.

'Dim fucker, someone's behind every dealer. Where would the fucking stuff come from?'

'Uneasy, though. You make me feel I'll get pulled into something – like Manchester.'

'A good discount,' he said. 'I'm famed for it.' There ought to be a placard behind him on the fire door, 'Reductions for Quantity, all items – H, C, E, Ganja.'

'Elsewhere it's – well, more comfortable,' Sally replied. 'Relaxed. My friends – they're deeply uneasy in case they're pulled into something. These are not rough-house people. These are people for socializing. Weekends. They can't handle menace.' A longish music break began, to get people into the bar, buying.

'No menace,' he said. He had one of those round, fat faces which could let part of itself slide down and become neck now and then, yet still have enough flesh to keep the face more or less a face, with nose, chin, eyebrows, the whole inventory undoubtedly present and more or less in exactly the right places, a genuine flair. It was obviously a great plus for him, but still not nearly enough ever to bring off a full deslob of his appearance. Sally decided no matter how hard it might be to get information, she would never fuck this, nor even half promise. Probably Esther wouldn't ask for that kind of approach, anyway, despite contempt for boundaries.

'What elsewhere?' he said.

'Oh, you know, elsewhere,' she replied.

'You pissing me about – doing hard to get? So, what else-where?'

'Elsewhere.'

'You won't get pulled into nothing with me. Nor your fucking friends. It's commercial, that's all.'

'Look, it's like this – you went *so* uneasy when I mentioned the guy on the tip,' she replied. 'Excuse me, but I had to notice. I wasn't looking out for it, anything like that, but I had to notice. So, are you tied up with that, one way or the other – with the people around that? That's bound to make you uneasy. *You* being uneasy makes *me* uneasy.'

'It's over.'

'Like you pretending you never even heard of it until I come up with the name. Like it can't be talked about, because you're in it somehow. That makes me uneasy. I don't think you'll regard this as unreasonable.' God, but such gorgeous user-to-pusher verbals!

'Tully,' he said. 'A dealer called Tully.'

'I told *you* that.'

'Girlfriend Pamela. Classy. Very cool. Three-fifty – that's a lot of C with the discount. You'd clean me out for the rest of the night. But all right. If you went motoring elsewhere, elsewhere wouldn't have that much on him if it's the elsewhere I'm thinking. What elsewhere?'

'Elsewhere. Obviously, the driving's a pain. I could do without it. But . . . but, you knew Tully? This is . . . like, sensitive for you? Sensitive, that's how it sounded, yes. I have this *feeling* you knew him. You can see I'd be uneasy and, with such slabs of uneasiness around for me and my friends, I'll settle for the driving to elsewhere,' Sally replied.

'You been using too much and are coming down now? This what makes you uneasy?'

'*You*, you make me uneasy, I told you. That's frank. Pardon me, but how it is. I like this club and the Jim O'Rourke but . . . I want you to consider, if I get uneasy because a guy's killed on a tip, that makes sense, that's not just uneasy for the sake of being uneasy, is it? This is not a guy just *killed*, this is someone given plenty of non-fatal knife prior – in a van, on the tip. How I hear it in the pub crowd, and as it showed in the press likewise, at trial time. The point is, nobody could *not* be uneasy when they hear something like that. It would be mad. If I heard someone stayed *not* uneasy when they heard of something like that, I'd be uneasy about that person's brain, because uneasiness would only be a sign the mind was working right, but no uneasiness would mean it was blotto.'

'What pub?'

'But then the way you go uneasy because *I'm* uneasy, even though when *I'm* uneasy it's only reasonable and right to get uneasy, this is going to make me *more* uneasy, and my friends. Bound to be. There are times when it's right to be uneasy. I mean, think, in the war, if I'm on an ordinary boat, like a merchant boat, and then suddenly out of the fog the battle-ship *Bismarck*. Standing on the deck looking at this battle-ship, I'm going to be uneasy, aren't I, and it would be right to be uneasy, seeing her guns?'

'What boat? This elsewhere guy – he's on a boat? Like a barge somewhere – living on a canal barge? I never heard of no dealer on a barge, not this area. What's he called, you say? Bismarck?'

'You're not stupid or for ever crack-smashed, so you can see this situation will make me uneasy. And I hear he was a big operator – Tully.'

'These friends – these *new* friends – parties, socializing – this going to be regular purchases?' he replied. 'Ongoing?'

'If I like the terms, if *they* like the terms, this would be regular. This is regular partying and socializing. What else? I mean, people enjoying themselves – people getting some good stuff to enjoy themselves with. I ask, what's wrong with that? They got jobs, so there's money coming in, so we want a party now and then, and socializing. No harm to anybody.'

'Coming up with three hundred and fifty, three eighty, just like that? Every how often?' The amount gripped him. No 'buy or fuck off', like last time.

'Often,' Sally replied. 'Look, we're earning it, working for it. Why not?'

'Right. You ask anyone – my discount, it's the best.'

'Well, I did hear that. This is important if it's regular. This could add up to a big save for us.'

51

'You said it *would* be.'

'What?' Sally asked.

'Regular.'

'Yes.'

'So, of course, a big save,' he said. 'You go elsewhere, you won't get that. Listen, I'm talking and talking to you now because . . . because, well, I value you as a buyer. That's how I am, considerate.'

'All right, I believe you, but I can't stand it when I'm . . . well, when I'm *uneasy*,' Sally said. 'Yes, I think that's probably the word. You familiar with that word, at all? Uneasy? Not to be uneasy – that's so important, I mean, unless uneasiness is the sensible thing because of the state of things. But if it is, then I'd want to get away from those things, wouldn't I? This is logic, but simple logic. So's discount important, yes, but to get no uneasiness, that is maybe more. Yes, more. We want to *enjoy* our parties and the socializing, and we can't if we're uneasy, even if the price is good. I hear he was a big operator – this Tully – and living in an avenue, two cars. If someone big like that is on a tip, multi-stabbed – I mean, someone who must have been good at looking after himself, if he gets a house in an avenue and two cars – I mean, if it happens to someone like that, this is going to make someone ordinary like me and my new friends – it's going to make us uneasy – yes, that's the term, I think – it's sure to make us uneasy, because we don't even know about looking after ourselves the way Tully did until he finished on the tip, and we don't want any nearness to that kind of thing, not at all. So, he *seemed* able to look after himself, but no good. And we don't even *seem* to know how to look after ourselves. We're not like that.'

'*Too* fucking big.'

'Tully?'

'*Too* fucking big.'

'But if he was big, he'd have his own people to look after him and he'd know how to—'

'There's bigger.'

'Bigger than a house in an avenue and two cars?' Sally said.

'Mansions. Acres. Paddocks. Bentley dropheads. Croquet. A personal library. That's *personal*, the library, not your council library. And genuine books. Hardback. Four-wheel drives. These are people beyond and beyond Tully. These are people who make Tully and other Tullys possible.'

'So, look, if bigger people are around, how is it you say Tully was *too* big?'

'And he talked. He was big but not big *enough*, not big enough just through business, so he needed more income and he talked.'

'Talked?'

'To police. Mentioned in the trial.'

'Yes?'

'And so he had to go. Talking like that – he could knock their business, really big lads' and ladies' business. Listen, there's grades in business, levels. There's the mansion level and there's a house in an avenue level. If you got paddocks and a croquet lawn and personal library with proper hardbacks in, many rare with proper illustrations, and someone is talking so you might lose the fucking lot . . . You see, they would *have* to take him out, wouldn't they? That's why they took him out, not because of the business as business, but because he talked. Survival. We've all got a duty to survive, haven't we?'

'This Tully? Did *he* have a duty?'

'But sometimes for one to survive, another has to go. This is nature. Think of a fox getting rabbits for its babes. You and your friends – no need to turn uneasy about Tully, because it was not to do with the *ordinary* business, but to do with him grassing. What you cannot – *cannot* – fucking have, if good business arrangements are running, with noble properties and lawns and vehicles to be looked after with money from them good business arrangements – what you cannot have is someone opening his mouth in a certain direction about such business matters. You heard of industrial espionage? Tully. This was negative, destructive, a blight on simple commerce. I don't want to speak evil of him, but sometimes it's got to be said.'

Sally already knew quite a stack about death from

whispering. Home in Cardiff, she'd once had a grass code-named Godzilla who went that way. Yes, survival could be competitive.

'The house in the avenue and the cars – these came from grassing, not just the business,' Mr Fire Doors said. 'To buy the house and the cars, *he* had to be bought. You cotton? *He's* bought, and with the money he's bought with he can buy the house and the cars and the lovely gear and stones for his Pam. Referred to as an equation, if you can grasp that. People wondered for a while before Knoll, of course, a house like that, still not the greatest but in a fair avenue, admitted, and with its own trees. They wondered if he took police pay, but they did not *know*. They did not know, so they did not act. They was beautifully fair with him. They let him go on and still on until they knew – that's *knew* – no question no longer.'

He glanced about. No buyers waited, so he could still work on her uneasiness. 'I'm not saying names, not as definite – I never would. Christ, do I *know* you to start giving you names, except you're somebody who buys, with friends who also want to buy? But think of, say, someone – a true businessman like Percy Blay – if someone, say, like Percy suddenly gets to *know*, I mean *know* – if someone like Percy gets to *know* Tully's talking private concerns to, say, Harvey Moss – called, of course, Harvey Handler – talking private concerns on a real steady basis, to be passed upwards by officer Harvey – well, if this gets *known*, someone like Percy – but obviously I'm not saying Percy for definite, this is just a name I picked out – I'm saying *for instance* Percy – but someone in this ballpark – Percy or some other – someone like that is going to have thoughts about keeping his property and the acres – I mean, grave thoughts about them maybe getting taken away from him and his woman and kids – or women – if he's put away and can't earn at full rate for years – all right, maybe running a business by phone and so on from inside, but not at full rate, it can't be – no, he's sure to wonder like this, and so he might ask a couple of available folk such as Barry and Gordon Ralph Chamberlain to get the van out and go up to Knoll with a mouth like Tully.

Only a simple trade ploy, for God's sake. It's just something that happens – has *got* to happen – but is over so quickly. Neat. Final. Except for the trial, yes, because they was careless, but that court and trial wouldn't reach somebody like Percy Blay, would it? Be reasonable. And so, no need for anyone else to be uneasy.'

Sally touched the roll of money in her pocket. 'It's three hundred and eighty pounds. Twelve grams?'

'Twelve?'

'Bulk purchase, and the price is down anyway. A flood of Columbian.'

'This is good stuff. You'll never get stuff like this elsewhere. And then the motoring.'

'I'll be coming every week, maybe twice a week.'

'Ten. You won't get more than ten elsewhere, *if* elsewhere's even got ten with him.'

Sally said: 'As a matter of fact, I think he—'

'And now, you see, it's all quiet again here, I mean in general, since Knoll. Things had to be put right, that's all. Now, today, tonight and tomorrow, and every tomorrow, there's no requirement to be uneasy, because that voice, Tully's voice, can't do unkind whispers no more. Serene. I get to church quite a bit. That's what I mean, things are settled and there's time for worship. This was a voice that *had* to be cut out of Tully, such as how a barber will cut nose hairs if they get too much – a man's barber, anyway, not Vidal Sassoon in a fucking *salon* full of fucking *stylists*, who'd be too *arty* for nostrils, I suppose. Sad for Pam and the kid – they got a kid – but that's how it's going to be sometimes.

'I can tell you, many conversations followed the death, but nearly everyone in this career said, regrettably Tully had to go, in that kind of unforgettable way. It had to be unforgettable, didn't it, because as long as it was unforgettable others would not forget it, meaning they'd never try the same talking aspect themselves? People get tempted to talk. It's not just the fees from detectives, it's power. Grasses get power – you can see that, can't you? And they like it. They can put people away the way a judge can. They can fuck up their

55

enemies by just a word or two in the right earhole. So when someone's trying to persuade them not to do it, not to get tempted, the message has got to be quite strong, such as Tully on the tip in that condition. Is it really three eighty? That will get you and your friends some really nice partying and socializing, and no need to be uneasy, of course not. And after a time, if you want to move on to H, like some of my, like, best quality clients now – many now, the new mode – I mean, select people in most probably custom-made shirts, like, e.g. chartered surveyors, lawyers, greengrocers of a wholesale calibre, utterly unstruck-off surgeons with no sign of the shakes yet – if you and your companions get the urge that way, this is all right, too.'

Now, several of those features which loyally stayed on with his face when most of it slipped down to his neck became useful and helped him give a really great peaceful smile. In any case, this smile was big enough to spread to the upper rolls of the neck area also, a jolly crinkling effect across the flesh. 'We call these times "post Tully",' he remarked. 'My grandad told me they used to say "post-war" in the last part of the 1940s, meaning things became good again and lightened up, eventually genuine meat in the pies. Like that with this "post Tully" era.'

'All right, ten,' she said. 'You talk good.'

'I'll need to get some from the car.'

'You're coming back?' The music began again.

'Wait. And then you got to go. You're stopping other clients.'

She waited. When he returned, he passed her two cigarette packets. She opened and counted two lots of five miniature envelopes. 'I was wondering how they knew.'

'Who?'

'Someone like, say, Bligh.'

'Blay. Bligh's the movie – the mutiny and bare-boob girls one.'

'How would he *know*?' she asked.

'What?'

'Tully had been talking certain matters.'

'Why?' It was back to shouting over the sound system.

56

'Why what?' she replied.

'What you asking for?'

'Still needing to know what sort of situation here,' Sally said. 'Someone like that, like Blay – if someone like that, in a big way, can just give the orders on somebody, this is a rough scene. There might be no real *cause*, just he felt like it. If he gets some idea about someone, anyone could be pulled into it. Acting like a shah or something, because of the croquet lawn and all that.'

'I told you, he *knew*. This would be only commercial practice. This would be proper justice, didn't I say?'

'But how do you know what he knew? You close to him?'

'Who?'

'Blay. Or Tully. I'm uneasy about that. If you could get pulled into something, the people you sell to could get pulled in. How it happens.'

'God, we've settled all that, haven't we?' he said. 'It's peace now, didn't I tell you? Someone like Blay – I mean, if it *was* Blay, and I'm not saying that for definite, I'm not – but someone like Blay gets information from everywhere. I mean *everywhere*. You understand me?'

'From the people Tully talked to?'

'From everywhere,' he said.

'Which everywhere?'

'Everywhere. Information's a commodity and of value, just like the stuff itself. It makes the stuff possible. Someone like Blay – I mean, if it *was* Blay, and I'm only giving you an example, aren't I? – someone like Blay gets top information. Has to.'

'How do you mean, top?' Sally asked.

'Top.'

'Top of where?'

'Top,' he replied.

'You mean, Blay got information about Tully *from* the top? They didn't want Tully any more?'

'Who?'

'The people he used to talk to in private. Top people,' she replied.

'But that's all gone now. We're all right, aren't we? You'll be all right. Your friends will be all right – the weekend parties, sharpening up on great stuff, believe me.'

Sally wanted to ask him more questions – about Tully and Pamela and what police victories, if any, came through the grassed information, but he lifted a hand to show it was over – *over*. The din made things too difficult, and she might be preventing other sales, though none would be on this scale. She took the three eighty in a roll from her pocket and turned her back on the dance-floor crowd to hide the moment when she gave it. 'I'm not even going to count this,' he said. 'I get the feeling you're someone who thinks long-term. You want to come back, so this is going to be right.'

'I keep wondering about Pam,' Sally replied, but he raised a hand again.

Five

Detective Sergeant Harvey Moss could, in fact, have gone into journalism or possibly even become an academic, but he chose the police. Wise? Christ, wise? There'd been an actual job waiting for him on a Coventry paper, with the good possibility of an internal move to London after a year. Or, he might have thought about a postgraduate degree in literature and a likely university post. An invitation to do research came, and the chance of a British Academy handout for fees and maintenance. Instead, he'd taken the graduate training scheme offering quick promotion in the police, and now here he was, on his way to . . . to where? Things grew bloody dark.

He decided he'd better make a few friendly telephone calls soon. Thank God he thought he knew where to ring. He must get some self-protection. No more than basic good sense, surely. No more than professionalism, surely. This couple of pushy, nosing inquiry women would obviously want to meet Justin Tully's former handler, and early in their trouble-making. Moss could certainly see why they had to be pushy and nosy. How else to do their job here – police on police, police giving police the treatment police usually kept for others. All right. Of course, of course, he accepted the necessity for this sometimes, and it might be better to have police digging than non-police. They'd know the difficulties of the game and be understanding. Would they? In fact, didn't the media beef that police scrutinizing police could be *too* understanding? If he'd picked journalism, he might have been writing leading articles along those lines now!

He wouldn't start the phoning yet. First, he needed to see these two working, see them direct and *in situ*. Moss had that kind of mind – happier with the actual, the concrete. This might be what had directed him away from the word-on-word of journalism, and from the high-grade talking to oneself of humanities scholarship. He'd thought he'd do a little private surveillance, confer some exclusive eye time. It could only be now and then. Moss had his own ordinary duties to deal with, and there were plenty. Occasionally, though, he would secretly follow one or both of them – at least, he *hoped* secretly.

Jesus, he found tailing hard. Naturally, he'd done the course, learned the techniques. He disliked blotting himself out, though, and bringing himself down to a nothing. The good gumshoe turned into anon. It didn't suit him to become the invisible man. He wanted to hang on to selfhood. Arrogance? Egomania? He did wonder. His university area would have been Romanticism – all that obsession with the capital I. Moss longed to be a presence and lately had felt once or twice he might be on the way. But to be regarded as someone, you at least needed people to know you were there.

All the same, unobserved he had managed to track Sally Bithron one grand summer day and, from a distance, watched her walk up the slope to around where Tully had lain, unre-constructable, in Knoll's last unreconstructed days as a tip. Moss stayed well back, because on open ground an observer stood out, especially a bad one who loathed being unnoticed. Although imported bushes gave occasional cover, she'd been trained in alertness and would watch them. Even spying from far away, though, Moss felt gripped, mesmerized, by her behaviour. It was sensational. She did more than just the routine location research, normal for an inquiry team. It seemed to him she played out for herself the rough events of the murder night, like a fully scripted piece of drama, taking all parts. God, he'd been blaming himself for too much ego. Perhaps this one didn't do too badly, either. He'diagnosed something rapt, trance-like, in the way she covered the ground and gazed around.

Moss loved the mad posturing and unnaturalness of profes-sional theatre, and went to all sorts – Jonson, Pinter,

Ayckbourn, Shakespeare, pantomime, Edward Bond, Congreve. He thought Bithron on the ex-tip resembled that Lady Macbeth sleepwalking scene, her imagination really busy, eyes staring, but staring at something so private. Her haircut and old-style grunge clothes made Bithron seem quaint, other-worldly. Did she *see* Tully, Chamberlain, Jolliffe? Did she hear them, especially hear Tully? The distance was too great for him to know whether her lips moved as she got dialogue going between these figments.

Street theatre he'd witnessed once or twice – but now, waste-dump theatre. Moss found it eerie, thrilling, uncoplike. They'd sent a dreamer like this to unpick his career and life? He felt flattered, enthralled. They must think he deserved more than a standard, plod investigation. They'd been warned he was formidable, a presence. *This Harvey the Handler, no pushover.* There would have to be plenty of imagination to complete the Knoll picture, even if Bithron had read the court transcripts. Oh, no question, she'd have read the transcripts.

He watched her lie on the grass briefly, at what would have been the tip top, where Tully died, ultimately. People around must think she fancied a sunbathe, or had passed out after plenty of something good. Neither. He knew she yearned for a kind of contact with Tully. This spot of ground could be the means, even though it had been transformed: still a slope but a smoothed-over, turfed-over slope, not jagged and eloquent with junk. Moss sensed she'd try to intuit herself into Tully's head on that night, imagine his words, collect his revelations. Crazy? Would-be ectoplasm? Yet Moss was troubled as well as excited. Would she manage somehow to invade such private territory?

He himself had grown close to Tully, in the way detectives sometimes did get close to grasses. Outside a love affair, you would find no more profound, core-to-core human relationship. Officer and informant became blood relations. That is, the grass's blood if secrecy failed, or was made to fail because the grass had somehow grown superfluous or a liability. Especially a liability. It could happen in so many ways. Always grasses strove for the safe point between having information and having *too much* information – like hitting a diabetic's drugs balance. Some art, grassing.

Yes, but a frail art. And so, Justin Tully dead and mutilated on the tip. A trade term existed for attachments that could grow between detective and grass, a disapproving trade term – the Stockholm Syndrome. It meant unhealthy dependence on the informant, even too much affection for him/her. The condition could turn dangerous. And now, did Sally Bithron, this girl from another, distant realm, believe that in some occult, second-sight style she could commune with Tully, dead, and find how the grassing set-up with Sergeant Harvey Moss worked, how it ended? This girl had a belief in herself or was half cracked, or both. He'd heard she would soon go on to the accelerated promotion course, the one he'd done himself more or less straight after university. She'd get there from the ranks, though. She must be gifted, and not just in the occult. Course instructors would like her. The mind that could ramble, soar, get outside itself, and more especially get outside traditional police thinking, was in fashion. Moss did all right on the course, but he had an idea they thought him a bit earthbound and banal for someone who knew Keats. *Get up there with the fucking Nightingale, Moss. Let's have some overview.*

As far as he could gather, both these visiting women had their unusual aspects. He felt himself entitled to a little harmless guidance from those who knew them, a few special briefings, as deep as he could collect. If this team meant to bite into his privacy, he could reasonably bite into theirs, couldn't he? Wouldn't he look a patsy otherwise? And so, yes, Moss would make several friendly calls: home-to-home, of course, no ear-flapping switchboards. What he had in mind went something like – *Harvey Moss here. That's it – DS. We met. I gave you a bit of line-out elbow in the inter-force rugby final. And you . . . well, we won't talk about that. But I think I'm still fertile! Look, Mike, I've got a bit of special curiosity re a couple of ladies from your patch. They're going to impinge somewhat here. I wondered if you—'*

Moss worried these two invaders might not know, or

sympathize with, the many rough, sacred and unholy complications of running a grass. Alternatively, for the sake of their cleansing role, they might *pretend* not to know or sympathize with the many, rough, sacred and unholy complications of running a grass. No question, they'd think Detective Sergeant Harvey Moss crucial to their investigations. All right, he *was* crucial, up-to-his-fucking-eyebrows crucial. He rated. He was substantial. He might not be much older than Bithron, but he had learned a lot very fast and had piled up experience very fast. It had seemed crucial to him to move out of literature's realms of gold and fully into the complexities of his job – sometimes harsh complexities. And so, Moss would do what any detective would if awkward interviews looked likely, he'd dragnet for profiles of the interviewers, find their form, chart their faults, look for something that might shake them a bit if they ultimately had to be shaken a bit to get them off his back. Not malice. Not even crude selfishness. No, no more than basic sense.

For now, he did a bit more tailing and got behind Esther Davidson and Bithron when they went out to Milton Avenue for a visit to Tully's partner, Pamela Grange, but learned nothing from this, except that they went. For fuck's sake, obviously they went. She could tell them all sorts, if she wanted to. She might be as vital as Moss, nearly. Possibly, Pam had pillow talk. Moss didn't. He stayed in his car for half an hour, uselessly watching the house, then withdrew.

He thought the kind of precautions he planned to take against Davidson and Bithron could well be seen as concern for the public – or did he kid himself? If the two visitors were allowed to work uncurbed, they might do castration damage on good policing here – while, of course, pretending they did it in the cause of good policing. Moss, although not especially cynical, had read some Machiavelli – that fifteenth-century philosopher with ruthless theories on how to hold power. All organizations needed their central hypocrisies, but no organization could admit it, and especially not one meant to safeguard righteousness, like the police. And so, when police behaviour in a case looked possibly imperfect, missionaries like Davidson and Bithron arrived to apply good dabs of purity, if they could. The high-pitched publicity that accompanied them comforted the country, and might even placate the country's media. But missionaries like Davidson and Bithron could turn out destructive by disturbing too much.

During the next week, he followed Bithron on her own twice to the Inclination club – less tricky jaunts than Knoll, because of street darkness for the approach, then crowd cover inside. She was young enough to look all right in Inclination, and so might he be, just about. In fact, her hairstyle and clothes probably took a couple more years off. Again he felt baffled. *She* would help Davidson pronounce on how he worked? Did Sally Bithron have the career nous? Staring at her, so kid-like beneath the laser lights, and so seemingly relaxed, he wondered, as he'd already wondered, if she realized at all – yes, at all – realized what running a grass like Tully in drugs country involved. Did she understand from *doing* it, or at least from knowing someone who'd done it – not via the wishful, sweet, Dumbo pieties of a manual or training course? Had she ever come across figures like Percy Blay? Had she ever come across people like a few of Moss's superiors at headquarters, with their intimate, indomitable special projects?

He had to guard himself against the possible clumsiness and cleansing zeal of these two investigators. Know thine enemy, then. The telephone calls should help. In Moss's three years as a detective, he'd learned above all about dossiers, records, past profiles – learned how much they mattered. You did not confine yourself to the here and now of a case. Get all-round and in-depth. Look at histories. Moss sometimes glimpsed the robotic, even stupid and potentially unjust factor in the drill, but habit had him and he went along. Habit had him because very often the routine did work. Paedophile offences? You'd soon know from dossiers the half dozen front doors you should beat on for likelies. Or, say you had to deal with a drugs gang shooting. A coded sign on dossiers covering that type of death showed whether you should immediately refer things higher, not poke about with inquiries yourself. Too much information could be . . . too much. Files might not add up to everything, but now and then they spoke a fine and damning tale – or told you to get lost fast and leave this tale alone. That might have its sinister implications, but sinister aspects to detection did exist. Grey, grey areas.

At the Inclination, hiding himself as well as he could behind other customers, he watched Sally talk with Peaceable Bernard Aix each time Moss was present, and almost certainly buy from him. *Get to be a customer, get entitled to some conversation.* The purchase might be heavy. At the most recent meeting between her and Aix, he had to go out to his car for what looked like extra supplies. *To court a trader, trade with him big.* Moss himself would be recognizable at the Inclination, of course, and could not risk approaching Aix when she'd gone, to ask what happened between him and her. Anyone Moss spoke to at length would be listed for attention and might be found soon afterwards like Tully, give or take a rubbish dump.

He would construct files, dossiers, for himself on Esther Davidson and Sally Bithron – unearth background, get home-ground sightings. During training courses and rugby games, he'd met people from their patch and other patches. He'd remained in touch with some, had a contacts book. In day-to-day policing, it was handy. You asked these acquaintances for information, and, of course, you gave some. Villains moved about, and this offered one way to keep track. Detection could be very word-in-your-ear. He'd make the calls soon.

People at the Inclination did not know Sally Bithron, and so she could chat away amiably to Aix, no rush. Would she have the judgement to know what to make of what he told her, supposing he told her *any*thing. Possibly she'd heard of those grey areas in policing – work spheres where right and wrong, law and criminality, means and ends, might overlap and seem to merge. But did this infant appreciate how disconcertingly grey, and darker than grey, grey areas could turn out? Did she know that once you slipped into a grey area, really into it, you might no longer have the power or skill to get clear? Did she realize that some brilliant, invaluable veteran detectives believed true policing had not begun until the grey areas went greyer and darker? The rest they regarded as on a par with helping old ladies cross the road, and netting stray dogs. Moss had made sure he talked to and listened to these old hands. He must ditch naïveté; essential if you longed to be a presence.

Moss took a look at Peaceable Bernard Aix's dossier and decided on a home visit early Sunday morning – wiser and safer than speaking to him at the Inclination. A *little* wiser, a *little* safer, and the best Harvey could manage. The profile mentioned regular church-going with his family, so Aix should be around, getting into a worship suit and locating his soul. Aix wasn't too bad a lad. Moss wished he could give him a comfortable, easy session in his own property and on the day of worship, but that would be difficult – *difficult*.

As he drove to Aix's place, Moss put his mind on to Bithron's boss, ACC Davidson. Of course, with her extra experience, Esther Davidson might appreciate all there was to appreciate about grey areas. But she held big rank, and, at present, had one big, exactly defined, promotion-potential job – to spruce up this patch. At such a rank and on such a job, she would begin from the basic proposition that policing could never, should never, tolerate grey areas. Or this would be her stated, official start point. All right, she, of course, knew they *were* tolerated and would be tolerated eternally, because without grey areas detection didn't start. Most probably she'd taken part herself in some grey area activity within the last year . . . or the last month . . . or on the day before she arrived for the inquiry? How else did you get to be and stay an ACC (Operations)? Not by helping old ladies cross the road or netting stray dogs.

But Davidson's stipulated role now, here, and on the tricky route to possible full chiefdom, must be to shine a hard and unwavering light on the Tully case. She'd aim to dispel all remaining shadows around his execution, and particularly in-house shadows. She might feel Moss lived among these shadows. She would *know* he did – a presence, but a presence in calculated obscurity. And she'd pretend to the Home Office, the *Guardian,* Old Labour flotsam, the Police

Complaints Authority, the civil liberties people, that, because of her unflinching brilliance, all detective work everywhere in future would become totally and eternally transparent, with no more shadows, and no more blown informants tortured to death on tips. Boom-boom.

And, OK, perhaps none *would* get tortured to death – on tips. Knoll might be a Tully special. But the rest of her glittering objective was questionable, of course, and, of course, she'd know it – know it in that very second-string, suppressed part of her head which dealt with the real and actual, not with show and semblance and official investigation OK-ness. As an official she would act officially. Her publishable report had to be fit for the archives in bound form, gold letters on the spine. Rites of purification must get kowtowed to, Whitehall, Parliament and Press given their sops. This also was what being an assistant chief meant. Boom-boom.

In the famous legend, Hercules had to muck out mountainously filthy stables never before cleaned. Well, good boy, Herc. Esther Davidson needed to do better here. First, yes, she must assure the populace, and the populace's leaders and media, that she'd given the scene an epic rinse. And after this she must claim that, although, in the nature of things, just as many arseholes existed as ever, things would remain now perpetually sweet, because she'd banned further fouling.

Aix invited him into his house. Moss said: 'Peaceable, although many would admire you for the risks you accept as part of your career, others might regard you as an outright fucking imbecile.'

'Look, Mr Moss, grand to see you, and I know Avril will be happy to meet you again, too, but she and the little ones are all ready for us to get along to St Mark's and they'll be coming into this room soon to see if I'm—'

'When I say risks, I mean the word entirely in a positive light, meaning you're not obsessed by dull, footling safety concerns, like somebody's fussy mother. There's a largeness to you, Peaceable. A largeness of spirit, that is. Audacity. I know some would call it rashness, but we'll leave them to their damn nerves, shall we?'

'As a matter of fact, it's quite a few years now since I

came to relish church attendance,' Aix said. 'The orderliness of the service, the calm. This is something I find I need. Those qualities – not always available elsewhere in life, I think you'll agree. In this day and age.'

'A policy of selling to more or less anyone. No fear-based, miserably cautious checks on new clients. That what you call them, Peaceable – clients, these apprentice junkies?'

'This is an orderliness that has been inherited by vicar after vicar through history,' Aix replied. 'Also bishops and so on. Termed the apostolic succession. You can feel it. Centuries. Like it puts you in touch with a tradition, plus, obviously, the dogma aspect, clearly based on many a piece of handed-down holy vellum.'

'Faith in humankind. That's what your drugs-selling policy shows.'

'Faith – oh, yes, I do believe in that.'

'Faith that someone who comes to buy from you at the club – a girl, say – faith that this scruffy-looking girl is what she seems to be and that's all,' Moss said. 'This is what I meant by spiritual largeness bordering on fucking self-destruct mania, Peaceable. The ability, wish, to take on trust, when trust is what you should be exceptionally mean with, given your game.'

'All right, some vicars look half-baked and slimy, but this is what they've *all* got, Mr Moss – faith. I'm so happy you mentioned it. This shows we're on a similar wavelength, you and I. Think of a padre in the battlefield, grenades every-where. *He* hasn't got grenades to throw back. He's what's known as non-combatant. So, what *has* he got? Faith. This is his, as it were, weapon. A collar back to front – what does it mean? We could look at it and say it's just a collar back to front, a bit of silliness, display. But that collar back to front *indicates* something. It indicates faith. What you could call a symbol. The collar itself is not important. Convenient, that's all. Obviously, the disciples probably didn't have *their* collars back to front – or any collars, being in bournouses – but this did not prevent them having faith. Only later, some archbishop, or like that, suddenly thought of the dog collar. This must have been a great moment. Such a moment is known in the Church as an epiphany. Like a glimpse of something vital yet simple.' Peaceable seemed suddenly in touch with jokes: 'For instance, they couldn't have a waistcoat back to front because of the buttons. Or shoes.'

'On the other hand, selling the way you do, Peaceable – the openness, the grand casualness – it can bring a problem or two, can't it? This has to be admitted.'

'Far be it from me, Mr Moss, to force religion on people, but, I mean, taking your own case – a young man with many a stress to handle in the CID, perhaps sometimes you also yearn for them quiet, soothing moments everyone needs. They can be found in church, Mr Moss, believe me. Stained-glass. I feel we all – all humanity, all colours, nations – we all got this urge to commune at times with one greater than ourselves. This, in fact, could be what makes mankind mankind, using that to take in women as well, inevitably. I don't see no evidence animals or sea creatures male or female have this awareness of an infinitely mighty outside force. A dog knows its master, yes, and might know its master is not a dog and is probably much taller and so on. But this is not the same as recognition of a creator, in my view – that outside force. Goldfish are fine and deserve to be looked after well, yet their minds are probably not on much beyond their bowl or pool. You, Mr Moss, you – I'm certain – would have such a sense of an all-powerful, controlling entity, such an outside force. Church would help you find that.'

'Girl about twenty-five, looking younger. Dirty old denim jacket, workman-style black boots, beige lace in one, string in the other, cash loaded. Unflagrant tits. Hair fair to mousy, cut by a certified madman in a three-minute remission spell of half clarity. Round face, nearly pretty. Decent arse. Turns it towards the crowd when paying you, not to invite or boast, but for discretion.'

'The church offers no cheap, flashy attempt to attract folk. Yet . . . original flagstones in the aisles, dark, shiny and at the same time soothing. They are blessed by centuries of reverent feet.'

'She's a cop lady,' Moss replied.

'You fucking what? I don't fucking believe it, Moss.'

'Of course you don't fucking believe it, Peaceable. If you believed it, you'd see what a prick of pricks you've been. It would wipe out the bit of ego and self-esteem you've hung on to, your trade and features regardless.'

'I know every fucking cop, men and women, in this domain, Moss. That's only basic professionalism.'

'Visitor.'

'Albert's never going to put a fucking stranger on a job like that.'

'Like what?'

'Like a fucking sting. Buying to trap me as a dealer.' Aix's voice almost left him. His grammar went shakier than during the church discussion. He tried no jokes. 'Christ, Albert Chave haven't been fucking moved or anything, have he? I mean, like exposed. This is tragic. He been got? You here as aftermath?'

'Albert's fine.'

'Yes, but fine how?'

' "How?" How do you mean?' Moss asked. 'Fine the way Albert's always fine. British fine. Part of a succession of fineness – perhaps not apostolic, but chief-inspectorly.'

'There been some change of fucking policy, Moss?'

'How do you mean?'

'Not that fucking zero tolerance I heard of, in New York, is it? Hit everyone for everything, agreements or not. The Inclination, by the fire doors – it's supposed to be all right, no interference. Like sanctified. You know this. They wouldn't send an outside girl to fuck up that. Not unless there's been a policy change, like I said. Some new broom with silver leaf on his cap. If there's been a policy change, I never been told or consulted. Albert been shanghaied to traffic? Anti-terrorism? That's all the fucking fashion suddenly. I got to be told matters like that. Look, I'm not told . . . if I don't get told, well, there's repercussions. I got a lot of dodgy knowledge about a lot of people, Mr fucking Moss.'

'I don't think she was sent. She just came. This is a roving girl. She follows her whims.'

'Her what?'

70

'Whims.'

'A kid does her own snaring? I don't fucking believe it, Moss. And where the money come from? This a kid with three eighty to play bait with? Am I supposed to fucking believe that? And coming back with more.' His voice was still poor but recovering.

'I *know* you've got a lot of dodgy knowledge about a lot of people. That's what she's looking for.'

'What?'

'What did you give her?'

'What commodity?'

'No, fuck commodity. What knowledge?' Moss replied.

'This was three eighty. Tens, twenties.'

'Looseners.'

'So how do you know about it, me seeing her? She told you? You in on it? Or I been grassed?'

'I watched.'

'You was there but she didn't know? One cop dogging another cop? I didn't see you.'

'The crowd hid me. Obviously, I stayed far back. Or not obviously. I need to see what she's doing.'

'Why?'

'I need to know what knowledge she made you leak.'

'Why?'

'Percy Blay, for instance. Did you talk about Percy Blay?'

Aix tried a small whistle, but mostly saliva and gasp. 'What – she's on that mission here to look at all you police boys and girls in the Tully case? I heard of that. That's *really* aftermath. No wonder you're fucking jumpy.'

'Percy's going to be pissed if you're talking about him to an officer.'

'This was in the papers. Outside force to investigate and report.'

'That's it. Outside force. Like God. *Just* like him. "Vengeance is mine, I will repay." Did she talk about Tully? Ask about Tully?'

'Nothing.'

'But you *did* talk a lot. Too tied up to look around and spot me.'

71

'Nothing. Just a matter of friends she wanted stuff for.'

'She asked about Tully quite a bit, did she? Kept on?'

'Nothing,' Aix replied.

'What angle?'

'What?'

'What angle on Tully interested her?'

'You're scared, are you? Of course. You, Tully, close.'

'What angle?'

'Her friends, weekending on something good, and with jobs, so payers,' Aix said.

'And then I suppose she asks who's behind it – I mean, who's behind Chamberlain and Barry Jolliffe. That the way it went? She says she needs to know, for ease of mind? Something like that? You gave her Percy's name? Christ, Peaceable.'

'You're *real* jumpy, are you?' Aix replied. 'Like I mentioned previous, you got stress. You ought to get to fucking church now and then, Moss. Experience a nave. Put something decent but not gross in the plate. It makes you feel better, like you're preserving the good, even if life all round is fucking pus.'

'I'm not going to speak to Blay, you don't have to fret on that. I'm not even going to speak to Albert. Definitely not. It's my own little saunter. At this stage. At this stage. You were obediently within your fire-door parameters, no disputing it. Sort of licence. She'd edge up to you, I guess, and say she wanted stuff but she heard things could be dicey here, not just police dicey, but dicey on a tip. So, she's offering a deal without saying she's offering a deal. The deal is, you talk to her about Tully and Chamberlain and Barry and Percy Blay, and she'll do a nice, heavy, regular purchase and not look for the commodity from anyone else. You'd have exclusive rights. My name come up?'

'The hymns, also, these can bring a balm, you know, Mr Moss,' Aix replied. ' "Hills of the north, rejoice!" – you ever sung that one? Tip top.' He hummed pretty well for a while. This did seem a bracing number. A weighty-faced man with good, jolly tunes was always going to seem cheery. 'Such hymns give you an idea of the scope of the world, and your own worries seem smaller because of scale. "Isles of the southern seas, deep in your coral caves, pent be each warring breeze" – that comes into one of the verses. This is what I mean by scope and scale. North. South. Then, "Lulled be your restless waves." So, we have a lovely tranquillity, even in the ever-moving ocean. Can't we learn from this, Mr Moss? These restless waves are a picture of our lives.'

'What they want to know, this visitor and her boss, is why Tully one day is all right, and obviously looked after – brilliantly looked after – and the next he's wrecked, on what you'd call a tip top. She'd probably think you could help her with that. Well, you probably *could* help her with that. As you say, dodgy knowledge. If you talked about Blay or all sorts of other names, this could give her a direction. That kind of thing at all, Peaceable? You offered names?'

'Some don't mind kneeling, and there are little cushions to help,' Aix answered. 'Truly fat cushions, perhaps stuffed by members of a holy order, if you'll pardon the phrase. Some knees need that – the fatness. You wouldn't get cushions in what are known as non-conformist churches, although it's not only for the cushions we go to St Mark's. Others just stay sitting when they pray. There's no rules about it. Many of the old could not kneel even with the fattest cushion, because of their bones at that age, and if they went down they'd never get back. You'd have, like, a scene there, people pleading to be helped, groaning and so on. Poor image for a church. This is not like one of them churches where they do healing, or they're *supposed* to do healing, and telling people that even if they get down on the cushion they'll be able to get back up on their own, because the minister will ask God to give them the outside force to perk up knees. This is an *ordinary* church, referred to as the Church of England because of the geography aspect, where the vicar probably been to Oxford University at least, with tutors and fives courts, and he realizes about older bones. He would never get people going on to a cushion if they did not want to. You're younger, Mr Moss, but if you'd like to stay sitting for the prayers, fine.'

Moss could put up with Aix's monologues on church

matters, but he needed to be sure Aix heard right and digested right what he'd just been told. Occasionally, with someone like Aix, the language had to become very straight, for clarity. Moss loathed having to threaten, but police work differed from checking metre in Keats's 'Hyperion'. Faced with Aix's evasive litany, it became necessary to do plainness. 'Listen, Peaceable, I don't want anything untoward happening to her via you or Percy or anyone else, just because I've told you she's an officer. That's not what this is about. I'm definitely not inviting that. You understand? Not some ploy. You can't clip *her.* They'd go fucking mad. They'd have to. All right, she looks like form five at the comp, but this is a girl here for the Home Office. The government. They'd *have* to get who knocked her over. Nobody could hide. This would be like God in Sodom and Gomorrah. You can go on dealing with her. See what else she says. See what else she asks. I'll visit again to discover what's come up between you. I'll enjoy a Sunday trip.'

'And then what you could call the social fabric side,' Aix replied. 'This is the thing about the Church of England. It's not just a religious matter, it's sort of so beautifully built in through history with the ordinary life of the—'

'Lead her on sweetly. Get what you can, yes? I'd be grateful for that, Peaceable. Listen, you let me down on this, and things at the Inclination could turn negative. It's only grace and favour what you've got there. It can be taken away.'

'Piss me about there, Moss, and you get pissed on yourself, count on it, you fucking two-timer,' Aix replied, discarding church topics again, as Moss had hoped he might. 'Knowledge, knowledge, knowledge. I'm full of it. Inclination fire door got what's known as "sanctioned outlet" status. This is time-established.'

All right, it's a rough life, getting rougher, and language sometimes had to suit. Moss said: 'I can't stand seeing someone with your sort of build – neck rolls, that kind of thing – I can't stand seeing someone like that knife-carved, Peaceable. Bulk has its own poignancy. And yet you got around, didn't you? An interlude some time with Pam Grange? You *and* Barry. Am I recalling right? Of course, it's possible it will never get out that you've been in thorough chats with an officer, but the way information can sort of somehow seep to people like Percy and his contacts – well, I'm sure you'll have heard of instances where—'

Aix's wife came into the room with a boy of about eight, a girl slightly younger, all dressed for church. Moss and Aix occupied Edwardian-style, high-backed armchairs in the Aix lounge, a large, square room, looking out through French windows on to the long, expertly ordered garden. It had a goldfish pool covered by netting to keep gulls and herons off, and a curved patio. Peaceable must have spent time watching the fish and trying to work out whether they wondered about God and large issues generally. He was the plumpish kind who would undoubtedly be upset if he saw a bird gulleting one of his personal fish, head first, that unthinking way they do, especially if his kiddies were with him when he saw it. All the lounge furniture looked Edwardian or Victorian and blended damn well. Rudyard Kipling would have felt all right here. Moss stood. Aix stood too. His wife was tall, heavily built, sharp-looking. 'I've been bringing some paperwork up to date and just popped in to see whether Bernard still attended St Mark's,' Moss said.

'Why is that in your paperwork?' Mrs Aix asked.

'But I've been detaining Bernard. Forgive me, Mrs Aix.'

'Yes, as a matter of fact, church matters, Avril,' Aix said.

'We aim for the rounded picture,' Moss said. 'One doesn't want a two-dimensional Bernard on file.'

'I think it's been an eye-opener for Mr Moss – my descriptions of the services etcetera,' Aix said. 'And hymns. I mentioned hymns. "Oh, safe to the rock that is higher than I." And others. Would we might see you at our services, Mr Moss. I'd really feel I'd achieved something if I could persuade you.'

'What's it all about, Moss?' Mrs Aix said.

'Well, I must let you get along now,' Moss said. 'Lovely to have met you again, and the children as well as Bernard, Mrs Aix.'

'What's it about? For God's sake, what?' Mrs Aix said.

'Family worship. That must be rare these days,' Moss replied. 'Rare, admirable.'

'You're not in the witness box now, you know, Moss. You could answer something straight,' Mrs Aix said.

Although it did pain Moss not to, he felt this was best.

'Harvey Moss. That's it – DS. We met. I gave you a bit of lineout elbow in the semi-final. Teeth OK? And you . . . well, we won't talk about that. But I think I'm still fertile. Look, Mike, I've—'

'Harvey? Of course I remember. Fast-tracker, right? Didn't you read us a poem of yours in the bar one night? "Up Tight?" No, more than one night. Encore. And encore. About cycle clips. Terrific.'

'You won't believe it, Mike, but I was trying *not* to be terrific. Understated? Banal even? The very ordinary given poetic treatment.'

'That right?'

'Terrific's been done. T. S. Eliot is terrific. "In my beginning is my end." Nobody knows what it means, so the kindly guess is it's terrific. I wanted to be *un*terrific.'

'Well, second thoughts, you may have hit it. This was so unterrific it sticks in the unterrific mind of someone like me – a mind so unterrific it can't get me on to fast track.'

'I had some favourable fluke. Look, Mike, I've got a bit of special curiosity to do with a couple of ladies from your patch. They're going to impinge—'

'Esther? She *does* impinge. That kind of girl. Yes, I heard she was up your way, Harv. She'll want to see you, will she? Well, of course. I read bits of the trial in the papers back then. You did a turn, didn't you? You were handling him – the dump deado, right?'

'Plus a DC – also due for fast-tracking. Bithron.'

'Sally.'

'She's doing some sniffing about,' Moss said.

'Well, yes, she would. Sniffing about is her thing.'

'So, I thought I'd give you a ring. Maybe get a pointer on what they're like – what they're like in general terms, you know? Just general terms, Mike. A context.'

'But you're in the clear, aren't you? I mean, nothing that—'

'You know how they can be on this kind of caper – doing the cleaner-than-clean. It's dangerous. All right, all right, they have to – that's the task. You won't hear me slag them off. Just to ready myself, that's all. Basic.'

'But you're spotless, aren't you? Nothing . . . well, dubious? I mean . . . I mean, if there was anything, it would have been jumped on at trial. They'd have thrown it out if you'd . . . If there was anything. You got convictions, didn't you?'

'Both went down,' Moss said.

'That's what I mean.'

'But now an inquiry.'

'It can happen.'

'Well, yes, it's happening,' Moss replied.

'She can be very fair.'

'Who?'

'Esther.'

'What's it mean?'

'What?'

'Fair.'

'That's what I hear. Fair. If you mention her name, people always say "fair" or "very fair", the way they might say "loud" or "pipe-smoker" about someone. Salient. The fairness in her attitude is salient.'

'You don't know her, not yourself?'

'Harvey, she's an ACC, a bit out of reach.'

' "Fair" meaning?'

'She'll listen. I don't say an open mind. Where d'you find something like that, except an operating theatre? This is a very senior officer, for God's sake. But, yes, she'll listen.'

'Does she know the variables?'

'Now, that's a new one on me, Harv.'

'Variables. Running a grass, there's going to be give and take, obviously. Things can't be crystal-pure. There are *variables*.'

'Oh, variables like that. We say accommodations. Plural.'

'Accommodations, yes. People have to be accommodated. Both sides. The grass has to be accommodated. *We* have to be accommodated. You can't just sound off a law and order fanfare and expect everyone to curtsey and bow. There have to be accommodations. There are *variables*. Is she one to understand that? How far can I talk to her as if talking to someone with . . . with, well, an awareness?'

'As I see it, Harv, every time a grass gets done like that, the fucking press hint he was fingered by us to please someone bigger. Someone crooked and bigger.'

'Me, I'd never be a party to—'

'Oh, I know that, Harv. You're a university type, aren't you? But the press, the media. They stir. Investigative and so on. Vigilance they call it, and their *duty*.'

'As long as she realizes – accommodations, variables.'

'What I really detest is when the papers say, without exactly saying it, that some grass had too much information on an officer, became a menace and so had to go. Smears.'

'But, broadening it, Mike, life outside the job . . .'

'Esther's?'

'And Bithron's. Not gossip. I don't mean intrusive, mucky gossip, obviously. But things that might show how they'd view a situation like this,' Moss replied. 'Their personalities. Indicators about personality. Touchstones? So I know how to face them.'

'There's some complications.'

'For whom?'

'Whom! There you are! I knew you were a college boy.'

'Complications for which?'

'Both.'

'Domestic?'

'Some complications.'

'Marital? That sort?' Moss asked. 'Not gossip but—'

'A tale around that both were *so* glad to get away for a while up to your realm.'

'Gay? Sort of elopement?'

'Just like . . . escape. Each.'

'From?'

'Complications.'

'Outside interests?'

'It's hard to get anything on someone like Davidson. This

is an ACC, for God's sake, as I said. Discretion she's bound to be *au* entirely *fait* with, now isn't she? She knows about covering tracks.'

'Married?'

'Pro musician. Bassoon. Artiste. They can be unpredictable.'

'Who?'

'Artistes.'

'But what – she's got something going outside?'

'Complications.'

'Messy stuff?' Moss asked.

'At the rumour level. Only. I wouldn't speak of it, except that you asked. You're not going to let it go further.'

'Thanks, Mike. Just for my personal knowledge. Putting them into a whole life picture. So, is this someone in the job?'

'Who?'

'If Esther's got someone on the side – someone in the job?'

'I thought this was the kind of mucky stuff you didn't want to know about.'

'Only if it has a bearing, obviously,' Moss replied. But, of course, Mike had it right. Once you began digging you dug on.

'This is an ACC, Harv. She'd be careful. This is someone who definitely knows about discretion.'

'Someone in the job?'

'Very much only rumour.'

'And there's something wrong with it?' Moss said.

'Wrong? Well, obviously, she's married, so—'

'No, I meant if she wants to get up here for a while – "get away", you called it. Something going wrong? Like trouble because of it? Possible break-up? Something like that?'

'I did say "get away" – that's the story – they both wanted to get away. Just a coincidence there's two, unless Esther heard about Sally having trouble and understood that kind of trouble, it being like her own, and picked her so *she* could have a break, too. They stick together.'

'Who?'

'Women. Women having that kind of trouble. Relationship trouble. They're tender with one another. Support. Mutual. Snuffling into each other's gin and tonic. But then you've got to ask yourself, what does it mean? *Can* they get away? All right, they put a couple of hundred miles between them and the complications. There's phones, though. There's the motorway.'

'And something similar for Bithron?'

'Off and on.'

'Also married?'

'Partnered. Non-live-in but fairly steady, I gather. Folk see her out clubbing alone, though. Pal Joey's.'

'Looking around?' Moss asked.

'So goes the tale.'

'Trouble there, too – with the partner?'

'I suppose they have a tension or two, yes, Harv.'

'Why she wants to get away?'

'Sally has run informants. We had bad trouble here with them, too. She'll know about grasses. The accommodations and variables. You'll be fine with Sally.'

So perhaps she'd understand grey areas, after all. 'How should I—?'

'Sally will respect your work,' Mike replied.

'How should I—?'

'Sally will respect your work – unless she and Esther have been told what to find. And, of course, they *have* been told what to find. Not find too much, of course – of course – but find *something*.'

'She looks driven, but also as if she's into . . . well, listen, Mike, into what could be, well, like . . . like fantasy. Like visualizing the past?'

'That's her. That's DC Sally. She's set for a big career. They've picked her out for zoom progress. Fantasy's known as lateral-thinking on the fast-track course.'

'I ran into it there.'

'I forgot. You're fast track, too. Are you in it? God, I feel left behind.'

'In what?' Harvey said.

'When she visualizes. Are you in the scene she gets?'

80

'This is the tip sequence, I think– the killing,' Moss said.

'Yes. Are you in it? I mean, are you in it *as she sees it*? Obviously, only as she sees it. Would I be talking on an open line about it if I meant otherwise, for God's sake, Harv?'

'So, is she the sort who *would* put me in a scene like that?'

'I hear that on fast track they're encouraged to let the imagination soar and roam. You'd know if that's right. She'd be brilliant at it. Free association. Get a bag of possibilities that way. Then test them out against fact. Just about the opposite of how most people see detection – working inwards slowly from clues, like Sherlock. What I understand, these stars – what Sally will be, and you are already, of course – the bright, bright, bright stars line up a range of feasibles and afterwards ask which clues fit. Liberate the brain. But the supposition is, these are very good brains to start with, or they wouldn't get picked for fast track. So, you and Sally, not me. When stupendous brains like this are liberated, they go straight to the answer by natural flair. Or that's the theory. Don't fret, Harv. If she imagines you on the tip in one of her dreamscapes, or makes you involved some other way in the death, this will be only one version among plenty. She'll have all kinds of theories. It will be revised in the light of likelihood. They just need a *portfolio* of possibilities. They feel ground down and confined without that, these detective stars. Well, listen to me telling you, a star yourself. But look at it this way, Harv – for fuck's sake, Harv, is she going to find pointers to confirm a handler had his own informant murdered?'

'Why else was she sent here? What's the inquiry *for*, Mike?'

'What are any of them for?'

'Never mind that. What's this one for?'

'Harvey Moss.'

'Harvey! Here's a voice from deepest history. At least three years.'

'Three years, two months,' Moss said. 'Not my choice. Thought I'd give a ring.'

'You've had some exposure. National press, indeed! That

tip killing and so on. A grass? I recall *Mail, Telegraph, Times, Sunday Times.* And that's only the ones I see. Wow. I've been boasting. I tell people I know you –bumped into you on a course.'

'A bit more than that,' Moss said.

'Well, yes.'

'A lot more.'

'But you know what that actress Margaret Leighton said,' she replied.

'Yes, you told me. All sorts use that quote, I expect.'

'"On tour it doesn't count." For us, on a course it doesn't count.'

'It counted for me.'

'Oh, it counted for me, too, Harvey. At the time. Don't make me sound just a casual bitch. But we had to go home, you to yours, me to mine. I felt it was best like that.'

'I didn't, don't. There's no mine to go home to now.'

'You had big things ahead. They must think a lot of you – handling such an important voice. Tully? That his name?'

'Look, Jane, this is still . . . this is still a going topic here.'

'Well, I heard, yes. Esther's up there, isn't she? And Sally Bithron. But safe, aren't you? It's grey-area stuff, obviously, but you're safe, surely. The trial went OK for you, yes? And the *Sunday Times* did their full investigative police-as-demons and you remained OK.'

'OK. But now an inquiry. These inquiries – if they can't find what they want, they make it up.'

'Grasses. Almost always trouble when there are grasses. You did beautifully in court, though, didn't you? Your stuff stood up absolutely. You'll be fine, surely? Some query on money? Suggestion of skimming? Well, *I* don't believe it. Not of Harvey Moss. Always, with grasses, these cash problems, and especially if things go sour. You had a controller, didn't you? Any handler has a controller. They're supposed to watch the finances. The controller all right?'

'Have you run a grass, Jane?'

'You want some unofficial stuff on Esther and Sally, do you? Why you ring after so long.'

'Just background. I've got to be able to look after myself.'

'Esther can behave half mad. Fuck and blind. It's an act, naturally. She'll fool about. She's watching.'

'I want to be helpful to the inquiry, Jane, obviously, but I've got to know how to keep things . . . yes, safe . . . your word – safe for myself. They could be in scapegoating mode. I've got to look after myself.'

'Sally, damn clever. Her love life is weird. There's some managerial figure called Pete. They live separately. She cruises some nights, as I've heard. There's like a . . . I don't know . . . what would you call it . . . like a mystical side to her. You won't hear that said about many cops, will you?'

'Mystical? I wondered about that,' Harvey said.

'You've seen it? She gets bored with the usual police ways and feels entitled not to be bored. So she'll . . . what? She'll turn . . . yes she'll turn a bit mystical, visionary. Apparently it's encouraged on fast-track courses, so she could be giving herself dry runs. And then Esther. She's got something going, so they all say. Married, but something going. Could be one of our lads. Consequently, a bit sensitive. Between her and him a great rank gap, perhaps. Possibly Esther's into S/M. Occasional wounds to nose, cheeks, forehead.'

'God – an ACC?'

'But Esther.'

' "Visit her face too roughly." '

'What's that?'

'Half a line from *Hamlet*. Who's the boyfriend?'

'Rumour only. I'm not doing a name, even for Harvey Moss.'

'How about you?'

'What?'

'Married? Anything like that?'

'Something like that,' she said. 'How about you?'

'I was waiting for you.'

'Oh, yeah?'

'Why not?' he said.

'I told you – at the time, I told you.'

'On tour, on courses.'

'Grand memories, though, Harvey. Fond. And so a real wish to help – short of getting into a name. Esther's husband

– Gerald. Musician. Nice but a temperament. Bow ties, including ochre. He could be trouble if there's trouble. Esther shows the stress sometimes. She and Sally both wanted the job up there with you – some space for a while.'

'Esther acts mad?'

'*Acts* mad. Her style.'

'And are you happy?' Moss said.

'If I was offering advice for coping with them, I'd say just answer straight, answer exactly as things are. Give them strict truth as you know it. That would be my first thought. But on reflection, this stinks. For Christ's sake, we're talking about police, and one an ACC going on chief, now there *are* lady chiefs. Is it so clever to be honest with someone like that? We all know what our leaders can make of strict truth. Still doing the poems? 'Up Tight'? Cycle clips? Thought-provoking, Harv.'

'No, I didn't want to be thought-provoking. Thought-provoking's been done. "Bird thou never wert" – Shelley about the skylark. *This* is thought-provoking. Not only is it not a bird when he hears it, it has never been a bird and nor has any other of the species. So, what are and were they? You can't bring that kind of high-powered conundrum out of cycle clips.'

'No, well, perhaps not exactly thought-provoking. But you get the *feel* of cycle clips in your poem. That's how it fixes itself on the memory.'

Six

Obviously, Moss had found a replacement grass since Justin Tully, and he telephoned late, one of those whisper and squeak calls on a boom-and-fade mobile that might mean something truly urgent, or might mean standard-issue panic. Moss had been into a fine, utterly blank, healing sleep, and it took him five seconds to realize who was talking, and then another five to feel civil.

'Can you get over here, Harv?'

'Now?'

'This is big.'

'After two a.m.?'

'Really big or would I . . . ?'

Moss waited. 'Would you what?'

'What?'

'Now and then you're inaudible.'

'Big.'

'Give me a hint,' Moss said.

'Could be a life. This . . . you . . . young.'

There were other words between that might have made sense of these three, but Moss didn't get them. He hung on to the last one. 'Young?'

'Yes. School.'

'Who? School? Do I hear you right? What school?'

'Yes, young, obviously. Harv, I don't want to . . . you'll understand, not on a cell phone.'

Moss was sleeping alone. It happened a lot. He stuck his legs out of the bed as a start in getting up. Fuck it, the call seemed more than panic. No pleas for help. And it had discretion: 'not on a cell phone'. Substance? Maybe. A maybe would do. Some grasses never came up with anything as good as a maybe. 'Are you safe?' he said. 'You yourself.'

'Best don't come into my street.'

It was always best Moss did not come into the street, and he never did. But he said, 'Right,' rather than, *Oh, thanks for the brilliant warning, Dick. I hadn't thought of that.* Great to see him careful, not a matter to be mocked. A comfort.

'Leisure centre car park.'

This time of night a vehicle there could be as plain a signal as parked outside Patterson's house. 'Right,' Moss said. 'Half an hour?'

'. . . excited, Harv. Really excited. I've got you something truly great . . . time.'

A weird mixture of the boyish and the parental coloured his voice now – parental bordering on the priestly. The whisper and squeak had been replaced. Typical. Moss had come across this sense of vocation in grasses before. Some spoke about their work like faith healers. A calling. A crusade. Of course, a few informants would be scared away from the job temporarily by Tully's long-drawn-out, ghastly death, some possibly for ever. Others saw a rosy employment chance. *The grass is dead, long live the grass, meaning yours truly.* Long live the grass, for a while, anyway. They'd heard of Tully's house, with its own pillars, in an authentically treed avenue, and about the cars and the sweetly dressed looker who lived with him and gave him a son. Some might guess these rewards came partly on account of secret conversations with a handler cop now and then, and these conversations could be seen as easier than banging your way into a security van, or even easier than arsonizing some club/casino whose owners had so childishly argued, and argued again, that they needed no protection, thanks very much. If the club needed no protection, how come it caught on fire when it didn't have any?

'Now you're definitely going to be there, Harv? When you said. I can't be hanging about on foot. They've got all-night security lights.'

Moss pushed back the bedclothes and stood. He wore silk pyjamas. His mother had often told him that to sleep in silk was not an extravagance but hygiene. He took notice of his mother's teaching on many topics, some to do with garments, some much wider. He would not say all mothers should be listened to, but his own mother had done a great deal of thinking, and tuned into many general knowledge programmes on radio and television. The properties of silk probably came up there. 'I'll be with you at two fifty.'

'Just sit still and be as vigilant as . . . and suddenly from nowhere . . . me, in your car.' Again the come-and-go voice resembled a kid's, and an oracle's. 'Don't be startled, Harv. Don't cry out with delighted amazement.'

'Right.' Dick Patterson adored the tatty arts of furtiveness. He took terrified pleasure from all grassing's hard, hit-or-miss disciplines. For him and many other grasses, they made the frame and basis of a faith. These thrills to the spirit were another factor that sucked grasses into the game and held them. Informants of Patterson's wholehearted, driven kind would regard Tully as someone who got slack about conceal-ment, or who failed on the perilous, wobbly balance between information and *too much* information. Admittedly, these added up to big errors, but errors Patterson and those like him believed could be skirted by noting how they arose, then applying their fresh, God-given talent.

Grasses sometimes came over as crawly and snivelling, but many had amazingly strong self-belief. That was part of what Moss meant by a calling, a vocation. *I grass therefore I am.* Destiny: compare Mozart, born into music, turning out operas as a child. Grasses knew that, although it took all sorts to make a world, it took their special sort to destroy by a nicely placed phrase or two the world of anyone they hated. Anyone they hated who could be parcelled and sold to the CID.

Moss got out of the pyjamas, leaving them, anyhow, where they fell. The floorboards had been varnished but looked grubby. Never mind. Although he respected his mother, he did not want to grow cowed by cleanliness and silk. Swiftly, he dressed in khaki chinos and a double-pocketed beige shirt. He thought these colours had class, relaxed class but still class, even after two a.m. This might be what a moneyed ex-company chairman who'd retired early to the Algarve would wear. Sunglasses and a bit of folding money for the bar and taxis would go in the pockets, easy to reach. Moss liked to give a confident image to grasses he ran. They had a right to expect that. Answering their needs could be complex. Because they had to trust you, you shouldn't seem too different from them. Because they had to reverence and fear you, you shouldn't seem too like them. Royalty encountered this problem, too.

He had a small, all-metal cosh with round head and a wrist strap, and put it into his trousers pocket before going out to the car. There was something crude about this weapon, about any weapon, and he knew his mother would hate to learn he carried it. She would ask whether this could conceivably be the proper outcome for his years studying great literature. He did respect many of her views and often consulted her, but she needn't hear of the life preserver. She would never really understand the situation. He hoped that, at two thirty a.m., his mother might be in bed and reasonably secure, wearing silk; whereas he had to turn out and see an informant in circumstances that could not be forecast. He drove towards the leisure centre pretty certain Dick Patterson would show. Dick considered himself a professional, a professional mouth. He and Pavarotti – both professional mouths, both singers.

As Patterson had promised, Moss didn't see or hear him approach until the rear door of the Peugeot gently opened and he moved in and lay out along the back seat. Moss kept facing forward. He felt glad for Patterson. If Dick showed such smart care at this admittedly basic level, it could mean he'd be prudent all round and might last. Informants craved the role, and, because they craved it, could more or less convince themselves they'd manage all right at the trade and stay intact by simple flair, just as somebody born to be a lion tamer *had* to be a lion tamer and remained sure right up until the teeth closed around him that he, personally, would never get his head bitten off. Adrenaline ran some folk. Natural informants didn't get pulled just by the earnings, though these could be all right, as Milton Avenue showed. For a few, it was not even *mainly* the earnings. They believed their contact with a detective and the whole grand law system carried status, but a hidden one, naturally. They had a secret power. They saw themselves as unofficial police. Naturally, Moss understood this ambition. Through clothes, footwear, overall appearance, and responsive behaviour, he tried to earn the regard grasses clearly felt for him and his occupation. He hated hanging about in salons, and so cut his own hair, but reckoned this was acceptable, once it began to get back into shape again after the first few days.

Patterson brought a slight smell of ganja and Imperial Leather toilet soap. Because Moss did not spot any approach until Dick reached his car, smell had to be uppermost. He always carried these odours with him. They were better than fear sweat. Moss could have identified Patterson from them. His breathing stayed virtually silent. He must have trained himself into good control, whatever his nerves and the effort in getting here. This lad wanted a future and would work for it. Moss found it comforting to believe – to *try* to believe – that intelligence and carefulness would look after Dick Patterson. Of course, if things went bad, nothing and nobody would look after him. But Moss wanted to believe in a definite, positive relationship between precautions and survival, although he knew that didn't always exist for grasses, or even often. You had to see *some* sort of sane, basic structure to life. Chaos, otherwise. And, remember this very unpleasant fact – Tully had never been less than thorough on precautions, whatever Patterson thought, and yet, just the same, the van came for him, to a spot where none of them should have been that day, and then drove him – this established, worthwhile resident of Milton Avenue – drove him to be rubbished on rubbish. Wasn't that chaos? Moss could feel confused sometimes.

'Telepathy, Dick,' Moss said.

'What?'

'Me and you.'

'How?' Patterson replied.

'I was in bed, of course, yet unable, indeed unwilling, to sleep, because some deep intimation told me you would call.' It became vital now and then to endorse a grass's belief that the link between him and Moss had its occult, magical factors.

This might help an informant who felt guilt about informing, and some could never fully shed that, despite the strange tug of vocation. For many, the guilt was a folk-feeling, pervasive, and went almost as deep as the urge to grass. They'd grown up with this potential guilt, and it had to be countered. Moss worked to confirm that the confidences between him and a paid mouth lay beyond ordinary control – had a kind of ordained, automatic element to them. He always let in some hefty vocab, such as 'indeed' and 'deep intimation', when he spoke of these lumpy topics. A lot of grasses expected big language. They felt it dignified the situation, like a judge's wig or priest's robes. Ransacking a cash van they wouldn't get any 'indeeds', nor during petrol attacks on a club. This way, grassing ceased to be despicable and took on quiet prestige.

'Something now, Dick? Tonight?'

'Not actually *now*.'

'Not actually now, but what?'

'To see the site now. I think that's wise, don't you?' The voice of a pastor again, patient, instructional, commanding.

The pride of informants in being crucial to a worthwhile officer helped them discount that raging, perilous contempt the crook world felt for traitors. Grasses naturally recognized some hate came as a condition of the career, the way it did for journalists or hospital managers. But just as there had always been takers for these jobs, so with grassing. Although occasionally an informant might have some sense of whistle-blowing public duty, in Moss's experience this was rare. Money and/or concealed glory and influence – these drew the dedicated whisperer. Such factors should not be despised. They were presumably what attracted people into espionage posts, too, and espionage could be an honourable, courageous, crucial game. George Smiley. Inevitably, the power applied by grasses would often be to injure an enemy by fingering him/her. An enemy or someone they envied. Generally the two overlapped.

'What kind of site are we talking about, Dick? We should be careful.'

'This is a school. It'll be empty. Didn't I mention a school?'

'How does a school come into it?' Moss asked.

'Into what, Harv?'

'Which school?'

'This is a school you'll want to get a really good look at, preparatory.'

'A preparatory school?'

'It *is* a preparatory school, as a matter of fact, Harv. Private and fee-paying. But I meant preparatory to action. That's what could be called a play on words, I think. Oh, yes.'

'What action?'

'Which is why I suggested now, although such an hour. Reconnaissance, you can't beat it, you know, Harv. That came in the trial, didn't it?'

'Reconnaissance by night?'

'Discreet. What does the head teacher make of two grown-up lads hanging about her school when the kids are there? She'd hit the anti-pederast button and your colleagues would come at a canter. We don't want them. Not at this stage.' Grasses believed in the holiness of one-to-one – informant to detective. *Just the two of us.* So, the Stockholm Syndrome took over occasionally.

'I don't expect you to bring money with you now for a fee,' Patterson said. 'You shouldn't feel bad about that, Harv, not at all. If I call you at two a.m., it's obvious you won't have access to the informant fund.' He giggled for a moment, the idea sounded so daft. 'I'm content to wait for settlement until the whole project is completed.'

'Right.'

'You'll think to yourself "Project! Settlement! Hark at him!"'

Yes. But at least Patterson could puncture himself now and then. 'Not a bit,' Moss replied. 'You're careful what you say, I know that.'

'But I think you'll come to regard it as a likely project when you glimpse the scale, Harv. What I meant when I said "big". Probably you thought this is me on a sales pitch, or an excuse for ringing so late and dragging you from your pit. No. Scope. Oh, certainly. Rely on me, do. This has range.' Moss started the engine. He wished he really believed that communion between detective and informant was fated and bound to be. Now and then he himself felt squashed by some of that famous, sticky guilt over such relationships. Obviously, they dragged the grass into appalling danger. Tully. Tully. Tully. Even if the grass survived, did his conduct degrade him? Did the relationship exploit a disgusting and pathetic frailty? At a film club showing, Moss had seen Victor McLaglen play that simple-minded, shame-filled stool pigeon in John Ford's famous 1935 movie, *The Informer.* Essay topic for Staff College candidates: *How would you counter the belief among some officers that grasses are shit and those who deal with them are shit and shittier?*

'Go right,' Patterson said.

His voice came from a slightly different spot and Moss suspected he was going to sit up. 'Stay down for a while yet, Dick. We still have to be careful.' He wanted to get that idea, that word, deep into Patterson so it became a part of him, at least until someone cut it out. Careful. Careful. Careful. Think Tully, Tully, Tully. Think enemy. Enemies.

After they had been driving a couple of minutes, Patterson said: 'All right now?'

It would never be totally all right. Cars were noticeable at this time of night. What else could it mean but grassing if someone who recognized Patterson and Moss spotted them – say, someone on their way home from a club, or a burglary? The Peugeot was unmarked, of course, but would be known. 'OK,' Moss replied. Sitting upright, Patterson could navigate. Moss drove out towards the eastern edge of the city. When not giving directions, Patterson wanted to talk. Grasses did. And they liked to ask questions. They had the rhythm and habit. It was how they collected information.

'These officers, Harv . . . ?'

'Which?'

'The ladies on a visit.'

'Oh, those.'

'They've got you worried?' Patterson said.

'Worried?'

'Left at the lights. I don't really understand what they're here for.'

'A formality.'

'Yes, but—'

'Home Office procedure. It has to be gone through, that's all,' Moss replied.

'They'll talk to you?'

'Most likely. A formality.'

'And to others?'

'Well, obviously,' Moss said.

'Talk to your bosses?'

'Most likely. It's a formality.'

'And outside?'

'Outside where?' Moss replied.

'Outside the force. I mean, that totter who found Tully. Stan Staple. They'll quiz him again? And Percy Blay? Or people like Peaceable Aix, with all the gossip through Inclination, and maybe close to Tully's girl for a while, even with a face like Peaceable's. I hear he's gone holy, off and on. And talk to Chamberlain and Jolliffe inside? And then Pam Grange herself?'

'No, this will be internal, to examine police conduct. Formality.' Moss kept it in mind that a grass was a grass. Despite all the sacred one-to-oneness of the informant-detective bond, these people had an eye eternally on the market and a mouth for the powerful – and perhaps especially for the *very* powerful. The chance to bring secrets to an assistant chief like Esther Davidson could seem exciting to Patterson. She owned true, stratospheric rank. Most likely he'd turn jealous if he heard Davidson's aide had found Peaceable at the club and got him talking. Of course, now Peaceable had discovered her identity, there'd be no more talking, but this might not matter to Patterson. He would still feel left behind, yearn to catch up. So, Moss had decided to edit. In grey area policing, full transparency could be a mistake. If Patterson had some extra secrets, or came by extra secrets in the future, Moss wanted them disclosed to him, not to Esther Davidson. Accordingly, he tried to convince Patterson that she would have no interest in his snippets.

'One thing I would never believe is you fingered Tully, Harv. Well, obviously. How could I work with you if I did?

I might be next, yes? Trust. Would it be possible for you – you, Harvey Moss – to betray a colleague?' He had that short laugh again, at the clear idiocy of the question. Moss did not mind 'colleague', and especially not if Patterson took some strength from it. Build these people. Plump up their egos. Save them from McLaglen collapse. Patterson said: 'Is that the sort of thing they'll try to do you for – for putting Tully on a plate? Second left.'

If they were making for a private school, Moss thought he knew now which one. 'Not a matter of doing me or doing anyone, Dick,' he said. 'This is just to draw an official line under it – close the books. A bit of bureaucracy.'

'It doesn't happen after every murder trial, though, does it?'

'Some.'

'Or what's a trial *for*?'

Moss could have done without the interrogation. But he stayed polite. 'Now and then some minor query afterwards. It does happen.'

'Like "justice has to be *seen* to be done"?'

'Right.'

'Twice? Say, to find how he came to be out on the beach that day, and how they knew it?'

'Some aspects still a little cloudy, yes,' Moss said.

'Too flash. Unquestionably too flash, Harv.'

'What?'

'Tully. Like, asking for it?' Patterson replied.

'He wasn't non-stop careful.'

'Myself, I'd always put most of it away – the money – towards a pension or health insurance, that kind of invisible asset. Invisible being the key term, you know. Invisible assets are the sort that are – well, invisible. They don't get people envious. People won't beat you up for your BUPA membership and, even if they do, well, you got BUPA to deal with the injuries.'

'You're careful, Dick. I know you're careful.'

'That knifing they gave him – it was to say, "So you think you can live in some fucking grand area through rat pay, do you?" I'm not arguing it served him right, Harvey. But understandable. Avoidable.'

'People can get slack. They think things have been all fine for so long they'll always be fine. They decide it's tedious to be careful. Understandable. But avoidable.'

'I'd never believe it was just that he'd become obsolete. That's another sick rumour around. You heard this one, Harv? But it's well known that when somebody who's helped the police, but can't help them any longer – well, it's known they get a new home and identity somewhere, so they can be safe. Don't tell me the police would hand a tout over to knives just to dodge a bit of expense. Relocation – this is a term you'll often come across in the press, and that's not to the crematorium. Supergrasses get relocation. It's only normal. Famous. Pull in here, Harv, will you?'

'Ah, Cheyne College.'

'You know it?'

'Heard of, naturally,' Moss replied.

'Day school shaping youngsters for those boarding academies like Harrow, Winchester, Eton, and less.'

Moss had been shuffling dossiers in his head since guessing it would be Cheyne. 'And I've often driven past,' he said, 'admired the architecture.' Someone eminent had a child here. That much he recalled, but couldn't get closer, so far. Perhaps several of the eminent. Jolliffe? Tully himself? Percy Blay? One of Blay's competitors in the trade – Luke Main, Steve Ivens? Peaceable?'

Cheyne was a fine spread of grey stone Victorian-style buildings surrounded by playing fields and clumps of woodland. You could set a child on the way to social acceptability here, even if you'd never bothered about social acceptability yourself. Of course, if you *had*, and had taken a respectable job, you probably wouldn't be able to afford Cheyne's fees for your kid. 'Who's here?' Moss asked. 'Tully's boy?'

'Good, Harv. Good. Good. Good radar.'

'Targeted?'

'Good, Harv.' Patterson came around from the back seat of the car and climbed in alongside Moss. Possibly all right. They had seen nobody and no vehicles for a while now. Almost three a.m.

'Who'll target him?' Moss asked.

'I wanted you to have a look at the terrain. OK, so you've driven past, but you wouldn't have noticed the layout, not in detail. Why should you? The layout might get to be important, though.'

'Tully's boy will be snatched?'

'People heard about big earnings in that trial, Harv, didn't they? Tully wasn't just drawing money from you and yours for insights. He had a lovely, protected business. *Very* protected, yes? There's the house, the cars. And what else is she sitting on? Maybe the law let you look at Justin's bank statements etcetera, but you wouldn't be able to see hers. The kid's still at this pricey school. Pam dresses catwalk. I don't hear she's been down to uncle hocking the rocks. Noticed the rocks? She's not shy with them. Stupid, you say? Diamonds, emerald, amethyst. Yes, Tully had a foul death, but it might not be adequate. You can see there'd be bad anger and envy if she's hung on to the profits, and who says she hasn't?'

'Take a kid?'

'I know it's not . . . know it's something beyond the usual, even for hard people, the hardest, but you've got to realize, Harvey, this is a grass's kid and a grass's lady. They're outside the usual. They're another category. As some folk see it.'

Yes. Another category. To describe the loathing like that must hurt Patterson. He had a lady. He had kids. He was a grass.

They had parked opposite the big, handsome, wrought-iron, open gates to the school. A short driveway led to a quadrangle with a tall central fountain, switched off now. The main buildings lay on three sides of the quadrangle, playing fields bordered by trees at the rear.

Patterson said: 'Pupils come out into the yard at break and they move between buildings for different classes, and to get to the gym. In the afternoons they go for supervised games on the sports ground. Why I thought you should see the layout, Harv.'

'When?'

'Soon. Or would I have you out here in the middle of the night now?'

'Soon being?'

'Soon's the best I can do,' Patterson replied.

'Who?'

'Many would be interested, wouldn't they, Harv?'

'Yes, but who?'

'I can't do that for you, not yet.'

'Not yet because you're tied somehow?'

'Tied?'

'Scared.'

'Not yet, because I don't know. But I'm listening.'

'If it's soon there might not be time to listen,' Moss replied.

'That's true, but I'm listening all the same.'

'Listening where?'

'Listening.'

'Listening where? Are these prime sources?' Moss said.

'Prime sources?'

'The people who'll do it.'

'These are *good* sources, Harv. I've never brought you gossip, have I?'

'It's vague, Dick.'

'We know the child, we know the school, we can guess the motive.'

'Kidnapping – these people don't do it,' Moss said.

'Which people don't?'

'Not part of the culture.'

'Which culture?' Patterson asked.

'Villain culture.'

'How else do they—?'

'This would be a public grab. They couldn't count on her to stay quiet and keep us out of it. They're never going to get near any ransom money. They'd know that.'

'I only tell you what I hear, Harv. My role, yes?' His voice was still patient, firm, full of reason. 'At the back the fields run into woodland, with paths through it. Anyone could bring a four-wheel drive up close. I've looked around.'

'You've been into the school grounds?'

'I wouldn't trouble you until I've done the rudimentaries, would I, Harv?'

'You've got to be careful.'

'Kids moving between buildings make their own way – no teacher with them. A straggle. The games periods in the fields do have staff around for coaching and reffing, but when children go out there and when they come back, they're by themselves.'

'You've watched this? How? Where from, Dick? You need to be careful. God, didn't you tell me the head would get suspicious?'

'Alone, I can be very discreet. Don't fret, please, Harv. I'm like a pro, you know.'

'They'd try other ways.'

'Other ways to what?'

'Make her shed money,' Moss said.

'How?'

'Threaten. Terrorize her.'

'Perhaps they have.'

'Have they?' Moss said.

'She's tough.'

'They have?'

Patterson shook his head a couple of times as though in despair and about to give up on explaining things to Moss. 'You want to think of it just as a money situation, don't you, Harv? Account book. This you can understand. You hate the notion – maybe fear the notion . . . can't take the notion that people would like to hurt anyone who belonged to Tully, just for the delight of hurting. Vengeance – you think that's only for opera. Not a bit. If there's money as well, that's fine. But the real objective is pain. One death isn't enough for Tully, not even with the foreplay.'

'So be careful, Dick.'

'I think you could be right – they'd realize a ransom payment is probably not on.'

'So, once he's taken, the child's dead?' Moss asked.

'It's *your* logic that says so.'

'The logic only applies if he's snatched in the first place, and I still don't—'

'Why I brought you out here, Harv. So you can see the setting.'

*　　*　　*

98

Moss went home and slept for a couple of hours before work. In the afternoon, he fiddled a little spare time and drove out to the school again. He did not believe Patterson. He definitely did not believe Patterson. All the arguments Moss had given him in the night applied, plus plenty more. Dick Patterson was a novice, might be too eager to establish himself, not just to get in line for a weighty 'settlement', but out of pride and the urge to excel. This did not mean he had manufactured a tale for Moss. Patterson sincerely thought his information good. But for a grass to put together the fragments he heard and saw and make a safe forecast would always be tricky. It demanded a lot of practice, and for now Patterson lacked that.

So, Moss asked himself why he had to go back like this. Although he could not believe Patterson's predictions, he found he could not forget them either. The precision and thoroughness of Dick's scan of the school – its geography, its procedures – badgered Moss. Perhaps Patterson had counted on that. Confusion again. Moss recognized it. One accusation Patterson had made stuck and gave trouble. Was he right to suspect that, because Moss felt so appalled by the idea of kidnapping, he discounted it? This would be wilful blindness, not logic. Moss had bleated about the 'culture' forbidding it. And he did think this true. But cultures could change. Had he kept up to date? Although he never minimized the hatred felt for grasses, was he stupid – yes, naïve – to imagine it stopped at the execution of the grass himself, didn't encompass his family, especially if the family looked loaded and his woman flaunted the gains?

For the kind of operation suggested by Patterson, a lot of planning and pre-watching would be needed, and Moss returned to Cheyne now to see whether anyone had observation under way in school time. Of course, he expected to see nobody. Certainly he'd see nobody. To use that term he'd given Patterson, this revisit was a formality, a *negative* formality. In the words of another police phrase, he wanted to eliminate the possibility.

He took the cosh. These people might be past the observation stage and the weapon could be very . . . Very what?

Useful? Relevant? But, for fuck's sake, hadn't he just been telling himself he did not believe all this – any of this? The grab of a child not merely violated the culture, as he understood it, but it would not work. He'd explained this to Patterson. Any sensible villain could see that, no matter how driven by rage. The trail must lead direct to people grassed by Tully, and the police would go after them, regardless of who gave the word for Tully's death. Mad to invite such risk. Impossible, and all Moss wanted was basic, formal, confirmation that no child-snatch could ever happen – could even rate consideration. Taking the cosh amounted to nothing more than a twitch. A formal twitch.

In the day, it was unwise to park outside the school and he left his car half a mile away and walked. At first, he did not approach the gates but found the rear way to the woodland and playing fields. Anyone watching might pick this spot. The woodland was not large and he did a reasonably swift search. He saw nobody. Patterson had it right about the paths: wide enough to take a jeep-size vehicle. But he saw no tracks in the soft soil to suggest someone had been driving here recently. He returned to the front of the school. It was three forty-five and parents began arriving by car to meet their children. The earliest lined up alongside the fountain in the quadrangle. The rest queued in the road.

Moss kept walking. He recalled Patterson's warning that the paedophile danger had grabbed public consciousness and the school would be alert to males hanging about nearby. He did not see any here himself, either. Moss grew increasingly sure Patterson's scenario must be only that – a melodramatic rumour he lacked the experience and brain to examine properly and dismiss.

Moss turned and walked back for a final view. Cars continued to edge into the quadrangle, pick up their load, circle the fountain and come back out. The fountain functioned now, one central, high, thin jet and two broader, smaller ones to the sides. Like all fountains, it suggested continuance, serenity, order – what went up came down and went up again. He could still spot no sign of anyone watching. Perhaps it had been absurd to trek out here, as he had suspected. But at least he felt reassured, comforted, more confident in his ability to weigh a tip-off. His fast-track brain could still fast-track, couldn't it?

He observed from near the turning to the side street where he had parked. A BMW pulled in alongside him. Momentarily, he closed his hand around the stalk of the cosh in his pocket. When he looked into the car, he saw Pamela Grange with a boy of about nine wearing Cheyne's grey and silver uniform. She lowered the driver's window. 'This your beat, Moss?' she asked.

'Is it yours?'

'What's on?'

'On?'

'The school involved?' she said.

'In what?'

'Whatever.'

'Is home time three forty-five every day?'

'Why?'

'I'd know where to find you,' Moss replied.

'Why would you want to?'

'The same time every day?' he said.

'Does that trouble you?'

'I wonder about it,' he replied.

'So, are you managing to block them out?'

'Who?'

'The lady snoops. The seekers after truth.'

'I haven't got much of that for them – or not much they haven't got already.'

'They seem to think *I* have,' she said.

Moss studied the boy. Undersized and underweight by a bit, most probably, pale with large dark eyes, deep forehead, hair also dark beneath his pushed-back school cap, unsmiling, quizzical. He gave Moss a good stare but then turned away and looked at the traffic as being more interesting. Eyes and forehead recalled Tully photographs, and his slight build. The boy's colouring was Pamela's, though. Tully had been fairer and fresh-faced.

'Can we give you a lift?' she said.

'My car's near, thanks.'

101

She pushed her head out of the window and dropped her voice. Moss bent lower and smelled a reasonable scent – 'Allure', maybe: 'Are you saying it's bad to do things the same time every day?' she asked.

'Can it be avoided?'

'School finishes at three forty.'

'And you have to get there, in the queue,' Moss said.

'You've been up to have a look, have you? What's happened?'

'Could you ask them to let him out ten minutes early?' Moss replied.

'They wouldn't like that. Rules. It's a stuffy place. What you'd expect. They're already worried about having him there at all – after what came out about Justin at the trial. Sins of the father. It's difficult. They've got their reputation to guard.'

'Or could he stay behind for a while?'

The boy turned and gave him another big, get-lost stare. He might be less well mannered than Tully. Perhaps he took that from his mother, also.

Seven

Sally driving an unmarked Volvo, they tailed Pamela Grange again in her BMW. Sally thought of this and similar earlier excursions as Esther's spasms. Instincts, Esther called them. Well, all right, you *are* the assistant chief, ma'am. Of course, Esther *would* believe in instincts – her own. She'd believe in anything that lifted her above the usual plain and sane qualities of a police assistant chief. She didn't want to be just a member of a force, however near the top. Esther in person and solo *was* a force. No question she saw herself like that – impulsive, ungovernable, dazzlingly, dazingly sporadic.

She'd said from the start that Pam might need protection, and now and then, spasmodically or instinctively – take your pick – she decided they should get out and give the girl some. Obviously, this exceeded Esther's proper role here. In an oblique, polite way, Sally had indicated that to her one day. 'Arseholes to roles,' she replied.

The protection could be *only* now and then, and for the rest of the time Pam and her son lived exposed to all the perils that Esther sensed existed here post trial, and which her and Sally's mission probably increased. As Pam had asked on their first formal meeting in Milton Avenue, why not let things lie now? To that, at least two answers offered themselves. First, Esther had her Home Office orders. Second, Esther would dislike letting things lie. She was born to stir.

The broken nature of the minding they could offer Pamela and the boy did not seem to trouble Esther. Continuity bored her. She'd feel tramlined. So, she made these now-you-see-it-now-you-don't gestures, however skimpy. But, naturally, she would not regard the occasional tracking of Pam as only a gesture, and definitely not skimpy. No, it sprang from a gorgeous, Estherian *urge* – irresistible, large-minded, chancy, would-be clairvoyant. Sally could more or less understand that. She, also, believed in acute post-trial perils here. Sally knew a precedent. Back home, she had dealt with another situation where the partner and child of a dead informant found themselves in danger after a court case.

And she accepted Esther's view that no local officer should guard Pamela. There were deep tales still to be told about the days before Tully's death, and Pamela could probably tell them. Or she could be violently stopped from telling them by people who wanted her silenced and/or punished as a part of Tully. At the interview in Milton Avenue, Esther and Sally had drawn next to nothing from her. That didn't mean nothing existed. Pam seemed the kind of woman a man would talk to. She seemed the kind who would demand to be talked to, and the kind who remembered what was talked about. But she was also a woman who knew how to clam. Later on today they had another interview scheduled which might be just as unproductive, this one with Chief Inspector Albert Chave, controller to Detective Sergeant Harvey Moss during Tully's fink career.

'Looks like the school run,' Esther said. 'Oh, God, same time, same route, every day. She should wear one of those seaside bonnets. Not "Kiss Me Quick", "Kill Me Quick".'

'Perhaps there's a plainclothes protection team with her and she feels secure. They wouldn't tell *us*, would they?'

'She feels *what*? Fucking *what*? Protection team where?'

'One of these. Or more than one.' Sally took a hand from the wheel and gave a small wave to indicate all the cars going in their direction.

'Did you see anything waiting at the house?' Esther asked.

'They'd be too clever.'

'Or joining her as soon as she left the splendid avenue?'

'They'd be too clever.' Sally stared ahead at the Citroën estate between them and Pamela. Two men sat in the front. Thirties? Forties? Capable-looking? Shoulders. Unscrawny necks. Sally always noted necks. Then she mirror-checked the people carrier behind. It seemed to contain three men and a woman – elderly? Too elderly?

'I don't like it,' Esther said.

'What?'

'Police protection teams. The idea.'

'No, I didn't think you would.'

'Protection teams get very close. They stick at people's backs, allegedly to protect. So easy for them.'

'Easy to what?'

Esther's body twitched big in the passenger seat. Her voice became absurdly gentle: 'Listen, Sally, I wonder whether you'd agree not to play super sodding dim with me? I don't need stupidity from you to make me seem intelligent. I can do without a foil. So easy for them.'

'If they were going to do something about her, wouldn't they have done it a while ago?'

'Who?'

'Listen, ma'am, I wonder whether you'd agree not to play super sodding dim with me? Whoever.'

'But which whoever?' Esther replied.

'Bent cop whoever. Villain whoever. An alliance between both whoevers.'

'There've been changes.'

'Which?' Sally said.

'*We've* arrived, of course. Some believed the trial closed everything. They might be panicked now. They've seen you're not someone to be messed about, Sally.'

'Listen, ma'am, I wonder whether you'd agree not to take the mick.'

'Couldn't. Not in my nature.'

'Which?'

'Which what?' Esther replied.

'Not in your nature to take the mick, or not in your nature to agree not to take the mick?'

'Right.'

'What you mean is, they've seen *you're* not someone to be messed about,' Sally said.

'They think I'm a comic music-hall turn.'

'Well, yes, but down the bill. Got a theme song? "It had to be me"? But there's a bit of something else to you as well. Many must spot that.'

'What something else?'

'A bit. Of something else. And not just the ACC insignia.'

'A bit, yes,' Esther replied. 'The ACC insignia *is* important, though.'

'It puts you one up on me.'

'No. More than one. Much more than one. Oh, God, Sally, this magnet school. Five days a week around three forty-five p.m. Guaranteed she gets more or less immobile in a queue for ten minutes plus. "Take Your Time To Kill Me Quick." Had a look at the Ordnance Survey? You're hot on maps, did A-level geography, I recall. Fields at the back. Woodland. They could come for her all ways. And/or for the kid.'

'Who?'

'Whoever.'

'People don't touch children, do they?' Sally said. Colleagues had told her this during the previous, similar crisis at home. She hadn't believed it then and didn't now, but she wanted Esther's view.

'Which people don't touch children?'

'I thought villains regard that as disgusting and beyond.'

'Which villains?' Esther replied.

'Who are you afraid of? Sometimes you talk as if it's CID people here, worried she'll spout about their dodgy business arrangements with Justin. Now you're saying it could be lowlife looking for ransom, or the worst sort of revenge.'

'There's a difference?' Esther became quiet for a while. Sally kept the BMW in sight. Then Esther said: 'You know, I didn't mind taking this job – to dodge the domestic situation for a few months. I expect you heard the scuttlebut. You'd be good at that. But can I get privacy up here? Negative. Anyway, I'm not sure any longer it's a happy move at all. Things are so . . . so shifty here, the whole scene. So wearing. So dangerous. So dark. Can I really bring light to it? We?'

'Which damn domestic situation?'

'So right. Yes, to get away from that temporarily,' Esther replied. '"Space" I believe it's called in the marital guidance jargon.'

'Moss has been asking people back there about you and me. I had a whisper.'

106

'Yes, I did, too. He would. Training. Do it to us before we can do it to him. I heard he's a brain, the kind who's actually read *Martin Chuzzlewit*, not simply watched it on TV. So why wouldn't he realize we were certain to find out he's been snooping? Well, he's young – trying to adjust fast to a tough trade and getting one or two things marginally wrong. Prat. Does his snooping bother you, Sally? Are you still not altogether committed to the boyfriend? Pete, is it? Nice, I hear, but ultimately . . . well, ultimately you wonder? Standard situation. Don't feel uniquely guilty at your inability to respond full-out. So, you get to Pal Joey's now and then. Of course you do.'

'You still seeing whoever on the side, ma'am?' Sally replied. "Whoever" can be a plural, I think, can't it? I don't want you rationed.'

'*Whom*ever, if we're doing grammar. I'm on the end of calls from both of them.'

'Which both is that?'

'What?'

'Your husband and someone else? Or—?'

'Lord, though, these bleating, imploring, man voices, by phone,' Esther said. 'Do you get them here, likewise? Claims. Recriminations. So much worse electronically, though I *am* touched a little. Like damned souls offered a single, concessionary call from hell – and, of course, they want to make it to me. I hold up one of these beautifully designed, state-of-the-art mobiles to my ear and what I get out of them is ugly, gasping disgruntlement and dim smarm. I detest possessiveness.'

'Well, you would, ma'am.'

'Because I'm a flighty, autonomous spirit, you feel? Crap of that sort?'

'Yes, that sort of crap. Pamela's joining the school queue.'

'Move in behind her.'

'Yes?' Previously, they would circle a couple of blocks and hope to time it so they picked Pam up again as she left with her lad, Walter.

'It's all right,' Esther said. 'I want to stay with her today. That's all – I just *want* to.'

'See? You *are* flighty and autonomous. Ma'am.' The

Citroën Sally had noticed earlier was still ahead of them, and now lay between the Volvo and Pam's BMW in the queue edging towards the school gates. Two men doing taxi service for a kid? Was this likely? The people carrier behind had disappeared from her mirror.

'Why should he want to pile up that kind of information about us?' Sally said.

'Who?'

'Moss.'

'They do,' Esther said. 'Custom and practice, learned at Nelly's knee. The process makes them mind-numb, like any habit – even someone as smart as Moss. It's why he thinks nobody would get in touch to tell us what he's been doing. People of dear Mossy's sort have heard information is power and so assume *all* information is power. No ability to select, despite his fine degree. It's a low-rank characteristic. Sorry. Not you. Anyway, you'll climb.'

'I did climb the ex-tip.'

'That's what I mean – so much thoroughness, creativity. Do you get calls, Sally? Pete? And so on?'

'But what about calls the other way? Do *you* call *them*?' Sally replied. 'Or one of them. This might reveal a lot.'

'What?'

'Which one you needed most to talk to.'

'I *have* wondered about it,' Esther said.

'What?'

'Well, the usual question – is there one I like to talk to in a good, sensible, comradely way, and one I like to . . . well, you know . . . get taken over by?'

'And have you produced an answer yet?' Sally replied. 'This would be a useful bonus from the trip up here – if it helped you decide.'

'A tricky one. How about you?'

'What?'

'Do you have to make calls? Who to? Just Pete?'

'Ideally, the one you like talking to and the other one should, in fact, be the same,' Sally replied. 'Sex manuals and advice columns in the press always insist on this. Trite? They forecast "relationship drift" otherwise.'

'Me, I don't see "drift" as a negative term,' Esther said. 'How about you?'

'What?'

'Sally, do you get something from casuals that the other can't give?'

'Should we warn her? Mention this dangerously predictable trip?' Sally replied. 'Or warn the school, perhaps. But we've no real authority, have we? This is not our patch.'

'Is it the very casualness that appeals to you?' Esther said.

'Would your . . . well, various connections think you wangled this assignment deliberately to dodge out on them – and so they feel deserted?' Sally said. 'Which one would feel deserted most? This, also, could be illuminating.'

'I'm more or less certain my situation back there would never get to violence,' Esther replied. 'Oh, more than more or less. Oh, yes. Not *major*, malevolent violence. Some heavy knockabout while romancing, yes, obviously, but not aimed to kill or even permanently disable. Blood on Chinese carpets is a bugger, especially the blue bits, as a matter of fact. How about you, Sally?'

'What would you do with them?'

'What?'

'The carpets.'

'Professional cleaning. Don't try it yourself. You'll make the stains worse and probably ruin the blue bits,' Esther said. 'You're into Chinese?'

'I meant dividing up household stuff if the marriage ends.'

'No man I've ever been concerned with was – is – an *expert* in violence – guns or knives or even martial arts. The other kind of arts, maybe, but I'm not going to get beaten to death with a bassoon. Almost certainly. How about with you and yours, Sally?'

'Yes, Pam's damn vulnerable here,' Sally replied, gazing about. She could have let her imagination cavort, but was scared what it might show of the future. Now and then, best stick with the actual. Things had stayed serene and routine so far.

'Lust is so damn democratic and undiscerning these days, isn't it?' Esther said.

'I still don't know whether I was allocated to you for this job, or if you calculatedly chose me.'

'Your partner – sound, unvain man, I gather,' Esther replied. 'He's presentable, about your own age, fit, and yet you have to prowl. It does put you in touch with that item, humanity, we spoke of, I suppose. Or certain parts of humanity. Yes.'

The BMW moved into the school forecourt and was out of sight for a short while behind the high perimeter wall while they waited in the road. 'You've done some research,' Sally said.

'I like to know what I'm selecting. And then my own position – similar. My husband has wonderful, lovable attributes, I'd never deny it. He's apolitical, kindly, unstable, non-golf, decent breath, sexually inventive, non-soccer, aristocratically ungenteel manners, probably faithful for much of the time, circumspectly savage, residual tap-dancing skills to almost professional level, can appreciate films by the Coen brothers, except *Hudsucker*, naturally – and yet there's this appallingly sad falling short.' Her voice went right down for a moment. '*So* appalling because inexplicable and unwarranted and unchangeable. He deserves better. Who else can hit me about in the way I want to be hit about sometimes? I know you understand, Sally. Children – would they have made a difference? I'm not certain. I'd still be me. He'd still be him. Identity – such a damned encumbrance.'

'"Deserves" doesn't come into it. That's the guilt you reproached me for. They don't *deserve* anything. They're about the place, that's all.'

'Yes?'

'What's the other like? Others?' Sally turned the Volvo into the forecourt. Half a dozen cars waited ahead. Three teachers supervised the pick-up of pupils near the school building's big main doors, as the cars in line took turns to collect a child. Then the vehicles rounded the fountain, went down the other side of the forecourt and exited on to the road. Exposure total, pace slow, perils foul.

'I don't ever hold it against him in the least that he's taken to wearing those fucking vermilion or ochre bow ties, depending on whether it's the weekend,' Esther replied.

'Who?'

'But one does have to ask oneself, would one have married him if he'd been into timetabled bow ties at that stage, the courting stage? Everyone has these imponderables in their lives. He stands well enough among bassoonists, I gather, can come out with an occasional smart joke – referred to a friend who missed the Honours List as persona non garter. He might have worked at it, mind. This is a fine, honest, intelligently brutal man who's been supportive to my career, but . . . How about you, Sally?'

'In a way, I suppose it's a kind of bravery, a sort of attractive arrogance, for Pamela to do everything as she always did – say, the regularity, forecastability of this car trip,' Sally replied. 'Foolhardy? Perhaps, but possibly admirable. It's her way of declaring, "I'll continue, no matter what happened to my partner on the dump." Normality – people crave that. They make themselves ignore, forget, the horrible breaks in it. This would also be a steadying factor with the boy, Walter. Pam radiates standard ritual to him, not dread or panic. Fine, don't you think?'

'So, should I feel self-blame for rocking a marriage, disrespecting a marriage and him?' Esther said.

'No guilt.'

'Certainly, I *can* feel it now and then. One is rejecting what one formerly prized, for reasons many would find incomprehensible, and which might be only fleeting. Illusory? But, then, doesn't Jung say it's a mistake to treat everything non-concrete, not blatantly "real" as an illusion?' She went silent suddenly and Sally thought she must have seen something to trouble her. It turned out to be only a pause while she considered and then disowned some of what she had just said. 'But, no, the reasons are not fleeting,' Esther stated. 'Chronic. Oh, God, yes, chronic. How about you, Sally? Yes, you feel that kind of guilt, too.'

'Or Pamela could have been given a hint she's all right – that nobody wants to hurt her,' Sally said. 'She's been told Tully dead will do. But is this hint reliable? Is one hint enough? How many folk are there around who want to get to her – villains, cops, both?' She watched Walter Tully as he waited for the BMW to reach him, while a Honda one ahead took its pupil aboard. The boy looked pale, too slight, insulated from the children and teachers around him. He seemed unbreakably patient, like someone who'd learned early not to expect things to turn out OK, or even come close.

Sally had been at a different kind of Victorian-architectured, grey stone school from this – a council primary and junior, built originally as a public elementary school after compulsory education arrived in the late nineteenth century. It had had no fountain. Just the same, she could still see the charms of this sweetly laid-out, fee-grabbing place.

'Looks a good lad,' Esther said, gazing at Walter. 'He probably sees some very rough days in a venue like this.'

'Venue like what?'

Perhaps Esther came up through the same sort of schools as Sally. It might be Esther's ferocious pushiness that made Sally assume the assistant chief did it all from no favoured background – plus, of course, her choice of Sally as side-kick. But could the State system produce Esther's committed, prancing, barmy, gloriously effective selfhood? She might have done some work on herself. Esther's voice these days boomed bourgeois-loud, strong with consonants, languid and full on vowels. When she'd remarked 'Arseholes to roles', the grandeur in the o sounds echoed royal broadcasts. Although Sally's dossier would be available to Esther, Esther's was not to her, naturally, so the ACC's background might stay mysterious.

She said: 'But whatever Walter has to put up with here, he shows nothing. The brave lad doesn't want to trouble Mum.'

'You mean, he'd be persecuted for having a dad dead on a tip top?'

'God, no. Prestige in that. It's dramatic. Kids love any kind of reflected eminence – would envy him. I know I would have, at *my* school,' Esther replied.

'Where?'

'But they'd hate his father as a grass. Against the most central classroom ethic, for heaven's sake, isn't it? This kind of prep school, and the ones they'll go on to. Oh, yes. It would have been true even at mine.'

'Where was that?'

'More so for boys. Omerta. "Never peach on a fellow."'

'That a quote from somewhere?'

'Probably,' Esther said. 'In my time, I've read a book. "Peach" meaning inform.'

'Is that so?'

'"Never peach on a fellow" is the only piece of advice any dad would think worthwhile for a lad entered here – plus, of course, "Don't hang about in the showers, unless, that is, you're the style of boy who does hang about in the showers."'

A woman teacher came down the line of cars, nodded respectfully to the two men in the Citroën then reached the Volvo. Esther lowered the window with swift and good affability.

'Yes?' the teacher said. She gazed in.

'Waiting,' Esther replied. 'But very pleasant, given the fountain view and leaded windows.'

'Waiting for? I don't recognize the car or—'

'Toynbee le Fèvre,' Esther replied.

'Who?'

'You must know Toy.'

'I—'

'Don't tell me you've lost the dribbling little sod again,' Esther said.

'You're police, aren't you?' the teacher replied. 'I can tell by the eyes.'

'Which?' Esther said.

'Both,' the teacher replied.

'Both my eyes or the eyes of both of us, Sally and myself?' Esther said.

'And your jaw. *Yours.*'

'Oh, jaws are only jaws,' Esther said.

'That's a custody jaw. That's an interrogation jaw,' the teacher replied. 'We don't really want your kind lurking, you know. The school must maintain a quality. You have your uses, probably. Maybe. The polity needs beadles, the establishment needs guardians. But not appropriate here.'

'What about the two in front?' Sally said.

'Look, let me ask you, is this something new, this harassment? Why do you have to dog her, and Walter?' the teacher said. 'Haven't they had enough?'

'Who are the men in the Citroën?' Sally asked.

'Citroën? Why? A ploy? School governors, come to check home-time arrangements – traffic etcetera, safety,' the teacher said. 'It's routine, twice a term. Don't pretend to be interested in *them*. I know why you're here.'

'How is it you're sure they're governors?' Sally asked.

'Because they are.'

'Anyone could tell you're a teacher,' Esther said.

'Leave Walter and his mother alone, you hard-jawed bitch, with your know-all, prop-to-the-governing-class eyes,' the teacher answered.

The BMW stopped and Walter entered. The car drew away. After it went the Citroën, without a child. Esther put the window up and Sally followed them. 'As a matter of fact, my husband used to like the line of my jaw, found it a turn-on,' Esther said.

'That teacher was just dumping routine abuse, like police and flat feet.'

'This was a while ago – the jawline and my husband.' Her voice almost disappeared again. 'A nice, touching memory, but only that, a memory. Sometimes I feel I'd like to get back to such pleasantries, but I can't, Sally. I've made them impossible.'

'It might be the general region of the body to interest him. Men *can* get obsessive like that. Jaws. Thumbs.'

'He knows he mustn't say that sort of thing to me any longer. Senses it.'

'Oh, yes, with some men it's women's legs and tits, clearly,' Sally replied. 'Then the behind is important to many of them. *Oh, quel cul tu as!* Or, Oh, such a bottom!'

'You do French as well, do you?'

'And it's not only men who find women's buttocks enticing. Didn't Colette say that where the back flows into the arse lies the true essence of a woman's beauty?'

'Do you read all sorts?' Esther replied.

Back on the road, the Citroën turned off at a junction, leaving nothing between the BMW and their Volvo. 'Perhaps they *were* school governors,' Sally said.

'That teacher had the feel of awkward truth to her. All the best unreconstructed Marxists get jobs in private schools.'

'How do you know?'

'They tell themselves they have a better chance of destroying the system from within – but not until they've retired and got their pension. I'm going to try to do something about my jaw.' She pulled the vanity mirror down and put her face up close to it.

'What can you do with a jaw, for God's sake, ma'am? Jaws are structural, for cracking nuts or gripping a bassoon. Not like hair or toenails.' The BMW cleared some traffic lights on orange. Sally had to wait. 'Accept. Make a plus of it. Project it as your best feature.'

'You think so? But how?'

'Write in to the *Sunday Times* style supplement and ask why it never does anything on jaws.' When they caught up with the BMW, it had drawn in to the side of the road. 'That's Harvey Moss she's speaking to, isn't it?' Sally said.

'A rendezvous? What's he doing on foot up here?'

'I stop?' Sally asked.

'No. Absolutely no.'

Sally kept going.

Esther said: 'Did you see? That fucking kid, head around this way, peering at us, knowing us, the big-eyed, blazered demon. You can tell he's the son of a . . . well, we mustn't get abusive about informants. We're nowhere without them.'

'In any case, I thought you liked the look of Walter.'

'There's a complexity to me, you know,' Esther replied.

'That right?'

'I can't be contained in some bland, steady, constant-as-the-northern-star persona – not with a jawline like this.' She held it up to the glass again, affectionately now. 'Yes, I'm fond of that boy, the nosy pup.'

'Let's talk Tully, shall we, Chief Inspector?' Esther said.

Chave gave an absolutely tolerant grin. It meant, What

else? Chave was middle height, plump but quick on his feet, not too readable. Chef, cinema manager, cop – if you had to guess. His dark suit seemed genuine wool, probably not Marks and Spencer but reach-me-down all the same. He said: 'I've brought my notes on that matter, naturally.'

'You were controller throughout the connection with Tully?' Esther said.

'From 1999 until his death,' Chave replied. He would be excellent in the witness box, voice unstrained, precise, face round, open, almost boyish, almost disarming. He still had all his hair – fair to mousy and short – and this helped with the youthfulness. He might go higher.

'And was Sergeant Moss Tully's handler for the same period?'

'Sergeant Moss proposed him for registration and Tully became an official informant from that date,' Chave said. 'Sergeant Moss was named as his handler, reporting to me. This is usual – the officer who finds an informant then runs her or him.'

'And I assume this relationship – informant, handler, controller – operated according to the national police guide.'

'Oh, entirely,' Chave replied. 'The chief and our Superintendent Notram, head of CID, as you know, were – are – extremely rigorous about that.'

'It's vital, isn't it?' Esther said.

'Vital.'

'Vital that, where policing moves into what are known, I think, as "grey areas", there should be very exact and clear rules of practice,' Esther said.

'Such precise and clear rules, in a sense, making these popularly described "grey areas" *not* grey, or at least less so.'

'This would certainly be the objective,' Esther replied, 'don't you think so, too, Detective Constable Bithron?'

'True,' Sally said.

Esther waited. 'Is there more?' she said.

'No, just "True," ' Sally replied. They talked in their room at headquarters.

'And yet, of course, because of necessary secrecy and,

possibly, a degree of *quid pro quo-ism*, the informant organization of any force is always going to have some so-called
"grey area" aspects,' Esther said.

'*Quid pro quo-ism?*' Albert Chave asked.

'Exactly,' Esther said. 'Dead right term.'

'*Quid pro quo-ism* meaning . . . ?'

'DC Bithron explains these technicalities so much better
than I,' Esther said. 'Word-flair when she wants to.'

'A certain give and take between informant and detective,'
Sally said. 'Possibly some blind-eyeing of certain of the informant's activities by the detective in return for tip-offs about
larger matters.'

'There. Beautifully put,' Esther said. 'A detective conniving
at selected offences as a kind of bargaining ploy – this is
what could be seen as "grey areas", I feel, don't you – and
what could be, and often is, treated by the courts as unac-
ceptable? Judges do their pompous and pious little nuts. They
think their fucking courtroom with its bum-sucking ushers
is life.'

'Quite understandably such behaviour gets censured,
because this is certainly not an arrangement approved in the
guide,' Chave answered.

'Ah, the guide,' Esther said, crossing herself.

'This would be an extremely . . . well, *controversial* practice,' Chave said.

'You've not run across anything like that?' Esther asked.

'Entirely at variance with the guide,' Chave replied.

'You've not run across it?' Esther asked.

'The chief and Mr Notram would be opposed to anything
of that kind, I think,' Chave said. 'I believe, in fact, the chief
had some personal input to the guide, and so is very keen
to see all its provisions properly observed. His, as it were,
baby, to a degree.' Again Chave gave that grin, affectionate
and indulgent now. 'We're proud of the chief here – his
contributions to national and, yes, even international police
matters. They give the force an added status, one which all
of us can feel and share in, regardless of rank.'

'A world dimension,' Esther said.

'So true,' Chave replied.

'Mr Notram as registrar of all informants and holding the documentation, you as controller, Sergeant Moss doing the day-to-day contact as handler?' Sally said.

'Day-to-day and more likely night-to-night,' Chave replied. 'As I'm sure you'd expect. Daylight's a liability.'

'DC Bithron's done a lot with grasses. She tells me that some experienced detectives – not necessarily herself – but some detectives describe the guide as total, high-flown, sanctimonious shit,' Esther replied. 'Have I got that right, Sally? Shit?' Esther really struck the final consonant.

Of course, Sally had never spoken to her about the guide. 'Total, high-flown and sanctimonious,' she said.

'Hardly,' Chave replied.

'Alternatively, window dressing,' Esther said. 'Is that right, Sally?'

'Total, high-flown, sanctimonious shit or window dressing, or an amalgam of both,' Sally said. 'Total, high-flown, sanctimonious shit *as* window dressing.'

'A collection of strict rules laid down for the judiciary and media to hear about and approve, while all competent officers deride it, ignore it,' Esther said, 'because they believe that, if they didn't, informing would be dead. They think the grassing game makes its own rules – has to, because all informants are different and have their personal objectives and crazes and superstitions and dreads.'

'The chief would be very disappointed if that were true,' Chave said. An idea hit him and his body perked up slightly, mind made flesh. 'For instance, I think of a book called *Black Mass*. I wonder if you know it, ma'am – factual account of an FBI attempt to get evidence against Mafia leaders in Boston, USA. To acquire this evidence, they enlisted local criminals as informers, and allowed them to pursue their villainy uninterrupted, including violence. They actually thwarted Boston police operations against these gangsters. This is the kind of disgraceful, chaotic situation that can arise if proper, regulated behaviour is not observed. Oh, yes, I'm happy, indeed proud, to say that here we'd regard the guide as binding, in all its provisions. Happy. That *is* the word. There is an easiness in the conscience because we know we've acted fairly, responsibly. I expect you've experienced this yourself, personally.'

Sally thought what would be good about him in the witness box was that, although he could chant gorgeous stretches of ooze, his lips never got flecked like a convulsion.

'Tully was one of the biggest traffickers in the Western World, wasn't he?' Esther asked.

'He did have drug connections.'

'He ran dealerships,' Esther said.

'There *was* some dubious activity.'

'Protected?' Esther said.

'We were building a case against him – wanted him to think he was protected, so he'd become careless. Textbook tactics. There would be several such operations current at any one time.'

'Building for how long?'

'It would be a considerable project, probably requiring a very long time,' Chave replied. 'Amassing.'

'Who?'

'Oh, us – amassing evidence.'

'Black amassing? Meanwhile, he's in a big house on Milton Avenue, runs two cars, one a new BMW, and has a lad in private education,' Esther said.

'You're so right, ma'am – to refer to it as "meanwhile". A *mot juste* if ever I heard one. Yes, only meanwhile,' Chave said.

'DC Bithron worries about informants growing too powerful,' Esther replied.

'Powerful how?' Chave asked.

'What makes DC Bithron anxious is that an informant might become so well-placed that any prosecution for his/her own villainy is impossible. She wonders whether this had happened to Tully. I think I'm describing matters right, Sally – about the basis for your anxieties?'

'The informant has negligible power – except, of course, over those he or she gives information on,' Chave replied.

'Take a far-out, hypothetical example,' Esther said. 'Imagine officers running a grass skim part of the fees intended for her/him and the grass discovers this. Or suppose officers were rewarded with kickbacks by the informant for making his or her business more profitable by victimizing competitors. These possibilities turn DC Bithron nervous. They would give the informant a blackmailing hold on the officer – *officers*. Courts and the Home Secretary go mad if they think detectives are on two salaries, even if the Home Secretary's on two himself, as MP and minister.'

Chave said: 'Clearly such actions on the part of an officer – officers – would be intolerable – illegal in the full sense of the term.'

'Money,' Esther replied.

'Money?' Chave said.

'The pay to Tully. This was your responsibility, as controller?'

'Certainly. The guide stipulates that as one of the controller's duties.'

'How would payments be made?' Esther asked.

'Cash.'

'Via Sergeant Moss?'

'Direct.'

'You would hand over the money to Tully face to face?' Esther said.

'That is the agreed practice here.'

'Where would it happen?'

'Certain mutually acceptable sites,' Chave replied.

'Hear that, Sally? "Mutually acceptable sites."'

'So what's your point?' Sally said.

'Would you expect them to be mutually *un*acceptable sites?' Esther replied. 'Mutually acceptable sites like what, Chief Inspector?'

'Car parks. Side streets. Vehicles would always be involved.'

'Tully would get into yours and you would shell out?'

'Usually like that.'

'Night?'

'Generally night.'

'A light on, so you could count and he could check?'

'I would have packaged the money before the meeting.'

'How would he know it was right?'

'He'd just know,' Chave said.

'Conversation?'

'Hardly any. Speed was important. He would not wish to prolong contact.'

'You'd thank him for the information, though?'

'Perhaps some thanks. But he was being paid, after all,' Chave said.

'Moss always present?'

'Invariably.'

'Sitting where?'

'Ma'am?'

'Is he alongside you in the passenger seat, so Tully has to get into the back and you turn and pay out like that? Or is Moss in the back so Tully can join you in the front, closer?'

'Detective Sergeant Moss in the back.'

'You drove to the meeting like that?' Esther asked.

'Yes.'

'You must have looked like a chauffeur. Would Moss talk to him?'

'Briefly. As I said, speed.'

'Was Tully happy to have the two of you there?' Esther asked.

'Happy?'

'He's outnumbered.'

'Yes, he seemed happy. He knew us both. And there was money.'

'Tully gave good information?'

'Oh, certainly. It led to many prosecutions.'

'Drugs?'

'All sorts. He heard a lot,' Chave replied.

'Were there, though, some big villains he couldn't, or didn't, or was told he shouldn't, inform on?' Esther said.

'We told him not to attempt anything that put him in gross peril. This would ultimately be counterproductive.'

'You varied the vehicle you used when meeting to make payments?' Esther asked.

'Oh, certainly.'

'What about Tully's?'

'Sometimes his own. Sometimes his partner's.'

'Wouldn't these cars be known?'

'Some risks are inevitable,' Chave replied.

'Risks to the grass.'

'They accept this. In return they get something that satisfies them immensely – prestige, as they see it. Plus wages.'

'How much?'

'The sums would vary.'

'Decided how?' Esther asked.

'The value of the information.'

'Yes, but how assessed?'

'Related to possible convictions, their importance and/or the prevention of planned criminal acts and the size of these planned criminal acts.'

'This would be for you to determine?'

'It *is* the controller's responsibility,' Chave said.

'These are difficult, imprecise areas, aren't they?'

'Experience helps. One gets to feel what is about right.'

'Subjective judgements?'

'Judgements. I'd prefer just to call them judgements. All controllers have to make them. As you'll be aware, ma'am.'

'And are the judgements always accepted?' Esther asked.

'By?'

'The informant.'

'A good relationship can be built,' Chave said.

'Are the judgements always accepted?'

'A good relationship can be built so the informant will trust the controller's evaluation of material supplied.'

'Would the informant always understand the criteria behind these evaluations?'

'If a good relationship has been built, the informant will trust the controller's evaluation and accept that the proper criteria have been applied.'

'How do you regard the repetition of these sodding brick-wall, gibberish formulae, Sally?' Esther asked.

'I wouldn't call it mind-reading,' Albert Chave replied, 'nothing so mysterious, but a kind of unspoken agreement will grow up about what this or that piece of information might be worth. A sort of recognized scale. The test ultimately is, does the informant come back with more insights for us?'

'Tully did?'

'Tully did.'

'Until Tully didn't and couldn't,' Esther replied.

'Tragic. Thank God we were able to get the people responsible – though, of course, there can never be adequate amends for his suffering and death.'

'And in the event of dispute?' Esther asked.

'Dispute?'

'Say an informant asking more than you, as controller, think is appropriate.'

'This is where the importance of the good relationship comes in,' Chave replied. 'The good relationship would enable that kind of gap to be bridged.'

'By bargaining?'

'Generally an informant will come to accept the advice of the controller on a matter such as price, if a good relationship has been established.'

'Bargaining?'

'The controller is in charge of public funds. These have to be dispensed judiciously.'

'And the accounting,' Esther said. 'I know DC Bithron is sometimes puzzled about how the accounting can operate when an officer pays money which, because the transaction is secret, cannot be covered by receipts. She's of a clerky disposition and thinks in terms of dockets, strict paperwork – that sort of thing. You're a docket person, aren't you, Sally, and would be first-class working in a shop or bank?'

'It's not something one could ask of informants – to sign receipts,' Chave said. 'A piece of paper like that, somewhere in the headquarters building – it would make them extremely on edge. They hear about a break-in at that most secure of secure Northern Ireland police stations, Castlereagh, and Special Branch documents about the informant organization removed. It's bound to cause general anxiety. And if they grow *too* anxious they'll cease to come forward with further material.'

'But you would record what you pay out from the fund?' Esther asked.

'Naturally, I enter all such disbursements.'

'Alongside the name of the informant?'

'Alongside a code name,' Chave said.

'Tully had a code name?'

'All informants do. It's not for accounting only. When they telephone here, they have to go through the switchboard, obviously, and they'd see security risks in that if they used their real names. Our switchboard operators are first-class, but civilian. Likewise, should the informant's handler be unavailable, another officer might take the call, and it would not be right for this officer to know the true name. Mr Notram, as registrar, keeps a list of code names against real names in a safe. This has to be totally watertight.'

'Was it?'

Eight

Sally went out again to Knoll and found herself defeated by it now. God, but this panicked her. She'd lost something, lost it. Knoll looked today like an urban rural park and only an urban rural park, its slopes, extensive trimmed grass, swings nicely ranged for size on levelled stretches, wooden benches, lemonade picnics, squawking, incommunicative carrycots. That's what Knoll *was*, of course – an urban rural park, grafted with smart environmental skill and civic enlightenment on to a rubbish dump. But Sally *wanted* the rubbish dump, mourned its loss. When she came here before, she could do the dump, recreate it in her head, and recreate the long, terrible moments of Tully's death, and those three dramatic people, not see as now only a load of actual, full-scale harmless nobodies taking their nice, tidy outdoor pleasures. Had her imagination shut down? Was she stuck with the wan here-and-now, the feeble real? Ploddism had her by the throat? Method and fact had wrapped her up? But method and fact hadn't taken her and Esther forward in this inquiry. Perhaps imagination hadn't either, so far, but she thought it had a better chance.

Walking up towards the Tully death area, she knew she must scheme a cure for this sudden mind-palsy at once. The way to do it seemed obvious. Sally decided to locate Stanley Basil Staple, that busy scavenger who discovered Tully's body on Knoll and told the police and then the court about it. Staple would be a link. Although he might be as actual and real and workaday as existed anywhere, he belonged also to that famed early morning tableau when a dump was a dump was a dump, not some irrelevant green, reclamation showpiece up for leisure time prizes. Obviously, he'd have moved his totting on to other tips since Knoll's conversion.

125

Sally could ask around for likelies and try to bump into him one dawn. The files contained plenty of newspaper photographs of Staple in the files, so she'd be able to pick him out from totting colleagues. The pictures showed a square, calm, moustacheless, genial face, which looked as if it had enjoyed so many happy previous finds on tips that even the discovery of a tattered corpse could not mess up these memories and depress him. She turned and descended to her car. The decision to trace Staple made her more optimistic, though she could still hear, from behind, happy, discordant yells of children on swings, or playing chase over the butchery spot.

She knew what pushed her brain back to things as they really were, and stymied her myth-making. Lately, the work had been like ordinary basic policing – tailing Pam, followed by standard, liberal-arts graduate abuse of police from the teacher, then a knotty, cloudy, slippery interview with Albert Chave. Esther showed she could do the basic stuff as well as occasionally cut loose and fly, and the change must have seeped into Sally, changed her, too, watered her down. The examination of Chave had become almost parody third-degree, as though Esther wanted to prove herself no music-hall turn after all. That ferocious hectoring – who sat where in the car, light on or off, who paid out, in what form? Left hand or right to take the money packet and did he wear a signet ring? – no, she didn't ask that but it would have been in line. Actuality reigned. The job dominated. People's jobs did dominate, didn't they: reduced them, confined them, categorized them, squashed them? Was it true of Pete and his 'executive manager' post at home? Poor Pete. And perhaps fact and the job had taken over Sally, too, as she watched and listened, killing that dreamier, thesping, fantasy side of her. *So, resist, Bithron. Get your feet out of the fucking concrete block, fight to the surface.*

At moments during the Chave session, Sally had seen what the teacher meant by an interrogator's jaw. When Esther's questions came at full pace, her face did get jutty, drifted a bit towards those Hapsburg contours. Perhaps early on her husband had fancied the pride and push of it. After all, Hapsburgs *were* royals.

126

'You're police?' Staple said when Sally found him one morning.

Christ, did she have an interrogator's jaw herself, a give-away? 'I'm not bothered what you lift from here,' she replied. He looked more worn now than in the newspaper photographs. Shock might take a while to register with him. They were on the lower slopes of a tip called Springfield Heights, a brilliantly authentic tip so far, with a tip's range of layered, authentic stinks, jagged, jumbled outcrops, foraging seagull teams – yellow beaked, yellow eyed. He carried an old blue leather suitcase with reinforced brass-studded corners, and showing large, faded but still colourful Rio de la Plata and Valparaiso labels, like a remittance man moving on. Sally didn't know whether he'd recovered the case today on the tip or brought it with him to take items. This was a case with weight, of another classier, statelier age, when porters existed.

'It's stuff people don't want,' he said, 'and would only get buried.'

'Right.'

'In a way my work is useful.'

'Turning discards into valuables,' Sally remarked.

'I'm only stealing from them dig merchants, you know – the what-you-calls.'

She wanted to help him out and offer *archaeologists*, but stayed silent. It would be easy and unforgivable to get patronizing with someone whose vocation was refuse dumps.

'Archaeologists,' he said.

'Plenty of other stuff for them, anyway.'

'So, what's it about then? Being here – you. If, like, I may ask. Of course, you're at liberty to. You got a right as much as me to tips.'

'Thanks.'

'This is democracy.'

'Equal opportunity.'

'But the trial's over, so why you still nosing?'

'You had a lot of press.'

'It's not clever.'

'What?'

'Words and face everywhere. There's some dangerous

127

ones around. Well, I don't have to tell you, being that your job got to handle them'.

'But only *finding* the body. A fluke.'

'Yes, only.'

'But?' Sally said. 'Who can blame you for that?'

'*I* know it was only finding the body.'

'But?'

'There are some dangerous ones around.' He had on paint-streaked blue dungarees, perhaps reclaimed previously here or at Knoll, and a terrific fit, though not remittance-man gear.

'The dangerous ones went to jail, didn't they?' Sally asked.

'Did they?' he replied. 'All? What's it about? Being here – you. I mean, if I may ask, although you're entitled.'

'Dangerous how? Why?'

'Sometimes it's not clever to find a body,' he said. 'To be the first there. People want to know how is it you managed to be first there, like maybe being part of it, helping him along to being only a body.'

'Which people want to know?'

'They're curious.'

'Business people?' Sally would have liked to use a fragment given by the Inclination's fire exit trader and ask, Such as Mr Percival Blay? But it might not be the kind of name to play with on a tip, and she didn't.

'Quite a few,' he said.

'But you explained in the witness box why you were there – the nature of your livelihood – early-morning activity.'

'Yes, I explained that. Who believes it? Does everybody believe it?'

'The court believed it.'

'Some people read in the papers that the court believed it, but this don't meant *they* believe it. Some think they see more than courts. Some think courts only see what they want to see. Courts want things tidied up. Courts are like tips. They tidy things up. They get nuisance people and nuisance stuff out of the way.'

'What does that mean – "see more than courts"?'

'Yes, see more than courts,' he replied.

'What then, what do they see?'

'I didn't say they see it. They *think* they see it.'

'Who do?' Blay? But, likewise, only an unexpressed thought. She said: 'What do they think they see?'

'If I can ask, why are you out here on a tip, this time of the morning, although entitled?' he replied. 'An officer.'

'Are you saying they think to themselves, "*This is a totter, and what do totters do, they tot, they pick up stuff*"?'

'I never touched the body.'

'You told the court that and the court believed you,' Sally said.

'Would I? I wouldn't never touch it, not a body like that.'

'This was accepted.'

'You say totting, but he didn't have nothing in his pockets when found,' Staple replied.

'No, I know.'

'Look, I don't mean when he was found by *me* there wasn't nothing in the pockets. I mean when the police came, and the others, and searched him.' His features tightened up more with confusion. They stood fairly low on Springfield Heights. The tip rose steeply behind him, and when Sally shifted her eyeline for a moment from his face, she saw two tattered mattresses, a cracked pink washbasin with a length of its waste pipe, and four or five big tyres. She could understand what he meant about archaeologists. Tips did portray a culture. Staple continued: 'Or no . . . When I say I don't mean there wasn't nothing in the pockets when I found him, I don't mean I *knew* there wasn't nothing in his pockets when I found him, because I didn't search his pockets, so I wouldn't know there wasn't nothing in his pockets, would I? This is obvious.'

'Yes, obvious.'

'But when the police came and looked at him they found nothing in the pockets. That's what I heard – nothing in his pockets.'

'Yes, how it was,' Sally replied. 'You said that in court.'

'Is that what it's about with you?' he asked.

'What?'

'You don't believe it? Your bosses don't believe it? You think maybe I got to some of his papers, his secret notes, and took them?'

'Papers? Secret notes?'

'Them pockets was empty when I found him. What I mean is, if they was empty when the police searched him, they was empty when I found him, because . . .'

'Yes, I get that. It's very probable the people who killed him also cleared his pockets,' Sally replied. 'Routine. In court they denied it. Who believed them, though?'

'This was a grass, wasn't it? He could of had all sorts of info in his pockets. That's obviously the trade of a grass – info. You think I've got it?'

'They'd want to get rid of that,' Sally said.

'If he was a grass, he could have a notebook or something like that in his pocket, with names and other things to tell his officer. A grass always has an officer, for meeting, talking, getting paid.'

'Oh, those two would be ordered to search him,' Sally replied. 'Yes, most likely. Make sure he had nothing harmful.'

'A notebook or something, like with their own names in it, or their chief's name.'

'Certainly.' Was their chief Percy Blay? Or was their chief possibly hired by Blay? But it might be slander to ask. And was Blay protected?

'Would they want to leave that there – a notebook?' He spoke it as simple logic.

'Not likely,' Sally said.

'I wouldn't be interested in his notebook.'

'Of course you wouldn't.'

'That's dangerous. In any case, I wouldn't know whether there was a notebook like that in the pockets, because I never looked in the pockets, not even for a wallet.'

'No.'

'If you find a body on a tip and it's been slashed and you can see it's been slashed, you know there's going to be a lot of questions, and so you don't touch nothing in case you get trouble.'

'I can see that. Does this happen a lot?'

'What?'

'Finding slashed bodies on tips.'

'Some would not of even reported they found a body, because of trouble,' Staple replied.

'You did well there.'

'You know them monkeys?' he replied.

'Which exactly?'

'I found some of them monkeys on Knoll once.'

'Which monkeys, Mr Staple?'

'Ornaments for, say, the mantlepiece. Plaster-cast. The three together.'

'Which?' Sally said.

'Paws over their ears and eyes and mouth.'

' "Hear no evil, see no evil, speak no evil." '

'Sometimes it's better – just shut your eyes.'

'You did well there. Didn't the judge say you did well – public-spirited?'

'He knew I could of been scared of trouble – totting *and* finding a body. Totting's not supposed to be legal. Well, you know that. But the judge said I didn't care about being found out totting and I told the police about the body. Like priorities.'

'You did *really* well.'

'Sometimes it's not too clever to get thanks from a judge,' Staple replied. 'Some people wonder what he's thanking you for.'

'But he *said* what for – for reporting the body, nothing else.'

'Some people wonder if it's really nothing else – what's, like, *behind* it.'

'Which people?'

'There are people out there, dangerous people.'

'What else could it be?' Sally asked.

'There's deals. On-the-quiet deals. I should think you know about deals.'

'What deals?' Someone must have thrown out a couple of hundred white plastic bags and the wind had picked these up and carried them around the tip. Many were now fixed on projecting bits of old toys, old furniture, old kitchen cookers, old lawn mowers. From a distance the bags reminded Sally of a famous scene in the film of *Oh, What a Lovely*

131

War, given a TV run occasionally. In that shot, the camera showed rank after rank of white crosses on First World War soldiers' graves. The idea pleased her. It was fanciful, a piece of imagination, an escape from the actual – yes, an idea. Brilliant. She'd made a recovery. She was not stuck with plastic bags on ruptured tricycles, the way the plastic bags themselves were stuck on ruptured tricycles: the crummy dominance of *things*. Things on things. The spiky, intransigent, dreary real. But she . . . she knew herself capable of visions again, her mind could go laterally, soar and provide private views. She'd been right to come to Springfield Heights.

'When I say deals – what's referred to as "behind the scenes",' Staple replied.

'Who's behind the scenes?'

'This is deals with the police. And then the police give a whisper to the judge, or a special letter, like recommending, and he says something nice and forgets about breaking the law totting. Well, I expect you've come across such arrangements.'

'What deals?'

'There's deals.'

'Did you hear somewhere he had papers on him – names, that sort of stuff?' Sally asked.

'Hear? Who from?'

'Was there a buzz around?'

'How do you mean, buzz?'

'Like, you know, rumour, gossip?'

'There was all sorts.'

'All sorts of what?' Sally replied.

'Buzz. If you call it that.'

'Papers? Names?'

'There'd be people out there, dangerous people, who might think Tully would be sure to have papers on him, and names, that sort of thing. Plus money. The buzz – what you call the buzz – this buzz said Tully always had a wad aboard. The buzz said Tully got paid cash and also kept cash to pay little folk who brought him them bits and pieces he could put together and make something to earn something fat from his officer. There'd be people out there – they would think, when a totter

132

comes along and finds a body, what do he do – they would think what he would do is he tots the body and takes everything, because that's what totters do – they tot – like a singer, if he hears his note on the piano, he'll sing, or a decorator, if he sees a wall he'll paper it. Then these people would wonder if the totter turned scared because he knew the body would be found when the men arrived for work, and first thing the law would ask is, who's out on the tip a lot when there's nobody else about? And the answer is: Stanley Basil Staple and other totters. So, he's in the frame. They're in the frame. So, some people might think that, to dodge this, he rings up and does the honest bit and says he found a body and he went through the pockets for identity, identity only, but the pockets was totally empty, swear to God. So, next, in the way they see it, the police come out and they think Stanley Basil Staple, being a totter, helped himself to everything in the pockets and then turned panicky and phoned in. They would know Tully always carried a stack. So the police say to this totter, if he'll hand over papers, anything like that, they'll forget about the money and ask the judge to be sweet to him because he been a help to the case. This is how some people out there might think it went. What I mean by dangerous.'

'But it didn't,' Sally said. Short. Definite. Bulging with trust. She took care not to make it sound like a question. Another go: 'But it didn't.'

'I never touched them pockets, but they might think I done a deal with the police, like – "Give us them papers and names, Stanley, and you can keep the loot." And, that way, I turn into a grass, maybe still doing it. That's how they might think, the people out there, big people. This is not clever. Tully gave tips and ends on a tip.'

'But it was a long time ago. If you'd done a deal like that, there'd have been action from the papers you gave. People would realize this.'

'Police sit on stuff, sometimes. They wait.'

She found she could visualize Staple at Knoll in gorgeous old junk-heap days, arriving where the body lay and standing over it, wondering how he should play things, maybe thinking about the pockets and then deciding the body and the pockets and Tully's watch had better not be touched. Or deciding the pockets *could* be touched. She imagined him bending to examine the wounds, and perhaps glancing about to see if any other early-bird totter spotted him looking at the wounds. His face would be kindly, sad, troubled then. Yes, she *saw it*. Suddenly, pictures could undoubtedly form in her head again, and she felt restored, beautifully liberated. He carried a mobile phone, but told the court he didn't use it, considering security. Instead, she saw him descending Knoll fast and finding a booth. He would dial the emergency number and be told to wait there until officers and an ambulance arrived. They'd send an ambulance no matter how clearly he'd said the man was dead.

'Have you had any trouble?' she said.

'What trouble?'

'Since the trial. Or before it.'

'I goes careful.'

'But I found you.'

'Yeah, you found me, and talking to me like this – that might not be very clever,' he said.

'Nobody around so early.'

'You sure?'

'They don't know I'm the police. I'm not local.'

'First thing they'd think is you're police. What else you out here for? It's not a tourist spot.'

'Yet.'

'What's a girl like you doing talking to Stan Staple on a tip at six a.m.? This is what they'd think. They've heard of women detectives.'

'This is ages after the body. Ages after the trial. You've had no trouble?'

'What trouble?'

'People asking you about papers, names, that sort of thing,' Sally replied.

'What people?'

'Well, these people you think are out there – dangerous people, you said.'

'Out there? Not all of them are *out* there. Some might be in the same building as you.'

134

'Police?'

'Tully knew a lot of stuff. That's what I heard after I found him. Stuff that could be difficult for all sorts.'

'So, have you had trouble – I mean from anyone – police, anyone? For instance, this might be the kind of topic that would interest somebody running dodgy businesses.' Mr Percival Blay? But who said Blay's businesses were dodgy – Blay Financial Management and its tasteful, memorable BFM logo? Could you prove it? Or was this part of that revived imagination?

Staple looked at her for a while and she saw what he meant. He meant *she* might be trouble, making him chat like this. 'I'm careful,' he said.

'People asking you about papers, names, that sort of thing?'

'Is that why you're out here?' he replied.

'What?'

'To ask me about papers, names, that sort of thing?'

'No – to see if people have asked you about papers, names, that sort of thing, and who they are.' Really, she came here to get some mind therapy, some imagination therapy, but it would be too tough to explain this. Wool. Flam.

'I stick to it – what I said all along, no messing with pockets, so no papers, nothing,' he said.

'You "stick to it". So, people *have* asked, have they?'

'I stick to that. It's been all right, so far,' he replied. 'So far. Yes, ages since, like you said. Some dangerous people out there would most likely know I didn't see no papers or names, because they told their boys Chamberlain and Barry Jolliffe to take all that when they done him.'

'Ah, so they might put the word around you're all right?'

'Yes, they might. But then somebody says, "So who's Staple talking and talking to out on Springfield Heights before brekker?"'

'I want you to be in touch with us if anything worries you. Anything.'

'*You* worry me, if I can say.'

She wrote some numbers for him. 'Where we're staying, my mobile and a separate line into headquarters.'

'Which we?'

'I'm Detective Constable Bithron. I work with an assistant chief, Mrs Davidson. Can you learn the numbers? Get rid of the bit of paper.'

'Like they did with Tully's.'

'Don't use general headquarters numbers.'

'You think this one's private?' he asked, looking at what she'd written.

'It's private.'

'You really think that?'

'Why? Have you heard some buzz they're listening in?' Sally asked.

'Who?'

'People in the building.'

'Police on police – that's the worst,' Staple replied.

'Have you heard some buzz like that?'

'If they send an assistant chief, they must think things are real bad.'

'Who?'

'Say the government. Them running the police.'

'You're exposed out here,' Sally replied.

'You just said there's nobody about.'

'If they *wanted* to be about.'

'I was all right. But now you – talking, if I can say.'

'How are locks and bolts where you live?' Sally said.

'Don't come there. Please. I got kids, you know.'

'Yes, I know. Three.'

'You got a file? Of course you have.'

'A newspaper mentioned the children at the time of the trial. A reporter wrote some background on you.'

'That's what I mean – not clever to be in the press,' he replied. 'Think of that Max Clifford.'

'Who?'

'With the stars and celebrities. Sometimes getting stuff into the papers about them, sometimes trying to keep it out. I got no Max Clifford.'

'And then, Tully had a child, as well,' Sally replied.

'He'll be all right.'

'Who says?'

'The buzz.'

'He's mentioned by name?' Sally said.

'If the buzz goes around about him and the buzz says he'll be all right, they got to use his name, haven't they, or nobody would know who they mean.'

'But if they use his name, it means someone's thought about doing something to him, doesn't it? All right, it was decided against, but someone's thought about it. Things might change.'

'He'll be all right.'

'How can you be sure?' Sally replied.

'The buzz.'

In the evening, she thought about ringing Pete, but decided against. Somehow, she still liked the distance. Well, no somehow, she knew how. The distance relaxed her, as it seemed to relax Esther. For Sally, distance meant her mind could travel and get rubbish-dump reveries. Pete would phone her occasionally, and she did not mind answering and doing a heartfelt tone to say she missed him. That was only decency and kindness. In any case, spells came when she *did* miss him. Of course. Of course. And spells when she wished she could miss him more. It seemed hard not to. But Sally drew back from initiating calls, for now. For now. Probably this reluctance would wear off. For now, she would hang on to peace, detachment, remoteness, dreamability.

In fact, she did not get peace. The phone rang and, after a good half minute's hesitation while she hoped it would stop, Sally picked up the receiver. She made her voice light, positive, responsive, loving. She reasoned that if Pete took the trouble to ring, he deserved this. 'Detective Constable Bithron? Percival Blay. It might be useful if we could meet and talk.'

'Blay?'

'Percival Blay.'

'In what regard?'

'I can possibly help.'

'Ah. Kind.'

'I expect you know of my business concerns in the area.'

'Forgive me. We're seeing a great number of people and I—'

137

'Percival Blay of Blay Financial Management.'

'As you'll probably realize, Mr Blay, I'm a stranger here and still catching up on names and other details,' Sally replied. 'Please overlook my ignorance, at this stage. Blay Financial Management, you say?'

'Always I sympathize with officers given your kind of task – placed in unfamiliar, perhaps hostile, surroundings and required quickly to make assessments, judgements. One recalls, doesn't one, Deputy Chief John Stalker, sent to Northern Ireland to investigate an alleged shoot-to-kill policy and encountering powerful intransigence and worse from supposed colleagues? You probably think of this comparison very often.'

Yes, of course, she did.

Blay said: 'Or of Sir John Stevens from the Metropolitan force, also sent on an inquiry into Northern Ireland security practices, and his office there actually torched.'

Yes, him too.

Blay said: 'But I'm sure that such enmity is not the case here. I refer only to the inevitable degree of isolation for investigating officers in another force.'

'That *is* one aspect of the work, I must say.' She liked it.

'I feel those of us living here, and therefore in touch with local concerns – we, as I see it, have a duty to assist you in your assignment.'

'Thank you. I'm making a note, if you don't mind. It's Mr Percival Blay of Blay Financial Management? That right?'

'BFM is my logo. You'll probably see it about.'

'Well, yes, I'll keep an eye. I will. B . . . F . . . M. And you feel it would be constructive to meet, do you?'

'Constructive, yes. It's a matter of—'

'Probably best not to do this by phone, Mr Blay. Can we make an appointment?'

She drove out to Blay's beautiful country house.

He said: 'I was amused, but, yes, also grateful, at the way you pretended never to have heard of me or my business when I telephoned. Grateful because you obviously meant this as a considerate act.'

'Did Stanley Staple tell you where to reach me?'

'I can't – but absolutely can*not* – I can't blame someone for duplicity if – and this caveat is a mighty, mighty caveat, Detective Constable Bithron – I cannot blame someone for duplicity *if*, as in this instance – if the display of ignorance about me and certain unpleasant rumours attaching to my name – if such duplicity is practised in the cause of kindness and the wish to, for example, protect someone's feelings – the "white lie", as it is fondly called – the "white lie" told to someone so as to guard that someone from the harshness, from even the cruelty, of too much frankness, too much truth. Perhaps, as a police officer, you'll regard this as a strange concept – "too much truth", although, of course, not all police officers are entirely sold on entire truth for the entire duration of their career. But, obviously, I don't refer to you in this, and you'll be wondering, can there be "too much truth"? To which I must answer, yes, some truths are best hidden away, or at least revealed with slow, tactful gradualness.'

'Sensitivity to the feelings of those around one is certainly a lovely quality, in my book,' Sally replied.

'And when one is, as it were, "on the end of it" – when one is the beneficiary of such consideration oneself, one achieves, perhaps, greater insight into that quality than if one were actually dispensing it to another.'

'Yes, in this instance at least, it might be better to receive than to give.'

'I certainly don't see it as disrespectful to the scriptures occasionally to amend a verse, as you have there, Detective Constable Bithron, in order to vivify a thought.'

'The scriptures can take it,' Sally said. She had the feeling he struggled with himself to keep the conversation grandiose and ducky, but that something different struggled for its ungentle chance and might win.

It won. He seemed to give up the oracular – for a while, anyway: 'Some might regard your show of unacquaintance with my name as typical, slimy police two-timing, based on the precept that you sods are trained never to let the public see what you know.'

'Obviously my phone numbers are not at all secret – the opposite, indeed. One needs to talk to as many folk as possible. But it just occurred to me that Stanley Staple might have drawn your attention to it, if there's some sort of working relationship between him and you,' Sally replied.

Niceness hurried back to him. 'I'd prefer to think that you – when you simulate no knowledge of me – I'd prefer to think that when you did that, it was entirely out of sweet-natured tact. You did not want Percival Blay to feel you might be prejudiced against him because you had received certain damaging reports, even before you and he met – damaging, that is, to Percival Blay. And so you acted uninformed. This was the behaviour of someone fair-minded and, yes, generous.'

'When you say Blay Financial Management, does that describe in full the nature of your businesses?'

'Yet in another way totally fucking absurd,' Blay said.

'What?'

'The unfamiliarity with my name.'

'We are available to talk to anyone,' Sally said. 'This is a policy very explicitly laid down by Assistant Chief Esther Davidson.'

'If you trawl the Inclination, as I hear, you're almost sure to collect references, aren't you? What else are you there for? That slack-gobbed sleeper-around, Peaceable Aix, near the fire exit.'

'He buys from you, works for you?' Sally asked.

'Aix will talk without thought of the consequences.'

'Oh, yes, we're available to speak to anybody,' Sally said. 'And if someone rings up and says he/she has material that could be to the point, we do not ask for details, or even an outline, then and there by telephone. As you know. ACC Davidson believes it is unreasonable to expect people to pass such material by telephone, unless he/she actually wishes to do so. And I endorse that. Perhaps this is what you mean by "sweet-natured tact".'

'Throughout that trial my name was never mentioned,' Blay replied. 'I think you can confirm. I'm certain you've searched the transcripts.' His voice suddenly hardened again. 'That would be the kind of dogsbody task someone of your rank would get on such an assignment.'

'I suppose that, in a sense, *all* businesses are concerned with financial management – their own if no other.'

'You'll hear the most filthy fucking whispers, not one of them backed by anything but malice and envy. If my name's not even mentioned in the trial, how can whispers like that be worth anything?'

'As is often said, life itself is—'

He worked at it really well and got a smile of cosmic affability going: 'In many senses it's a true privilege to welcome you here to my property, Detective Constable Bithron, and, when my wife joins us in a moment, I would like, if I may, to show you some of the more interesting features of the building. Much of it is sixteenth century, you know, including the archway and corridor from west to east wing and the chimney breasts in both the small hall and the gallery alcove, as we call it. We are not manic about the past, I hope, but where present comfort and convenience can be achieved alongside preserved aspects from another time, we both feel there is a duty to ensure those aspects are indeed preserved.'

'Property has a dual significance, hasn't it, the same as, say, clothes and/or fountain pens?' Sally replied with a warm conversational tone. 'There is that basic comfort and convenience – to have a roof, to be warm inside a coat, to be able to write a cheque and provide oneself with funds. But then there is also the historic, the environmental and status aspect to property – this latter especially. A house can become, as it were, an extension of one's identity. Likewise, we might expect a coat to give us not merely protection from the weather, but style, and a pen to allow us more character in the up and/or down strokes than a mere biro.'

Blay remained quiet for a while, the smile tidied away. 'What I have to try and work out when dealing with nimble fucking unknowns like you, with your mad, smarmed spiels and prole clothes, is whether you're heaping up secret information – that is, *supposed* information – yes, *supposed* information about Percival Blay, and then making out you haven't got an idea who he is, his logo unremarked, so he will be lulled and friendly when you're talking to him, and more liable to say something unguarded, stupid, incriminating. This would go for my attitude to your boss, Esther Davidson, also, clearly. I'm sure you will appreciate my uncertainties, Detective Constable Bithron, and sympathize. I can tell you are someone very quick to sympathize. Empathic is certainly a term that would fit you well. I welcome you into our home, yet you could be the most treacherous fucking daisy this side of Skegness.'

'Or take a house like Tully's in Milton Avenue,' Sally replied. 'All right, it doesn't have the murky old grandeur of this, but wouldn't it say to anyone interested that here was a boy who must have all kinds of income sources? Detached, portico pillars, burgundy stone patterns for the drive. How come he could go on grassing and grassing and spending like that and nobody does anything about him until his informant career's been running years? How was it arranged? Mysteries of this kind can appear in life, as you'll know, Mr Blay, and there may be business pressures, social pressures, that prevent questions being put about them. But because you have accepted me so genially into your spruced-up ruin, I do feel emboldened to ask.'

'Oh, I definitely welcome the purpose of your task, yours and AC Davidson's, in this area. You, coming from elsewhere, will be able to look on matters here with a freshness and absence of preconception perhaps not available to some others. It's a considerable privilege to receive you into our home.'

'How was it that—?'

'I suppose when I come on the phone to you you think, *I know this fucker's sly game: he's keen to get in first and pre-empt. He realizes we'll want to talk to him, so he asks for a meeting himself – acts unworried, confident, lays on the fruity verbiage.* You people can't see anything as a simple, friendly move, can you?'

'How was it that—?'

'All right, back where you come from, I'm told you go out solo looking for it in clubs. And report says this Davidson has big marriage complications. I, personally, don't feel it proper for one of our local detectives – Moss – to start inquiries into those matters. But I understand it occurred. Why I telephoned. I wished you to know that such inquiries have been made and that I deplore those tactics.'

'How would you discover this? Who talks to you, Mr Blay?'

'Ah, here is Charlotte now,' he replied. 'Detective Constable Bithron and I were discussing the brickwork of the chimney breasts, darling. I know she longs to see them. But we decided to wait for you, since your commentary on such topics is so much more knowledgeable than mine. Although only a detective constable at this juncture, she's been chosen for an accelerated promotion course, I gather, and I can certainly see why.'

They had been talking in what Sally thought a delightful, large, first-floor drawing room, its leaded windows westerly and open to the early-evening summer sun. The room contained three red leather armchairs and a chesterfield, also red leather. Sally and Blay sat opposite each other in armchairs. He wore a blue-black, lightweight single-breasted suit, grey tie on a white shirt, and black shoes. He was short, slight, delicate-featured, brown-eyed, fairish hair in retreat, but not too far yet. Sally knew him to be fifty-one and might have guessed somewhere near to that. When he worked at it he could look extremely well disposed and tranquil, the kind she would not be at all surprised to hear fixed things so he stayed totally unmentioned in a murder-and-disfigurement trial.

They both stood to greet his wife, and Blay made intro-ductions. She was the same build as Percival. She had on a dark skirt to her ankles and a black, high-collared top. When *she* smiled now, she kept the smile on duty for quite a time, open-mouthed and wide, and Sally felt it would have reas-sured many who wanted to think the best of people. Her hair was silvered blonde, and her nose short, straight, not aggres-sive or doughy.

'Come,' she said, turning. 'We'll reverence the famed masonry, shall we, and then return for some hospitality? You're here to see how the hell Percival kept his splendid little self out of the Tully shit, are you? My Perce has *such* flair. People revere him. I don't feel this is too strong a term. Hence, we can live serene and safe in our redolent property, no ugly, heavyweight minders about, no electronic alarm paraphernalia.'

Nine

When he could arrange the rest of his duties to give him some space, Harvey Moss continued watching Cheyne School at home time, and waited until he saw Walter Tully safely into his mother's car. Now and then, hanging about like this, Moss did wonder whether he should make so much of Dick Patterson's information. Right word, information? Guess? Rumour? Invention? Dick remained a babe in grassing, his reliability unproved.

But Moss wanted no preventable risk to Tully's boy or the boy's mother. God, wasn't there enough pain about already? So, a school patrol for him when possible, and hard luck if he looked like a loitering paedophile. Moss stayed outside the gates and picked points on the road from which he could watch the queue of vehicles move up towards Cheyne's big main doors and the fountain. In some ways, of course, the regularity frightened him. It also comforted him a little, though. Things continued. Sweet normality put the squeeze on.

Pamela spotted him, alerted by their unplanned meeting previously. Although she did not smile or wave, he knew her eyes reached him two or three times each day he got there for the pick-up drill. No sex in the eyes as far as he could make out. He would have settled for friendliness, but saw not much of that, either. The child's eyes reached him, too. He remained as impassive as his mother. It was the kind of blank kid-face you expected suddenly to turn hostile and stick out its tongue. Walter didn't. Naturally, they'd talk about Moss, and Pamela would probably attempt some explanation for his presence. It might even be the right one. After all, this lad realized things could turn dangerous – had been

made to realize things could turn dangerous. He should understand the need for protection. Is that what Moss was, he
wondered. He did have the little cosh in his pocket.

It didn't trouble Moss that they saw him. Perhaps his
continual attendances would convince Pamela things could
still turn dangerous. The drawback to having a BMW, and
waiting in a quality car queue outside a piece of pleasant
old architecture with a fountain, was that she'd experience
that lulling factor which Moss himself sometimes suffered
from. Things continued. The normality syndrome. This scene
felt and looked too nice for brutalities to sneak in. Just the
same, Moss's obvious anxieties might make Pamela think of
ways to vary the pattern, though he did not know how, unless
she withdrew Walter from Cheyne, at least for a while. Moss
would approve, but thought it unlikely. For Walter's sake,
she seemed set on rebuilding a routine, and Moss could
sympathize. Possibly, though, she'd start taking different
routes to and from school. This would be only a slight
improvement, but an improvement.

He had another reason for feeling glad they noticed him.
He required, yes, *required*, Pamela to see that, regardless of
what had happened to Tully on Knoll, Moss would never
write off the family. *Could* never. Through Chief Inspector
Albert Chave and the payouts, Moss had helped establish
the Tullys as they now were – the avenue, the education, the
vehicles, the decor – and he did not believe the survivors
should be abandoned just because Tully was gone.

No – get more bloody positive. Moss considered Justin
Tully's death made care for Pamela and Walter an even greater
obligation. This came from a very personal impulse based
on very personal guilt, not official police custom. Moss had
decided he must make up to them as far as he could for their
loss. That loss was down to him, wasn't it? Was it? Possibly
the blame should be shared, but he must take the biggest
slice.

He found himself unable to dodge or ignore this. The
discovery brought no pleasure to Moss, and he did not regard
himself as a more wholesome, more *caring* person because
of it. Conscience could be damned inconvenient and entirely

impractical, maybe unprofessional. The past lay irrecover-
ably sunk in unfathomable water. Just the same, conscience
would not let him escape via all these negatives, and kept a
cruel grip. Partly this must be his mother's fault. She had
kept on at him as a child to locate his conscience and give it
a look-in. Partly it must also come from his time with all those
big Victorian novels he'd had to read, and their obsession with
moral problems, and the proper outcome to moral problems.

Escape. He loved that as a notion. Only a notion. But he
longed to fight free for a while from all the hard actualities
of the post-Tully scene. This also might be his fiction side,
perhaps his poetry side. He wondered if Detective Constable
Sally Bithron, here to help with the investigation into him
and others – more bloody actuality . . . he wondered if *she*
had the ability to escape now and then. What else did the
strange theatricals on Knoll tip mean? He envied her those.
They smashed that dull, necessary dominance of the accurate, the factual, the notebook-able, the data-fucking-base-
able. He'd learned in his so-far short career that police forces
possessed elaborate, brilliantly sensible, well-meaning tables
of regulations and procedures, and that officers who let themselves get hog-tied by these stayed low or lowish – and moved
righteously and sluggishly at this level towards their long-
service medal.

Why not slip out to Knoll himself early one morning and
see whether he could bring off something similar to DC
Bithron's mind flutters? He'd be happy to do a bit of drama.
She had obviously been trying to recreate the past – recover
it from those dirty depths. Bullshit, of course, but perhaps
she drew something helpful from fantasizing. And was it
really bullshit? What about those crime re-enactments the
police officially staged when they felt stuck, hoping to get
at the subconscious memories of potential witnesses, cops
in the roles of victims? *Cameras! Action!* If Moss could trick
himself into the same sort of make-believe contact with the
past as Bithron's, he might loosen that motherly, Dickensian,
unforgiving half-Nelson kept on him by conscience. He
wanted to see – re-see – the detail and sequence of Tully's
death, and its true motives.

Fuck it, why unforgiving? Grasses understood from the start, didn't they, that carelessness or betrayal or office politics might kill them at any time, and especially politics? *We didn't promise you a rose garden, except as a fragrant burial ground.* They still chose the job. The money was danger money. They realized this. Tully had certainly realized it – had often talked intelligently, matter-of-factly, about the perils and how he countered them. Grasses became grasses because they got to know things, and one of the things Tully got to know was that he might have a jolly job for life, but life could stop short, or *be* stopped short, more likely. To Moss, his precautions had always sounded sensible, although, naturally, Tully could not foresee every possible peril. Nobody could. The office politics side was always going to be complex and shifting and secret. Big careers, big egos, big pensions, had to safeguard themselves, didn't they?

Moss went out to Knoll at first light, hours before the park opened, scaled a fence, then climbed slowly up towards the Tully spot. As he walked, he had time to think how totally idiotic this expedition was. The place gave him no revelations so far, not one. His imagination stayed where it often did lately, somewhere totally and maturely and correctly suppressed, if not defunct. How the hell could he have felt jealous of such lunatic posturing in Sally Bithron? Escape from the limitations and roughnesses of life might be possible, but the means generally came in bottles or small plastic-wrapped packets, not solo amateur dramatics. And when escape *did* come, it was very temporary.

Eventually, nearly up at the approximate site of Tully's torture and death, Moss had a surprise and thought at first that Chief Inspector Albert Chave, his controller, had opted to try the fantasy treatment for *his* problems. After all, Chave's problems might be big and dark. He'd already been in to see the investigators, Davidson and Bithron. Had he felt they were trying to nail him? Perhaps he deserved to be nailed. Possibly when Moss went in to see them, he would feel they were trying to nail him, too. They were here to nail someone, or more than one, weren't they? Yes, nails, not whitewash, would be their work stuff.

147

Wearing civilian clothes, Chave lay on his right side near toddler-style swings, those chirpy symbols of clean-up on what had been a dump and an extermination ground. Chave's face was away from Moss, but he recognized the solid physique, short tow-coloured hair, navy suit and tight, neat, black non-flat-foot shoes. Another here to recapture, if he could, that agonizing night? Moss felt it would embarrass Chave to know a subordinate had seen him communing like this with the voodoo world, and did not call out. Nobody who knew Chave would expect such mysticizing tripe from him. The approach by Moss had been reasonably quiet, so Chave might not know he was observed. Everyone had a right to some private daftness, rank no bar. Moss moved a little way back down the slope. Half-grown bushes had been transplanted in the new park and he found cover behind a hydrangea. He hoped that if Chave stood suddenly and began to descend, he would use a route away from this bush.

Chave did not stand suddenly, or at all. After about ten minutes, when there had been no movement, Moss began to revise his assessment. It had been barmy for him to come out here hoping for an inspired and favourable glimpse of truth. Was it even more barmy to suppose someone like Albert Chave would act on a similar hope? Chave definitely did not do fantasy. His personality always stayed as laced-up as his feet in those beautiful narrow shoes. Moss left his cover and began to ascend the slope again towards him. As he grew nearer, he saw that Chave's right arm was bent towards his face, and this angularity and the utter stillness of the body alarmed Moss. He did call out now, and had no response. 'Mr Chave? It *is* Mr Chave, isn't it? Taking a breather after the climb, sir? Yes, steep. And the sun's already pleasantly warm, isn't it?' Or had emotional pain caused by nearness to the execution venue caused him to black out? But Chave did not do emotional pain, not about policing. Chave did not do blackouts.

Why should the angle of the arm trouble Moss? It looked as if it or his hand were administering something to Chave – say food or make-up, or aftershave or a bullet. It turned out to be a bullet, and Moss must have sensed this from the start. Was there something about Chave which had seemed right for a bullet lately? When Moss stood over him and looked down, he saw that not even the most lavish make-up applied by the most skilled operator could have disguised the derangement of Chave's features by a one-shot in the mouth, and he would be needing no food or aftershave. It was not one of the largest calibre pistols. Without as yet reading the maker's name, Moss thought a .32 Charter Arms Undercover. Anything bigger and the recoil might have thrown the gun yards. The butt was still in Chave's hand, though, and the short barrel still between his lips.

Moss had wanted a rerun, hadn't he? Now here it was – not a rerun of the killing, though, but Stanley Basil Staple's discovery of the Tully corpse. If this were a suicide – and of course it was a suicide, for God's sake, what else, what else? – if this were a suicide, Chave obviously had a message to give. Why else would he have staged it here? 'Staged' – was that a heartless, flippant way to describe the death of someone Moss had worked with and been on-the-job trained by? But what other term would do? Chave had deliberately come out here to finish himself. His message concerned Tully. Yes, well, develop this . . . Chave's death must signify something about the way he, the controller, had dealt with Justin. As to staging, Chave evidently wanted to exit on a final line about the grassing set-up here as he had known it, and helped run it: a curtain – curtains – line.

Moss felt anxious as well as sad. Although Chave's choice of place itself spoke a theme, there might be another dispatch somewhere, more detailed, more specific. Did the chief inspector have a farewell note on him? Moss felt he ought to get a look at it, if so. He had worked to this senior officer, and if the senior officer had not been managing things right – if he had been managing things self-centredly, fraudulently, corruptly – Moss could get hit by fallout now. People about to top themselves were not always careful or wise in what they wrote by way of farewell. Possibly those two women would make something damn rough for Moss from a note left by Chave. Yes, this pair must have frightened Albert. Chave didn't usually do fear, either, but perhaps the stresses he'd run into were beyond anything he'd known before.

Moss decided he'd better search Chave. This would be grossly wrong, of course. It would put him a moral peg down from Stan Staple, apparently – a *legal* peg down. In court, Staple said he did not search or scavenge the body and the court went along with that. Credible? Delicacy might be fine in some situations, an undoubted plus, but it could slip into timidity, paralysis. Moss would not indulge it now. He liked to think he had discovered in these last few years how to take hold of a situation and act. All right, Staple had shown delicacy, so he said, but Staple was a rubbish-dump scavenger and likely to stay stuck at that. As a matter of fact, there had always been a certain delicacy about Tully, too. It helped make him a top grass – one who could accurately evaluate information and who didn't overload Moss with trivia. For Justin, delicacy had been a positive, a skill. On the other hand, you'd think folk like Staple had ditched most scruples, most delicacies, when their work station was a tip. Moss thought Stan Staple probably *had* ditched them, whatever he told the court. Moss had never believed Staple's tale.

But that was Staple, that was Tully. Now, he had to concentrate on Chave. At first, Moss bent over him and tried to get at his pockets without disturbing the lie of the body or the lip grip on his gun barrel. After all, this would be how Chave wished to be remembered – the pistol in his mouth, and a sure-fire, fairly noble, goodbye-to-all-that. Insolent to take this from him. Delicacy did matter here. Chave had arranged an I'll-carry-the-can gesture so his family and colleagues might think of him as worthwhile, even though he lay dead on a former tip and in a copycat situation. He had hoped they need never feel ashamed of him. There could be a valid grandeur of spirit about suicide, and Moss felt he should guard against accidentally resetting the body in any position that suggested Chave had been done by others, not himself. Moss knew it would have enraged Albert if people believed villains existed smart enough to leave him dead on Knoll as a chortling parable: *We can do it to Tully and we can do it to Tully's paymaster as well.*

Chave had believed not quite passionately that law and order must always win, even if the means turned unholy now and then. You could see this grand confidence in the flexibility of his walk, and in the imperturbability of his features. Moss hoped he'd been able to keep that imperturbability when questioned by Davidson and Bithron. Possibly not, or would he be here like this now? But he might have kept up that appearance somehow until this weary, defeated close-down. Had he been thinking of the ancient Romans' and of Rommel's manly suicides? Moss must not mess up Chave's image, whatever others might do, and however much his image when alive had been phoney.

In the search, Moss would look only for any death letter, and possibly Chave's keys, in case it grew necessary to go through his car in an extended hunt for last words. That must be parked somewhere near the base of Knoll, though Moss hadn't seen it when he arrived. There might be awkwardnesses in getting at three or four of Chave's pockets, because he lay on his right side and one trouser side pocket and possibly a back pocket would have his weight on them, as well as an outer pocket of his jacket and maybe an inside one. This last possibility could be the real drag, because if there *were* a letter, he would most likely have put it in that breast pocket. Formal, important papers often did get allocated there. Moss dreaded that he might inadvertently shift the body so the revolver barrel slipped from Chave's mouth and needed to be stuck back. It seemed very much the coarse thing to do to a chief inspector, even when dead. Moss recalled that scene in *Godfather II* where the young gangster, Vito Corleone, finishes off an odious extortioner by shoving a gun in his mouth. Not appropriate for Albert Chave. To earn its name, the Undercover's barrel was only two inches long, and would not be very secure as it now lay, especially as some teeth might have been blown away.

Moss considered the possibility of a note to be high. Chave had always been very clear and explicit in conversations with Moss, sometimes more than sufficiently so, in his view. To kill himself where Tully died might be regarded by many as an adequately clear and explicit signal. 'But you, sir – *you*

151

– would not be content to leave matters so ambiguous, though vivid, I feel sure,' Moss said, as he began on the easy-access pockets first. He could do this standing, but crouched. Talking to Chave in a voice somewhere between banter and arse-licking helped Moss part forget the foul impertinence of rifling his suit. In any case, ever since he had followed Bithron up here, this place seemed to have become a setting for the madly far-out and theatrical, and, at present, some conversation with a dead man seemed all right, the way King Lear talked to Cordelia's corpse.

'I wouldn't wish to be misunderstood as to why I'm keen to read any final thoughts, sir. I'm certain that even in the state of extreme tension which must have been yours when you decided on this finale, you would not commit to paper material that might endanger the careers and/or lives of colleagues more than they are already endangered. I, personally, have nothing to dread from any letter, except that grey-area doings, even when carefully described, might give these two investigating ladies a chance to twist, exploit, distort. These are their fucking *métier*.'

On a scale of one to ten, with banter as one and arse-licking at ten, Moss guessed his tone to be about eight or nine. But he thought this OK, given Chave's rank and honourable death. 'I definitely shall not destroy any such letter, regardless of its revelations, but I think I'm entitled to see those parts of it which might feature my work and so on with Tully, because the investigators will be made aware of such matter, no question, and before seeing them I need to check what special information they have. I believe in information. Well, so do we all, obviously. Tully was information. Information and the getting of it somehow, anyhow, is why we're out here now, Mr Chave. Of course, it's possible I would be notified of any material relating to myself which might be provided by a farewell note from you. I cannot rely on this, however, as you'll understand. Should someone at headquarters, or more than one, wish a full shit load to fall on me rather than himself, themselves, from this investigation he, they, might choose to keep your letter confidential – except, that is, from those who can drop the full shit load on me, Assistant Chief Davidson and DC Bithron. I have some personal information about them, it's true, as self-protection, but not nearly destructive enough at this stage. Hardly anything, really.'

As Moss had feared, the left jacket pocket and trouser pocket provided not much: some cash, his keys and three .32 cartridges. 'Did you think you might miss, sir, with the chamber's six, or do only partial damage?' This was preparedness in Chave, devotion to a purpose. This was consummate, calculating despair.

To get at the inside pocket, Moss now lay down and aligned his own body behind Chave's on the ground. Moss felt unwilling to get close face-to-face, because the blood and fragments were on that side and he had to make sure he picked up none on his clothes, although he'd respected Chave pretty well, or what he knew of him. The position he took would not look lewd or romantic, should someone see him cuddled up like that to Chave from the back, because, obviously, they both had trousers very much on and no vigorous movement would take place . . . Anyway, no one *could* see them in this seemingly intimate attitude, because the park did not open until ten a.m., and the day of the dawn Knoll totter had passed. Folded in against Chave's back and behind, Moss reached over the chief inspector's left shoulder and pushed his hand gently under the lapel of the double-breasted suit.

'You were a mentor to me, Mr Chave,' he said. 'I mean, your knowledge of the grassing game, its indispensability, its subtleties, its beauties, its pitfalls, its pitfalls, its terrible, innumerable pitfalls. But I felt always thirty per cent sure you would never fall into one of the pits yourself . . . No, make that twenty-five.' Moss's fingers closed on a decent-sized piece of folded paper jutting up from the inside pocket, and he drew it out. Then he gradually disengaged himself from the body and stood. He looked down to make sure the effective little gun barrel still lay nicely settled and meaningful inside Chave's mouth.

Ten

'Dead how?' Sally said.

'We get there. Soonest. Before anyone can rearrange things,' Esther said.

'What things?'

'Indicators.'

'To what?'

'Yes, indicators.'

'Dead how?'

'In the open,' Esther said. 'Like a rerun.'

'Of what?'

'Move.'

'Who'd rearrange things?' Sally said.

'Move.'

Sally saw off half her scrambled egg and wrapped the rest in a serviette. She downed her tomato juice. They went out to the car. Sally put the blue flasher on the roof for speed. She drove.

They had been eating breakfast together at their hotel, trying to recover from all that cracked boisterousness in the night, when Esther took a mobile call. 'Right,' she said. 'Thanks, Jamie. This is what I call true cooperation. It will be remembered.' She put the phone back in her bag, then swigged off a cup of China tea, jammed two pieces of black pudding into her mouth and stood. She looked appalling, not just her cheeks, gross around the black pudding, but the rest of her face as well, after such a violent night carry-on. 'Someone who might be Chave is dead on Knoll. Someone who *is* Chave. How I heard it just now – "Someone who *might* be Chave" – that's just journalism pretending to care for accuracy. We go,' she said.

'Who says?'

'*I* damn well say. Off your arse, Bithron.'

'No, not who says we go, who says he's dead?'

'Jamie – the local paper's crime man,' Esther said. She had cuts on her right cheek and forehead from those small-hours tearaway episodes, and a swelling and vivid discoloration over her left eye. Two flaps of skin on one of the cuts jiggled like tiny flags in a mild wind when she chewed or spoke.

'A reporter gives you tip-offs?' Sally said.

'I've done a couple of meets with the media, trawling for unpublished Tully stuff, getting myself known, fraternizing, ingratiating – that sort of thing. They're impressed by assistant chiefness. Will crawl. Long to oblige.'

'Lovely for you.'

'So, Jamie's a contact now, you see. Plus, of course, he aims to stir for a story – wants to get me, an eminence, nosing about and causing bother. Somebody in the parks department rang their news desk.' She seemed unworried about the defacements, but this couldn't really be how an ACC eminence investigating another police force and visiting a three-pip man's corpse near kids' swings ought to look.

Sally said: 'I wondered if—'

'Just drive. Those sods will swarm around him like maggots or the Red Cross.'

'Which?'

'Either.'

'No, I meant which sods will swarm,' Sally replied.

'People concerned.'

'Which?'

'There'll be a lot of people concerned about the death of a chief inspector in an environmental area.'

'Yes, but which?'

'Which what? Area? I told you, Knoll.'

'Which people?'

'People who are concerned,' Esther said.

'Concerned how?'

'Closely.'

'Closely in what sense?'

155

'Yes, a close sense. You've hit it.'

'Because of grief?' Sally said. 'His family?'

'Ah.'

'What?'

'I hadn't thought of that,' Esther replied.

'What?'

'Grief.'

'You hadn't thought of grief? Somebody's dead, for God's sake. Grief's likely, isn't it?'

'Yes, possibly grief in addition. Yes, there could be a slice of grief. Someone like Chave might be entitled to that.'

'In addition to what? How did he die?'

'Wondered what?' Esther said.

'What do you mean, "wondered what"?'

'You said you wondered if . . . If what?'

'I wondered if we should agree an explanation for your facial injuries, ma'am,' Sally said. 'I think they'll be noticed and intelligently discussed. Not favourably discussed.'

'What we don't know is whether the voice at the parks department also did nine-nine-nine, meaning a full emergency turnout there.'

'Like maggots or the Red Cross?'

'Kid, why not try to get beyond doing echoes?' Esther replied. 'You were sold to me as a bold thinker and creative dreamer as well as a sex quester in clubs.'

'Only one.'

'What?'

'Club.'

'Sorry. Clubogamy,' Esther said.

'Surely, the voice at parks would have to report the death properly, as well as calling the press. It could be obstruction otherwise.'

'Yes. Damn,' Esther replied. 'What point?'

'What point in what?'

'What point making a tale about the nicks on my face from those little set-tos last night with Gerald?'

'I'd say they're more than nicks.'

'Gerald's not a trained fighter. He plays the bassoon.'

'More than nicks. As you said, all sorts might be out here

on Knoll – death of a senior officer. Top-echelon people will turn up. And an eye lump like that – they'll spot it, mention it to one another, speculate jointly. This is not good for your . . . well, dignity, aura. A trickier matter than, say, finding your jaw strange.'

'We should say I walk into doors?'

'Unfamiliar ground, the hotel. You might have.'

'But staff saw what happened, didn't they? Night porter. Assistant manager.'

'They're trained not to gossip,' Sally replied.

'Are you retarded? It'll be everywhere.'

'What *did* happen?'

'That's the thing about relationships, isn't it?' Esther said. 'You'll have noticed, I expect.'

'What?'

'Closenesses. One sort or another.'

'Getting your face thugged in a four-star hotel room is closeness?'

'I said one sort or another.'

'Which sort was that?'

'And, after all, this is only an attack by a soft-handed professional musician.'

'Attacks. Have you had a good look at yourself?' Sally replied. They were getting near Knoll. Esther stared around, obviously searching for vehicles, more blue lamps, and uniforms and suits on the slopes.

'If we *are* first to Chave, I'll want to search the body,' Esther said.

'My God, you can't do that. Tampering. Not even our ground.'

'Do you know what the job is here?'

'Interfering with evidence would—'

'Do you know what the job is here?' Esther replied.

'Of course I know what the fucking job is here, ma'am – I'm part of it, aren't I – aren't I? – but just the same—'

'I'm telling you now – a pockets forage, at least pockets – yes, I'm telling you now so you can look away when I do it. I don't want you compromised, your saintly detective con-stableship. I don't despise ethics, and you've got some. Any

157

comeback, we say you were scouring elsewhere – very elsewhere – at the time. Don't worry, we'll keep you wholesome.'

'We *can't* be first, can we? Someone found the body.'

'I mean first. You know, *first.*'

'First police?'

'Would *you* let one of this crummy cohort get to a piece
of evidence ahead of you if you could stop it? Esther replied.
'Wouldn't you call that dereliction, in view of our brief here?
Do you think I look derelict? No, don't reply to that.'

'The body being a piece of evidence?'

'Listen, Bithron, never pull taste on me, all right? You
needn't think, because of a fucking husband-inflicted eye
welt, I'm short of taste.'

'So, who's the "one of this crummy cohort" that I wouldn't
want getting to a piece of evidence first?'

'One of this crummy cohort.'

'Police?'

'Chave had a good speaking manner, but he might still
say more when he's dead,' Esther replied.

'Well, if he can, he's saying it. To them. See?' They had
reached a parking spot from which the swings up near the
top of the tip were visible. A crowd of adult figures stood
grouped without much movement around one spot and gazing
down at the ground. There were possibly some uniforms,
though distance made certainty impossible. There'd been a
nine-nine-nine. 'They must have left their vehicles on the
other side of Knoll,' Sally said. She could make out tape
slung between trees to keep the public back.

Esther stared up towards the swings for a while, and the
urgency slipped slowly from her. 'Not much there for us
now, would you say? They'll have been through everything.
Everything. If you'd motored instead of gabbing . . .' She
pulled down the vanity mirror and studied her damage.

'All that'll clear up totally in ten days, or a fortnight at
most,' Sally said. 'In my view, a good chance of no permanent scarring, except that gouge near the nose, which might
retain a blueish, yellowish redness, like some old piss
artist.'

'Thanks.'

'How about your body? Nothing's broken. Not obviously. That's a plus. Ribs? Any pain when you breathe?'

'And yet there were damned rewarding moments as well,' Esther replied.

'I made it more than moments.'

'That's what I mean about relationships being complex.'

'What?'

'Many imponderables.'

'How do you feel you're placed now, after all that in the night?' Sally replied.

'Placed?'

'As to relationships,' Sally said.

'I'm sorry about any disturbance.'

'Someone gets into your room, there's bound to be . . . activity, ma'am. Is that the kind of romp pattern you like – the cruelty, tenderness, bad-mouthing mix?'

'Some pretty disgusting language from Gerald and me?'

'Was there?' Yes. Sally said: 'Conversations in those circumstances can sometimes leave ordinary politeness and so on behind. Should we get up the slope now?'

'What circumstances?'

'Yes, circumstances like those.'

'Tell me how it seemed to go last night then,' Esther replied. 'It's a haze. I'd appreciate your insights.'

'Oh, just a bit of clangour, and then the finale. Interesting to meet Gerald. Yes, interesting. Of course, his shirt and collar had been ripped half off by the time I saw him, but did he arrive wearing one of the bow ties?'

Esther finished at the mirror and, sitting back, closed her eyes. She would be short of sleep and possibly a little in shock still. Sally turned and recovered her scrambled-egg package from the back seat. She had brought no cutlery but unfolded the napkin, held it out taut between two hands and bent down to eat the mound, like an animal at a stall or someone snorting coke. 'Do you want a bit of this?' she asked. Esther didn't answer, might be sleeping. Sally ate all the egg and felt OK about it, ungreedy, especially as Esther had the black pudding. Afterwards, Sally rolled up the napkin and used a clean section to get rid of breakfast fragments

159

around her mouth and on her forehead. They might still go to join the posse up there with Chave when Esther felt ready, and it could obviously be regarded as unrefined and showy if one of them had thump marks on her face and the other bits of food.

Sally sat back and tried for a few minutes' doze herself after the rough high jinks and disturbances of the night. Her insights, as Esther called them, were much fuller than Sally had said. She and Esther occupied rooms alongside each other in an hotel of good construction and soundproofing, but just before three a.m. Sally had been woken by serious noise through the wall from number seventeen, Esther's – definitely not television or radio. As often happened, Sally had been into a terrifying, throwback dream about ticklish questions in her final examinations at school, this one, '*All Dryden's work after* Absolom and Achitophel *is a tentative yet documented testament to the short-legged grace of the Sealyham terrier. Discuss.*' In her dream, she'd been trying laboriously to mind-scan *The Medal* and *Fables Ancient and Modern* for examples. The din from seventeen had yanked her into consciousness, and she escaped this daft farrago. 'Thank Christ for the shindig next door and a slab of actuality,' she muttered. It shook her that she could *crave* actuality now.

Things seemed OK and she could concentrate on the uproar. There was some shouting: a male and a female voice in spells of loud argument and possible cursing, but not screams. Also, Sally had heard what might be fighting and falls and breakages, a man's groan, as from a knee or foot in the balls, then a stretch of near silence until the yelling and violent fracas started again. The words of the cursing she could not make out properly, but intonations suggested that famed terms like 'dickhead', 'mother-fucker', 'arsehole' and 'slag-marchioness' came up a few times.

Obviously, the situation gave Sally problems. Lying there, she wondered whether Esther had been out and brought back an acquaintance – acquaintances. Both she and Sally had night keys to the hotel and it would be easy to smuggle in a friend – friends – when there was nobody around reception. Esther did disappear some days and some evenings. It

160

might be concerned with the investigation, it might not. She wasn't required to account to Sally. She never even mentioned she'd been out, though once or twice Sally had spotted her from the window as she left. Sally wondered, while listening in the night, whether it could be that things in seventeen were going more or less as Esther had planned and needed. An ACC must tire of all the kowtowing and civility she'd get normally – people *impressed* by assistant chiefness, as she described it, *crawling, obliging.*

Sally had thought that maybe in those quieter times between the hullabaloo sessions, very nice *closenesses* were under way. She put her ear to the wall, trying to work out what went on. She did not feel obnoxious or furtive – or only tolerably obnoxious or furtive. As Sally saw it then, evidence was needed for a decision: should she get to Esther? After all, another possible explanation for the rowdiness existed. Had a violent intruder – intruders – penetrated the ACC's room, probably to get at her on account of the investigation? There did not seem much purpose to that, but they were on a strange patch, with its own grim processes. Or had Esther only been enjoying some quaint love life, routine to her? Wouldn't it be naïve for Sally to go rushing to seventeen with an offer of help when, in fact, the ACC and her companion – companions – were simply running through romance prelims? Sally had prayed, *Oh, God, let her be safe – mad or hormonally avid, perhaps, but safe.*

In the car now, Esther snored once then woke up and immediately opened the passenger door. 'Come on,' she said, and swung herself out. Sally followed. She had not slept. They began to climb.

'What did you think of him last night?' Esther asked.

'Who?'

'My hubby. The musician. In my room.'

'Will he be able to play? The knuckles on his right were in a mess.'

'He doesn't know a thing about landing a punch.'

'I still say he did all right,' Sally replied.

'He can become so insanely jealous – enough to get him travelling all that distance. Well, as you saw.'

'Jealous of whom?'

'Me,' Esther said. 'The job. The status. I'm taking a police force apart. I'm in touch with the Home Office. He's piping away doing Gounod at the back of a nothing orchestra. He'd love to be in a career where he can scare people, too. His lips are the strongest bit of him. Who's he ever going to scare? I mean, who outside? So, he tries to scare me. He has to bring me down to his own piffling level. Or try to.'

In the night, eventually, Sally had heard hotel staff gathering outside seventeen, drawn by the hubbub. It was then she decided she could intervene. The night porter had a pass key, but they had seemed scared to use it, afraid of what they'd see. Sally took the key from him and opened up. In the delay, Esther and Gerald must have dressed. 'You both looked wonderfully *soigné*, I thought, except for the rips and swellings on your skin, and Gerald's shirt and collar,' Sally said as they climbed Knoll. 'Of course, I didn't know it was Gerald until you told me later. But definite tap-dancing potential could be discerned in him, so perhaps I should have guessed.'

'It was debatable.'

'What?'

'Would it seem more odd or less for people to be fully dressed at three a.m.? We decided to put clothes on. After all, Gerald wasn't supposed to be in the room, was he? He's my husband, yes, but no hotel guest – not booked in. They wouldn't have approved.'

'He just turned up?'

'He'd gone back before dawn. Orchestra practice. In many ways he's conscientious.'

'Turned up why?' Sally replied.

'No, it can never be a full escape up here, can it?'

'Oh, can't it, can't it? Please. You make me miserable,' Sally said.

'These people believe in motoring and persistence.'

'He must be devoted.'

'Oh, God, oh, God, yes. Don't go on about it. Please. Please.'

'And yet the violence,' Sally said. 'Is that standard? Or

special jealousy? You said jealousy about your job. But is it more? Does he think you might have got something going for yourself here, as well as back home? That's unjust. I mean, about something here. Obviously, back home is different. Is that why he marked your face – to put others off?'

'The artistic side. Mostly he's equable and sweet and creeps about behaving like he deserves better from me for his loyalty and happy, vassal temper. And, OK, he might. But occasionally he'll really cataclysmically flip, the way they do, his sort. Last night. That's why I say artistic. If your life is music, you can get to a state where you don't care about sneaking into distant hotels and tapping on your wife's door. It seems trivial after Schumann. Of course, the sods had told him the room number when he rang previously. So, they should have expected uproar, shouldn't they?'

'True.'

'If you let a husband know how to find his wife – what else but savagery and the ruination of furniture, Sally? Let's be reasonable.'

'True.' Halfway up the slope, they paused and sat on a rustic-style bench. Now they were closer, they could do some identification of people near the swings.

'Their chief constable himself,' Esther said. 'And Notram, head of CID. Yates. What did you think of him?'

'Who?'

'Gerald, of course.'

'He looked like someone a woman should leave,' Sally replied.

Esther snarled, twitched her head, and threw both arms in the air at the shrieking obviousness of this. 'Oh, yes, yes, but apart from that?' The sudden movement of her face made bleeding from the nose gouge restart big. 'He didn't try to grope you, did he – you in a dressing gown? Did he? But he has this ludicrous faithfulness to me, the tame oaf.'

And Sally knew of similar dud faithfulness. They resumed climbing. 'Through a wall, Gerald's voice seemed pleasant,' she replied. 'Sort of a confident burr to it. I could imagine him saying "twist" in pontoon.'

'His lips weren't always like now, believe me. It's because of the woodwind, nothing fruitier. But I hate a stoop.'

'Some stoops are all right, as long as they're not lopsided.'

'We should be careful,' Esther replied.

'In what sense?'

'I don't want to get flung out of a flophouse hotel like that with TV pictures of it happening and an "Assistant Chief Constable Davidson" caption, plus discreetly worded, vicious statements from the management.'

'It's four-star.'

'They get three for no open sewers. The other means a fridge.'

'What do they say about the trashed furniture?' Sally asked.

'Publicity pinpointing that, or if we were told to leave – this would not be a plus for officers holding an investigation into possible police misbehaviour.'

'You're the only one who'd get thrown out. I'm all right.'

'So far.'

'Did Gerald say he'd return?'

'That's what I mean about being careful,' Esther replied. 'Listen, suppose they send a smashed dressing table to the repairer and leak the word that it comes from an investigative police officer's room – this is a bad reflection, Sally. All right, it's shitty, matchwood stuff, but all the same. There are people who'd be very willing to spread smears based on incidents of that kind – suggest we are not fit for such work, undermine us.' Blood from the pit in Esther's nose continued to gush and she tried to catch some of it by pushing out her lower lip. This was not good. It made her look very Hapsburg. Her azure blouse and black skirt took bad staining.

'Will Gerald come back?' Sally replied.

'A beautiful little weapon, the Undercover,' Esther said. They had reached the body and stood at Chave's feet. Sir Lawrence Matrinbanks, the patch's chief constable, and Superintendent Angus Notram, head of CID, were talking a little way off, but now walked back to speak with Esther. A police photographer took shots of Chave from several angles. Inspector Yates directed him. He must have other jobs besides watching Esther and Sally.

164

'This was a man with some terrible burden, yet who gave no indication of it to colleagues,' Matrinbanks said. 'There's nobility in that, I feel, whatever the nature of the burden.'

'He brickwalled Sally and me, that's a fact,' Esther replied.

'What was he hiding – what, what?' Matrinbanks said. 'The location tells us something, of course – of course. But too little. This might be the answer to your investigation, Mrs Davidson, mightn't it?'

'What might be, sir?' Esther said.

'This terrible death,' Matrinbanks said. 'Yet now we can never know it, the answer. He has taken it with him.'

'An answer how, sir?' Esther asked.

'Some secret factor in his dealings with Tully as controller?' Matrinbanks said. 'Some factor which made Chave feel shame and guilt to the point of . . . To this tragic point.' He nodded towards the body, a brief, sad, conclusive movement.

'This death could, in effect, mark the close of your inquiries, couldn't it, ma'am,' Notram said.

'How come? You think he did it to put all the rest of you in the clear?' Esther replied. 'Albert the Martyr, Alby the scapegoat, carrying everyone's sins into the wilderness?'

'An awful, impenetrable sense of blame must have held him,' Matrinbanks said.

'But perhaps warranted, sir,' Notram said.

'Perhaps, perhaps,' Matrinbanks replied.

'Is there a letter?' Esther asked.

'There can be no search of the body until the photographer has completed and the scenes of crime team noted all details,' Notram said.

'How was he discovered?' Esther asked.

'An anonymous call to the parks department, who at once alerted us,' Notram replied.

'We would certainly have notified you during the morning, Mrs Davidson,' Matrinbanks said. He was grey-haired, fifty-seven, with a large, genial face like someone decent and honestly rich in the televised *Forsyte Saga*, Sally thought. He wore a lightweight, grey single-breasted suit, the trousers

165

tucked into black wellingtons for the walk up Knoll. Confidence shone from him – the firm way he stood, the slow, bull-like, lord-of-the-pasture head movements when he looked around Knoll. Even if you did not know he was a chief constable, you'd have guessed he did leadership. Sally could not believe in him altogether, and made no real effort to. For her, his voice sounded over-assured, like an act. She had heard detectives use that tone when giving very rehearsed, cooked-up pieces of evidence in the box. She had done it herself.

'How did you find out about the death so soon, ma'am?' Notram asked.

'Sally is in touch with many a source,' Esther replied.

'But which source?' Notram said.

'This is quite a reliable source,' Sally replied.

'Well, obviously,' Esther said. 'We're here.'

'It might help us to know how the information came,' Notram replied.

'One of the reasons I brought Constable Bithron with me on this assignment is her known ability to acquire reliable sources quickly in a setting entirely strange to her,' Esther said.

'I'm extremely happy you should be here so early, Mrs Davidson,' Matrinbanks said. 'You will be present when Mr Notram searches the body after procedures are attended to. This could be important, in view of your investigation, should the investigation have to be wound up as a result of the suicide. It's crucial that everything connected with a misfortune of this kind be transparent.'

'May I ask, who arrived here first?' Esther replied.

'Luckily, we have a drill for dealing with this kind of incident,' Notram said.

'Good. Who, under this procedure, would have been here first?' Esther replied.

'I am notified of such an incident at home, if necessary, as on this occasion. I came immediately.'

'How long before the scenes of crime folk and so on, and the chief, arrived?' Esther asked.

'Not many minutes, I'm glad to say. The drill worked admirably,' Notram replied.

166

'But, of course, someone had been here ahead of even you, Mr Notram,' Esther said. 'The anon who told parks.'

'We would like to contact him, as we would like to contact Detective Constable Bithron's source,' Notram said. 'This would make for a completeness.' Tall, strongly built, he had a symmetrical, square, unadventurous face. His nose had been broken and very capably repaired. His eyes were grey-blue behind thin-rimmed glasses, and could suggest sincerity. He wore a velvet, navy fedora, dark woollen trousers and a brass-buttoned, navy-blue, double-breasted blazer in fine condition. He seemed to Sally like someone who would know how to look after friends, but might not have many.

'Skin snags like these you've noticed on my face could come to anyone who leads a normally positive sort of life,' Esther said. Blood from the nose wound had congealed nicely now into a neat rectangle, and her lips and teeth seemed completely free from stain.

'One reason our control room didn't inform you at once about Mr Chave was that we'd heard you'd had a difficult night at the hotel and felt you should be allowed to rest late, ma'am,' Notram replied.

'But I think we should reassure Mrs Davidson that this word from the hotel did not come in the nature of a complaint, despite the splintered furniture and disrespected silk sheets,' the chief said. 'It was just an example of concern for you by the manager, and we were, as a matter of fact, very grateful to be informed.'

The photographer finished and moved away.

Notram said with a fine, generous smile: 'The hotel manager is perfectly understanding and knows he would look narrow and even foolish if he made a fuss about a mature lady – not to mention your rank as an assistant chief – if he made a fuss about such a lady entertaining a male in her room, with some noise and admittedly regrettable, but accidental, rubbishing of fitments.'

'Especially the male being, of course, your husband, Mrs Davidson,' Matrinbanks said. 'Domestic clobberings are hardly the province of a hotel manager, nor, probably, of the press, and certainly not when they are heartily consensual.'

'Oh, quite,' Notram replied. 'I would have mentioned that, sir. This hotel-room meeting was clearly in the nature of a reunion, and some exuberance was sure to ensue. Well, good, here's Detective Sergeant Moss now. He's been trying for a trace on the anon call to parks.'

Sally watched Moss climb towards them.

'Inevitably, Harvey Moss will be distressed to see Chief Inspector Chave like this,' Notram said. 'He and Moss, of course, worked a great deal together as controller and handler. He's been told of the nature of the death, but first sight of his former colleague is certain to stun. We must give him a little while to compose himself.'

Moss approached and stood near Matrinbanks gazing down at the body. 'Oh, God,' Moss said.

'Easy, Harv,' Notram said.

'I know Sally here wouldn't want you going the same way, Detective Sergeant,' Esther said. 'No matter what private knowledge you shared with Chave. Take you out as well and she'd feel the investigation was *really* fucked, wouldn't you, Sally?'

Sally said: 'Well, I hadn't actually—'

'Feel it was *really* fucked, wouldn't you, Sally?' Esther said. 'Don't be concerned about these marks on my face, Sergeant Moss. They're insignificant compared with a .32 bullet up through the mouth and into the brain.'

Moss remained for another minute looking at Chave. Moss stayed very still, as though dazed. Sally thought his reaction could certainly come from shock at first sight of an admired colleague dead, or disabling sadness, or terrific play-acting.

'As far as I can see, pre-medical, pre-forensics, this is a genuine suicide,' Esther said. 'I don't know what Sally's view is. She can be sceptical.'

'In fact, there's a story attached to the marks on Mrs Davidson's skin, Harv,' Notram said, 'but not one we need to elaborate now.'

'Detective Sergeant Moss is the lad who's been snuffling about in our domestic and otherwise states – Sally's and mine – at home, isn't he?' Esther said. 'Sally's hurt, I know. Is it, well, *material* that she saunters out now and then clubbing, for heaven's sake? *Material?* And it's only *one* club.'

'Did you get anywhere with identifying the caller, Sergeant Moss?' Sally asked.

'These inquiries are proceeding,' Moss replied.

'Perhaps now Mr Notram could search the body,' Matrinbanks said.

'I won't attempt to remove the gun from his mouth or hand,' Notram said, 'on account of rigor and no flexibility in the fingers. We must wait for relaxation.' He held a folded sheet of plastic and spread this flat near the body. Then Notram knelt and began to go through Chave's pockets, placing whatever he found on the plastic. Sally saw some coins, .32 bullets, a bunch of keys, a wallet containing paper money and credit cards, a police warrant card, two handkerchiefs, no letter. 'We must look in his car and possibly his home,' Notram said.

'Yes, surely he would want to tell us why he's done this,' Moss said.

Eleven

Some Home Office magnifico was coming from London to talk to her, Esther said, arriving any day.

'Is this good?' Sally replied.

'You retarded?'

'You asked that before.'

'Did you reply or are you too retarded?'

'All the same, it *could* be good, couldn't it?' Sally replied.

'How?'

'They like the way you've been handling things and fancy a private briefing on progress – confidentiality, your and his ears only. If they didn't think you'd managed some progress, they wouldn't send.'

'He wants to shut us down.'

'You *know* this?'

'You heard Sir Lawrence, didn't you?'

'But that's only Sir Lawrence. Obviously, he'd want any inquiry shut down: slurs his princeliness. God, our staff have only just reached full strength.' Esther's administrative people occupied an adjoining room. Yates had looked in on them, offering help. Esther told him to stay away.

'The Home Office grow scared,' she said. 'A chief inspector kills himself in clarion circumstances. Suddenly, things look worse than they thought. An inquiry might unearth God knows what. Too much information.'

'But there isn't,' Sally said.

'There could be if we persist. Are allowed to persist.'

'*Can* they shut us down? This is a government thing, isn't it – the inquiry?'

'So is the Home Office a government thing. You hadn't realized that? Governments don't like to run government

170

things that can hurt *them* – the government. If a government thing looks likely to do them – the government – damage, it will become a government thing to stop the other government thing. This is a thing known as good governance.'

'How much of a magnifico?'

'Who?'

'The HO magnifico.'

'Civil Servant. First Division. Not necessarily Oxbridge these days, but at least Warwick. Quiet but niggly intellect: Senior Principal or Chief Tea Boy or Head of Unit, that kind of rank,' Esther said. 'Intuitive – meaning that if he's ordered to take a look at us, he knows this signifies take a look at us and terminate us.'

'Your face isn't too bad at all now – and it's only days after,' Sally replied. 'Except for the nose gouge. In sun, its colours glint like the finest wreath. Best if you hug shade for sessions with the Home Office. But any luck and he'll think it's only the start of syphilitic nostril collapse.'

'I've bought a masonry hammer in case Gerald comes back after this batch of concerts. Brahms mostly. He'd expect me to equip myself. Musicians think point, counterpoint. Short shaft for a small bedside drawer.'

'Oh. If . . . Well, if it resulted in his injury or death, plus, unavoidably, an investigation, the shop where you got it will remember you. Your nose disturbance fixes you in people's minds – I mean, that as well as general likeability and dash, ma'am, naturally. Or perhaps you paid by cheque or credit card, so identification would be even simpler.'

'I don't know whether Notram would keep the letter secret or pass it to Matrinbanks,' Esther replied.

'What letter?'

'On the other hand, if the letter implicated Notram in some rich dirt re Tully, he's certainly going to destroy it, isn't he?'

'What letter?'

'You heard, did you?' Esther replied.

'What?'

'Christ, Sally, did you hear, though? Astonished? Would that adequately describe what I was?'

'Did I hear what?'

'Notram.'

'What?'

'The sod's built a complete system to guarantee he's personally present at all sensitive, potentially embarrassing incidents first, and can get rid of anything awkward. This lad is set for a rapid rise to staff rank.'

'Or the letter could implicate Matrinbanks,' Sally replied. 'Notram might keep it then.'

'For pressurizing?' Sally said.

'Flashy, unseemly term. As security in case Matrinbanks ever tried to stick all the blame for losing or betraying Tully on Notram.'

'Pressurizing. Blackmail?'

'Of course, a maid cleaning the room is sure to report a hammer to management,' Esther replied.

'Anything happen, it's going to look very premeditated. Why *masonry* hammer. An inherited family trade skill?'

They were in their special office. Esther brought her fist down on a table. 'Blows from a masonry hammer do a wider sort of area.'

Sally said: 'I agree with you, ma'am, that if someone picks a flagrantly posturing death like Chave, he's sure to provide also a written spiel about himself. Self-annihilation is only the denouement. He'll wish to show the world his first four acts as well. There *has* to be a multi-page letter somewhere.'

'The Home Office wanted it one-to-one, private, myself and their emissary,' Esther said. 'I told them two of us are on this inquiry and he'd have to speak to you and me together. Colleagues. I won't have discrimination by rank.'

'Nice. If shit's flying you'd like to make sure you don't take the lot.'

Esther said: 'In someone else's realm I hardly think we can approach Mrs Chave pre-funeral and ask to search the house for a suicide letter, hoping – well, more than hoping, confident – hoping/confident it blackens at least Notram and possibly Matrinbanks enough to keep the inquiry alive. It would have to be upper ranks to impress the Home Office.'

'I thought you said they intended shutting it down because suddenly someone's scared we *will* blacken upper ranks.'

'But if a letter did exist and we had it, they couldn't close us, in case there were leaks and it looked like suppression of the truth. Now listen, Sally, I'm probably against any plan by you to break into the house one night for a look around. No, don't argue. I'd prefer you didn't attempt that. In any case, those two, M. and N., will have been over to his place by now and done a rummage, quizzed and browbeaten the widow.'

'It's a difficult trick – how to interrogate someone like Chave effectively but without pushing them to despair and suicide,' Sally replied. 'I can't see you should reproach yourself too much. I don't know what the Home Office is going to say.'

No, she didn't, not about either of them.

Sally telephoned Pete at work back home. She needed some non-police, dispassionate talk. Some advice. Pete had a management post and a lot of management training. *So, show me how to manage, Pete – how to manage when it's Esther not me who is the manager.* Of course, in a way it was unfair to use Pete like this when she had a problem. She enjoyed this inquiry job on strange ground because it gave her escape from a stack of complexities, Pete being one of them, and more or less major. Although they'd been together months, Sally remained unsure whether she wanted permanency. They still did not live together. She preferred it like that, and so she wondered whether there was something missing. On this trip, she had time to think about it. Escape. Just the same, though, she occasionally needed to get a view from Pete on some work problem. He brought a different kind of mind and training. They could help. So, Sally told him the situation now, looking for counsel.

'I'd better come up there and see you,' he said.

'Well, no, that's—'

'Not something for the phone, really, is it?'

'Just a bit of guidance,' Sally replied.

'I'd need to know the whole setting to make an informed judgement.'

Informed judgements were what managers hoped to make, and believed they did make. 'I've just described the setting, haven't I, Pete?'

'I need to *be* there, *feel* the detail and atmosphere. Context, ambience, are so germane. If you think there's a letter somewhere from this man – Chave, you say? – Chave – a letter would seem crucial. It could explain the whole Tully – Tully, you say? – the whole Tully matter, including his death.'

'The letter, suppose it exists, is undiscoverable.'

'I suppose your boss, the assistant chief – Davidson? – I suppose she's really pressing you to find it. In his home? Is that what's troubling you?'

'Look, Pete, Esther Davidson's definitely against housebreaking.'

'Of course. She's an ACC. She must formally state that. Did she say she was against before you suggested it? That's how the most accomplished leaders plant the idea – then can disown it and you if there's a cock-up. Havard Business School's got a twelve-month course on how to make sure underlings carry the can. And so has the police staff college, I bet.'

'Esther's not one to—'

'Yes, she'll expect you to make a real trawl.'

'How could you do it – spend time here?'

'I'm owed some days. I'll come at the weekend.'

In a way, it thrilled her, this readiness in him to travel immediately and help – try to help. 'Pete, have you been waiting for a call like this from me? Me turning sort of needy.'

'Could I know the Home Office would get awkward? You did say the Home Office?'

'Among others. I'm wondering whether you see this as a call that's apparently about work, but really to do with . . . actually *not* just about work.'

'Is it?' he said.

'Like an invitation.'

'To?'

'Like an invitation,' Sally said.

'*Isn't* it about work?' he replied.

'It *is* about work, but you might think it isn't.'

'So?' he said.

'I'm not sure. The hotel's become something of a problem, owing to—'

'Shall I stay somewhere else? Why not *both* stay somewhere else? Only a couple of nights. Would you be missed?'

'I have to be near her,' Sally said. 'She could give herself grave trouble. She's got an unorthodox side.'

'Oh, really?'

'Flamboyant.'

'Gets them big promotion – as long as it works,' Pete said. 'That's supposed to signify a bold, unfettered, inventive mind. True even for police, most probably.'

'I should be available, to enforce restraint.'

'God. What trouble?'

'She gets harassed and might react stupidly. I mean, stupid beyond. Jail stupid.'

'God.'

'Pete, we're on to something evil here.'

'Of course you are.'

'What's that mean?'

'It's about an informant, isn't it? So, there'll be evil aspects. You know that from previous cases. Ever read *The Friends of Eddie Coyle*, or seen the film?'

'But really evil, Pete. Supremos included.'

'As ever, I should think.'

Yes, it elated Sally that Pete should offer to come. And depressed her. Elation? Well, he wanted to see her so much he'd do the miles, stay for days. And it would all happen after one phone call, and a phone call apparently only asking for some job chat, no plea to visit: sign of a true relationship, surely. She mattered to him. Pete heard her voice and wanted her. Brilliant. Elation? It had to be.

Depression? The darkest. It had to be. Pete was one of those deep, enduring complications in her life – yes, deepest deep – one of those enduring complications she'd felt the need to run from for a time. Perhaps she'd wanted to run as a way to end it altogether. Now, had she wilfully concocted an excuse to make him show up? Did Sally hope, know, when she phoned him that, whatever the stated reason, he would hear her whistling an invitation? *Lover, come back to me.* The idea hurt. She felt weak, deceitful, unkind.

Esther said you could never really escape, and when her husband showed up it meant she had it right, didn't it? Nobody would say her face looked like escape, more like a totally botched break-out on barbed wire. After the call to Pete, Sally saw Esther's miserable view as even more right. By ringing him, she had smashed hopes of lasting escape, and, suddenly, the real, the dismally actual, trapped her again. Here comes Pete – Pete restored to a chief place in her life. Yes, the unyieldingly actual. There was the hardness of a hotel wall against her ear, and there was the hardness of a masonry hammer. There were those very obvious and measurable skin furls adrift on Esther's features. There was the stupid, dangerous prospect of housebreaking. There were Notram and Matrinbanks, thick-shelled, solid figures in a foggy landscape. There was that clever, efficient, emergency structure built by Notram, and perhaps benefited from by Matrinbanks. There was the kid in the grey stone school.

Sally had that urge to dodge out of it all again for a spell, give her imagination a medicinal whirl before Pete and the Home Office arrived and brought everything fully back to the inflexible and hazardous. She needed drama, longed for projections. And didn't Albert Chave dead look the rawest and richest of drama? His situation drew her, as bells drew church-goers. She felt she must mock-up the chief inspector, *in situ* on Knoll, destroyed, a mouth full of gun. Would she get subliminal revelations from this? Of course she wouldn't get subliminal revelations. Her theatricals did not bring revelations of any sort, but they brought excitement and a short sense of dodgy in-tuneness and supernatural fellow-feeling. Perhaps one day she might get an insight from some fantasy sequence, a bit of sudden, inexplicable lateral thinking, which would help solve . . . Solve what? Solve whatever needed solving at the time. But it had never happened yet. She did her performances because they satisfied her and gave the illusion of mind-freedom – seemed to liberate her eyes from the rough uglinesses of the assistant chief's injuries, and to liberate Sally's ear from crunched-up, sneaky duty against a flock-papered hotel wall.

Before the park opened next morning, she went out to Knoll, scaled a fence and climbed up again to the area where Tully and Chave were found. She had no .32 Undercover revolver, but had bought a short-barrelled imitation pistol in a toy shop yesterday afternoon. Near the children's swings, she lay down on her side with farewell-the-world, ceremonial style and slipped the gun muzzle into her mouth, her right hand closed around the butt, a brave finger on the trigger. She shut her eyes and tried to get rid of Sally Bithronness and metamorphose into Albert Chave.

Did he fire immediately he had lain down, or think for a while – ponder, doubt, possibly reminisce, the gun already in his mouth, or maybe still in his pocket or held against his side at this stage? Sally kept the barrel between her lips. This had to be the guts of the script. The toy was plastic and she realized she could not get an identical metal experience to Chave's. That hardly mattered. After all, bigger differences existed, such as, this gun had no bullets and she wasn't going to blow a gap in her palate as route to her brain. She was doing fiction, needed a prop, not an authentic weapon. It worried her slightly that the toy could have poisonous surface colouring to give a steel appearance. The makers probably did not realize someone would want to imitate a police suicide with it, and so might swallow additives.

What was in your head, Mr Chave, when your head could still hold anything? Sally thought the question but then gave a small, enraged snarl around the gun barrel. No, not *your* head, Mr Chave. She had to *become* Chave, if she could. What's in *my* head? Why am I doing this? Why is the hard steel of a .32 six-shot against my teeth? Sally waited for the answers to present themselves. Had the interrogation by Esther haunted him? Was there something he felt ashamed of in the death of Tully – something to do with money and/or treachery, or/and complicity? That above all – complicity. Had he felt unable to consult upwards about his plight, because he knew upwards to be as involved and mucky as himself – as himself and Harvey Moss? She asked the questions but did not attempt to reason answers. Intuition should do that. The impersonated Chave must provide them. Get a fucking mystical move on then, all right?

Had self-disgust and fright in Chave grown intolerable? Which? Where is it documented – words and punctuation, clarity, tragic heartfeltness, not just the vague sign language of this slope? Of course, Sally realized she hadn't got anywhere in trying to suppress herself and borrow that other identity: she continued to think 'he', 'him', 'Chave'. Her damn detective ego wouldn't rest or remove itself.

A hand closed firmly, carefully, unviolently over her own hand holding the gun, pulled irresistibly at both and drew the barrel from her mouth. For a second she did not open her eyes. Was this *it*? Had she, after all, reached an other-worldly experience? Someone, something, from the beyond had intervened? Stanley Basil Staple said: 'Ah, imitation only. I thought so, but didn't want any risks.' He released her hand.

When Sally did open her eyes, she saw him standing near her and gazing down. She realized now why the grip on her and the gun had been so strong and precise: this was a totter's grip, the fingers of someone used to picking out what he wanted, and only what he wanted, from tips. A gun in a mouth would be easy for a man with that kind of job skill.

'Why are you here?' Sally asked.

'I—'

'It's no longer a dump. What can you find?'

'I come sometimes.'

'Why?'

'Oh, with respect, miss, perhaps it's the same sort of reason as yours,' he replied.

'What's mine?'

'I think you want to act it out. One death or the other.'

'Do *you* want to act it out, one death or the other?'

'Not quite that. I'm tugged here now and then, you know.'

'Why?'

'The moment.'

'Which?'

'The moment – finding Justin Tully. Not something I can

178

forget. It's there, all the time. So, occasionally I have to come out here. Like to a grave? No flowers, but a little helping of grief.'

'Yes,' Sally said. 'Did you talk to Percival Blay about me, give him my number? No harm, but did you?'

'He said he had some information and would like you to visit,' Staple replied.

'You're in touch regularly?'

'Just some bits of information now and then. Anyone can just pop in to his place – no security, no staff. Well, he doesn't need no security, of course. He's looked after.'

'Is he?'

'Very. I think it's natural,' Staple replied.

'What?'

He waved his hand around. 'Grief.'

'Yes.'

'In the court and when I was questioned by police, they're asking all the time, am I absolutely sure I didn't search the body, meaning thieve from it, like, because I'm a totter, that's *all* I am, so if there's a body, I got to tot it. Like I don't know about nothing else – namely, I don't know about regard for a body. All right, I know the lawyers and police got to ask these things, it's their job, but . . . And so, days like this, I'll forget totting and the dump and I'll come out here and just think about Tully. All right, it don't *prove* nothing, because nobody don't know I do it – except you, now. But I need it, that's all. Afterwards, I feel quite a bit better. Like communing? That the word?'

'Yes. Oh, yes, communing.'

'I'll be back at the Springfield Heights tip tomorrow. But this is like a little escape.'

Escape, escape. 'Exactly.' Sally sat up, the gun still in her hand. He hadn't taken it from her, once he confirmed from weight and texture it was a toy. He remained standing near. He wore a dark suit, white shirt, dark-blue tie and black shoes, none of it found on a dump. He dressed formally for these tribute visits. Tully might have appreciated that.

'And then the other body,' he said. 'This is the one that interests you, is it – I mean, the gun in your mouth?'

'Because it's more recent.'

'You were . . . you were, like, trying to get in touch? You reckon, if you got a gun in your mouth, you'll be Mr Chave?'

'That kind of thing,' Sally said.

'Do they train you for that?'

'Who?'

'Say, the police academy.'

'For what?'

'Getting to the dead. Most people don't realize the police try this. They think it's all blue lights and cuffs.'

'There's some of that,' Sally said.

'Did you get to him, reach him?'

'Who?'

'Chave.'

'It's just a game I play.'

He squatted down alongside her, as if wanting to say something confidential. He whispered, though there was nobody in sight. 'I think I can discuss special matters with you, special *private* matters, because we're similar. That's how I see it, anyway. Both out here because we're caught by the past.'

'Communing', 'caught by the past' – some phrasing for a totter. 'Yes,' she replied.

'I can trust you.'

It was not a question. 'As long as—'

'At first, I got to admit it . . . at first, I thought . . . well, intimacy being carried on. It's got to be said.' Normally, his square, largish face looked imperturbable, but he showed real agitation now.

'Intimacy?'

'I couldn't see the gun,' he replied, 'not at that juncture, because I was too far off and on the wrong side.' His voice had risen to half normal and stayed at that.

'This gun?' Sally held up the imitation.

'The real one.'

'Chave's?'

'When I say intimacy, you don't expect that kind of thing in daylight in a park so early. This would not be consenting adults in private, would it? A park is not private. The thing

180

about parks is they're for the public. All right, this was before the park opened, but it's still not private, not really. That's what I thought then.'

'Who?' Sally asked.

'All right, they seemed to have all their clothes on, but they could of been just starting. The woo stage, couldn't they? Foreplay in garments. I didn't want to get close. It's, like, embarrassing. But *they're* close, obviously. The one tucked into the other, like spoons. I thought maybe he was muttering nice thoughts to him, his mouth up by his ear. I'm still looking from behind them, so I still can't see the gun.'

'Who? One was Chave?'

'I couldn't be sure, not at once. But I saw a lot of police because of the Tully case, and I thought Mr Chave and Detective Sergeant Harvey Moss.'

'Lying here? Was Chave dead?'

'I suppose he must of been dead. But I didn't think that then, did I? I thought intimacy. When I say "intimacy", you know what I mean? Pleasuring? I thought maybe they had to come out to that Tully region for extra kicks. Sex can be funny, you know. What gets people going.'

'Oh, yes. Yes.'

'This might be called a rendezvous. For instance, "Meet me, do, at Knoll park when the morn is young." Love talk has stuff in it like that – "morn".'

'And when did you see you were wrong?' Sally asked.

'He reaches around him, like, over his shoulder, like a good embrace, I thought, like the beginning of things.'

'But it's something else?'

'He's searching him. In a while, I realize, he's searching him. This is not romance. Not nipple-rubbing, excuse me.'

'Moss searching Chave when Chave's dead?'

'This is a police officer doing to another police officer what a lot of them thought I done to Tully,' Staple replied. 'Don't tell me this is not what's referred to as ironic.'

'And did he find anything?'

'He gets something from the inside pocket.'

'What?'

'Paper. Folded.'

'Like a letter?'

'It could of been a letter. Should it of been a letter? Is there a letter missing?'

'Anything else?' Sally said.

'He stood up. I could see him properly then, and it was Sergeant Moss. That one – he won't believe I didn't take nothing from Tully. He's always on at me, even now, so long after.'

'He'd got what he wanted from Chave?'

'The sergeant stared down for a while. I didn't know why. But afterwards I thought it must be to make sure the body looked like it had not been touched, and the gun stayed OK in his mouth. Then he went. Luckily, there's these new bushes, aren't there? I'm behind one, out of sight.'

'Did he take the letter?'

'In his own pocket.'

'Did he read it?'

'Glanced at it. He had to get away, didn't he? This is someone in a park with a body. He didn't want to be seen with that. You could tell, the way he went down fast. Read it proper later.'

'You?'

'When he'd gone, I waited. I waited a real while. I mean, I still didn't know Mr Chave was dead. I still had not seen that gun on the other side of him. I did not want to go up to someone who's a chief inspector of police and let him know I had seen intimacies, even though it was not the full intimacy – I knew that by then, because definitely no trousers off. Well, Mr Chave never moved, obviously. So I come out from behind the bush and go nearer. Then I can see the gun and the damage and I can tell he's dead. I was sure of that, or I wouldn't of left him, honestly. But I did not want more of that Tully carry-on – the questions. You understand? Look, miss, I say again, I'm telling you this because – because we're, like, the same, aren't we, coming out here to get some contact with them who passed away in bad conditions? I do think I can trust you. I got to speak about it.'

Sally stood and Staple straightened up. 'Did you do an anonymous nine-nine-nine call about Chave?' she asked.

'Nothing. You never know what they can find out these days, with them electronics. The voice. Or where you're phoning from. It's all recorded, you know. Well, of course you know. You're in it. Did somebody ring nine-nine-nine, then?'

'That's how some police got here so early.'

'Moss? After, when I knew Mr Chave was dead, I felt real, real bad about thinking he'd been up to outdoor intimacy on a murder site for bonus thrills. This is a poor way to think about a body, especially a senior police officer.'

'I can't get rid of the notion you *did* empty Tully's pockets,' Sally replied.

'I guessed you thought that.'

'Yes, mine's only a guess, too. I don't get magic disclosures, not about anyone.'

'They'd be *really* useful in your work, wouldn't they?' he said.

Twelve

Esther and Sally had scheduled an interview with Harvey Moss for the afternoon. They were in their allocated room at headquarters around lunchtime, preparing material, when the hotel manager phoned saying that regrettably they would have to leave his premises, owing to riotousness the previous night in seventeen, the unwholesome state of the sheets and now a masonry hammer. 'I'd like to think I'm tolerant, but it's the cumulative aspect.' Sally took the call. The manager didn't have their direct numbers, and had come through on a very buggable general switchboard line. Not too good, really.

Across the room, Esther worked on at a computer, seeming to ignore the conversation. Because of the angle Sally viewed her from, Esther's head and profile were outlined vividly against the screen, and her jaw seemed absolutely fine and, at present, near to unobtrusive, nothing like what it had been when catching blood. She had a longish face, not over-refined or scrupulous-looking even when undamaged, her skin reasonably fresh. Back home, when Sally used to glimpse her around headquarters, she had decided you could see faces of Esther's type in many a location other than nicks. Women with comparable faces would make them up almost casually and appear dashing just the same. Men still found Esther worth looking at, most probably.

Sally said in a friendly tone to the manager: 'Mrs Davidson had and indeed *has* no intention of damaging the structure of your building. I know I can speak for her on that.'

'We have to think of you as a unit, I'm afraid,' the manager replied, 'since both bookings are police bookings. Although the trouble had seventeen as its epicentre, I'm afraid I must ask you to go, also. Please quit the rooms by sixteen hundred hours.'

'I've never previously heard of a white, British-born assistant chief constable evicted from an hotel for a masonry hammer.'

'Both of you. If you do not comply, your luggage and possessions will be removed from the rooms and placed in store.'

Sally said: 'Should Mrs Davidson's husband come back at night, reasonably expecting her to be in seventeen, there might be a shocking and uncontrolled intrusion upon whomever replaces her, especially if he leaves the lights off, for secrecy in entering, or because he's self-conscious about kinks. Mr Davidson is by nature normally very docile, but can flip. He has a musical side, not just the bassoon, but tap-dancing.'

Esther picked up an extension and listened in.

The manager said: 'This might sound harsh, even unfeeling, but the injuries to Mrs Davidson's face are upsetting for other guests at mealtimes, plus what can only be called some lack of etiquette with food. There have been complaints. Better is expected from a high-ranking officer.'

'Oh, that!' Sally replied. 'We got an emergency call about a death near children's swings, for heaven's sake, and had to reach there fast. I'm sure you can see the difficulties. Anyone in her position would have dealt similarly with black pudding. These people who complained probably have ordinary, fairly slow-moving lives, and would be able to deal with breakfast at a more leisurely rate. This is not to criticize them, merely to point out a difference.'

'Davidson here. You married?' Esther asked.

The manager said: 'Mrs Davidson, is this at all—?'

'Are you?' Esther asked.

'I was,' the manager replied.

'Well, you'll obviously understand a stressful occasion like last night's,' Esther said. 'Spouses with what is referred to, I believe, as "their own agenda" can suddenly break character pattern. My hubby is placid when with a properly laid out score in front of him, but life will sometimes depart from the ruled lines. Some might even say *too* placid, which is

185

why he can't get top-class zing into his bassooning and is stuck with an also-ran band.'

The manager said: 'I really do not see what—'

'Dead?' Esther asked.

There was silence for a second. Then the manager said: 'My wife? Some years ago.'

'If you'd only had a word with me about that earlier, I certainly would never have let Gerald carry on as he did,' Esther said. 'Gross behaviour when there's been tragedy, even a while ago. A musician's foibles is one thing, but disrespect something very much else.'

'Well, thank you,' the manager said.

'The thing about Gerald is that, although normally stolid and affectionate, he reads too much,' Esther said. She continued to keyboard Harvey Moss data one handed as she talked.

'I've heard of people like that,' the manager replied. 'Reading can be an undoubted benefit, as say the classics or through Scripture Union, yet—'

'Do you know *Crash* by J. G. Ballard? There's also a film – opens with rimming. The movie has lots of arse generally, both genders, in fact.'

'I don't think I've come across this work,' he said. 'Because of hotel duties, I can't get to the cinema as often as—'

'Sally will give you the full summary. I'll say now only that it figures people who are turned on sexually by wounds – car smashes, mainly.'

'My wife was killed in a car accident,' he said.

'This would give you personal insights,' Esther replied.

'I'm sorry. I don't—'

'Gerald's very into *Crash*. Not just the rimming. The whole notion of erotic injuries. If you're buried in the middle rows of an orchestra with a fucking bassoon for half your life, you'll want the occasional extravagance, won't you? I'm not saying I married him because of these personal ways, but even when younger he would occasionally look about for deviances. Sheets will get rumpled a little and so on, given this fluctuating personality, won't they? I'm sure your bed linen was not always impeccable before your wife's death. If I may say. And yet Gerald can do a solo from Mozart

186

or Brahms and keep a very decent melodic continuity, even a narrative line. Sally here – my colleague – asked quite a bit about the hammer, so you're not alone with your queries. I'd hate you to feel absurd.'

'Not just that it's a hammer, but a *masonry* hammer,' Sally said.

'I like nice things,' Esther replied, 'tools as much as other artefacts. I expect you do, too, Mr— But I don't think we know your name.'

'Cosmeston.'

'What Cosmeston – if I may?' Esther asked.

'Edward.'

'I'm Esther and Sally's Sally. I feel first names are more suitable when a relationship is warm, don't you, Ted? We might get kicked off this job, anyway, in which case I'll certainly be out of seventeen and back into full-time conjugal see-sawism, but, if we stay, some informality between the three of us is surely best. That implies no special demands on you. Sally's come round to my view of the masonry hammer. She's sure it will speak conclusively to Gerald, should he show again, aren't you, Sally?'

'The maid was not prying – not, that is, *seeking* this hammer today,' Cosmeston said. 'Well, obviously. How would she know a hammer might be in the room? She wished to put some papers from the bedside table into a drawer while tidying and simply came across it.'

Esther had pictures of Moss on the screen and leaned forward to study them. She put a finger delicately on one of the left-side profile and followed the line of the back of his head down to the neck, probably only phrenology rather than sensual. She might feel she'd had enough of that last night. 'I'm not going to get angry, Ted,' Esther replied. 'All hotels encourage their staff to sniff into guests' stuff. How you complete customer assessments. For myself, I certainly don't say you've been asked by any outside interests to case our rooms, although we're dogged by damn ganged-up, self-protecting, powerful, roughneck enemies here. No, as I see it, poking around by hotel staff is just routine – though I don't know how Sally will view things. She can be suspicious and unforgiving.'

187

'I'll explain to the maid that hammer's in the nature of a talisman, a lucky charm you like to keep close during difficult missions,' Cosmeston said.

'I'd be glad if you would. "Talisman."' Esther's voice hugged the word. 'So exactly the term. If it troubles the girl, ask her to stick my hammer under the Gideon Bible, but not completely under, in case I have to get at it quickly,' Esther replied. 'And with its shaft at the drawer's openable end, please. Gerald, when he's in a fit, loves to bring surprises. Well, as you've seen.'

'Your wounds?' Cosmeston said.

'I'm going to do all I can to keep blood off the pillow-cases,' Esther replied.

'Please, please, don't fret about such trivialities. We want all staying with us to feel utterly at ease.'

'Thanks, Ted,' Esther replied. 'Sally and I are delighted we've cleared this small misunderstanding.' Cosmeston rang off. 'I can sympathize with him, the dear lout,' she said.

'Can you?'

'Oh, *I* wouldn't mind having someone like me in one of my rooms if I were a hotel keeper, and I don't suppose you would, Sally, but—'

'I'm not sure. I'd want a breakages bond in advance.'

'This doesn't – certainly doesn't – mean Teddy Cosmeston has to love it,' Esther said. 'Listen, Sally, I'm going to be nice and tender with Moss. These are sensitive people. Cosmeston just now, and also a man like Chave – chirpy-faced and possibly rotten, yet proving he's capable not just of despair, but of a wise yearning for the dark, and is alert to death-scene pageantry.'

'I say again, you and your questioning didn't actually kill him,' Sally replied. 'You're *entitled* to scare the spit from people. It's your role here.'

'There's a poetic appearance to this boy, Moss.' Esther pointed with her thumb to the pictures. Her hands were delicate for someone with her sort of rank. 'He could be just as rotten, of course, but I don't want any more grandiose self-immolation gestures, especially with the Home Office lad on his way.'

'We dispose of the Home Office, don't we?'

'Dispose of? How? Does that mean anything at all, I mean anything *at all*, prat?' Esther replied.

'No, of course it doesn't. I just thought I'd talk big. You seemed to need a boost, what with the scagged skin and your guilt over Chave.'

'Guilt's a plus, not available to everyone.'

In the afternoon, Moss came in, and Sally thought, yes, he did look a bit poetic, if poetic meant having eyes that seemed to see more than was on show to be seen. All right, she herself knew she liked to see more than was on show to be seen – or liked to kid herself she saw it. He wore a good grey suit, dark-blue shirt and silver tie, as though due to get into the witness box at a big trial. Esther said: 'This is a bad time for you, Sergeant Moss, an aftermath time, in view of Albert Chave's death. Sally and I both appreciate that. We're grateful for your attendance now.'

He nodded once, a small, for-Christ's-sake-get-lost kind of movement. To Sally it looked as if he had decided not to be smarmed or charmed into saying anything but what he wished. Perhaps, in any case, he'd been briefed on tactics by Yates or Notram or even Matrinbanks. Maybe Moss could put a whole dynasty in the muck if he gabbled. 'You'd like me to talk about Tully,' he replied.

'Is that acceptable?' Esther asked.

'I wouldn't say I had a choice.'

'You'll have heard we're likely to be pulled off this inquiry because of Westminster poltroonery,' Esther replied. 'You could probably stall. Chave did.'

'Do I want you going from here thinking I'm shit, even if you can't do anything about it, because the Home Office arrives and finishes you?'

'Why?' Esther said.

'Why what?'

'Why exactly don't you want us to think you're shit, Harvey?' Esther replied.

'Because I'm not.'

'But do you care what we think?' Esther asked. 'We rate?

189

I don't believe so. You got rough reports on us from a phone campaign to our patch, didn't you? You destroyed us before we arrived. Sally's sex activities are so damn flagrant and unkempt.'

'Yes, I care what you think,' he replied. 'There's a woman and child concerned. 'You might see me as responsible for taking Tully from them.'

'Well, I imagine you did,' Esther replied. 'You signed him up, didn't you?'

'I mean, took him from them by doziness or self-seeking or worse,' Moss said.

'That's what would have been in the Home Office mind when they sent us here, yes – betrayal, calculated or accidental,' Esther replied. 'Not just about you – the whole sacred line: handler, controller, registrar, chief constable. Now, though, we find HO doubts, HO night sweats. So, where are we?'

Moss said: 'What you'll want me to give you is an account of Tully and me right through from his recruitment.'

'Is that acceptable?' Esther asked.

'Have you ever brought a grass into play?' Moss replied. He put his unplumbable gaze full on Esther. Sally saw him smile, and brilliant joy suddenly stocked his mysterious eyes, as though he could not keep buttoned up the thrill of that high triumph when he recruited Tully. And as though he knew Esther and Sally would understand, and respond with him. 'This is to pluck somebody out of all the filthy loyalties and fears of crookdom and bring him/her to see that the duty to safeguard order and help it flourish is the greater call on their loyalty, cancelling fear.'

'Yes, oh, yes, it can be like that,' Esther replied. She spoke quietly, but with almost the same fervour as Moss.

'We have to believe in it,' he said. 'Now, God stand up for grasses!'

'Yes, we do have to believe in them,' Esther replied.

'There's ludicrous contempt for the informant, and not only from villains. Some police despise informants, even while using them.'

'The Judas fallacy,' Esther said.

'Organized crime is becoming *so* organized that the informant is often the only way to break it,' Moss said. 'The informant *is* detection.'

'Certainly,' Esther replied. 'You're an intellectual?'

On her way up to ACC she might have brought informants aboard. Listening to Moss's rhetoric, this canonization of the grass – all grasses – Sally wondered how laboriously it had been prepared or inculcated and what it aimed to divert them from. She wondered, too, if Esther felt actually as much in harmony as her voice and tone said. Sally had run informants. They were helpful, no question. Always, though, she had feared that grassing could destroy their souls, not convert them to glory, as Moss believed about *his* informants. Said he believed. Admittedly, this had not stopped her, though. Perhaps Moss had it right, then. And perhaps Esther, with her big, trained brain, could see this. *Talk to me, Mr/Mrs/Miss Grass, talk to me, talk to me, tell me what I could never find out myself. You are my oracle, my whistleblower, my inspiration.* Did grassing, in fact, rate as the sly and shady and honourable and proven basis of detection and, if so, why not take thorough, glorious pleasure in it like Moss? Yes, why not? Why not? Because people like Tully got murdered as a result of it, and left a wife and child ripe for similar. Confusion blitzed Sally.

The investigation room had a couple of deep armchairs, and Esther took one, legs nicely together. Moss took the other. Sally sat at a desk with her notepad. 'Tully was just a street-level pusher when I first came across him, selling mainly ecstasy but possibly some coke and H as well, though very small-scale, no real list of clients,' Moss said.

'You could have done him, all the same, but didn't?' Esther said. 'You had an arrangement?'

'This is standard,' Moss replied.

'Of course,' Esther said. Sally heard no irony.

'What's gained by squeezing someone more or less insignificant?' Moss asked.

'Zero Tolerance sounds smart and determined, but might not be altogether wise,' Esther said.

'Except as PR,' Moss said.

'Probably,' Esther replied.

Moss said: 'I could see Tully wanted bigger money. Even then he had ideas about buying a prestige house and getting his kid into private schooling. I felt he might try something violent for heavy cash – robbery. I told him he could earn with us instead. At first, he didn't fancy that. Not many of them do. I really got a friendship going. Really. It couldn't be too public, of course, but we'd meet and talk about all sorts – general, harmless stuff. He'd discovered galleries and painting. I wouldn't risk going with him to look, but I learned up about people he liked – Gauguin, Renoir. He bought prints for when he had a nice house. I didn't tell him prints were *infra dig*. He would have been hurt. I wanted things between us easy and good. And, in any case, I liked him. I had run up against a lot worse villains, even in my short time. Eventually, I came back to the earnings plan and said it would help me and him if he could try to get into one of the really big drugs operations.'

'Like Percy Blay's?' Sally said.

'Exactly,' Moss said.

'Of course, someone like Blay would be scared all the time of infiltration,' Sally said. 'Watchful – although he can afford to be so casual at home.'

'Tully took it gently,' Moss replied. 'He had a gift. He was a natural.'

'You did brilliantly,' Esther said.

'*He* did brilliantly,' Moss replied.

'The preparations,' Esther said.

'It couldn't have happened without,' Moss said.

'He edged up in the Blay hierarchy?' Esther asked.

'Yes, *edged* – the word. He showed them bit by bit how he could expand his trade base within their network, build customer dependence and bring in the gains. He got their confidence.'

'And it would help that you were blind-eyeing and protecting him,' Esther said.

'The agreed strategy,' Moss replied.

'Agreed how high?' Esther asked.

'Agreed,' Moss said.

'How high is important,' Esther said.

'To you,' Moss replied. 'I didn't need to ask how high. My superior was Chief Inspector Chave. I talked to him, took his directions, and that would do. Normal in such an operation, I believe.'

'Obviously, none of that detail could come out in the trial, because Blay is still at liberty and uncharged,' Esther said.

'We'd have had court privilege, but we didn't want to throw accusations at Blay too soon. We're still amassing the case against him.'

'Just as you were amassing the case against Tully, while using him,' Esther said. 'Anyway, does the build-up against Blay allegedly go on, despite Tully's removal? Allegedly, yes.'

'He gave us so much, but not quite a case against Blay. There was a lot of other material—'

'We've done a chart on Tully-related convictions,' Sally said. 'Impressive.'

'The Crown Prosecution Service wants real likelihood of a result before it acts, especially against someone as powerful as Blay,' Moss said. 'I'm bringing on another grass now. It's slow.'

'Yes. Is he/she safe?' Esther asked.

'We do all the security. They can never be totally safe, can they?' Moss replied. 'I think it's wonderful when they come over, but I also feel a grim responsibility. It's why I worry about Pam and the boy.'

'Would Blay have known you'd collected almost enough from Tully for charges?' Esther said. 'Is that why Tully had to be taken out when he was?'

'It's possible.'

'Almost certain?' Esther asked.

'It has to be possible,' Moss said.

'How might Blay have discovered that?' Esther said.

'I don't know as fact that he *had* discovered it,' Moss replied.

'Does it seem a reasonable explanation?' Esther asked.

'It's one possible explanation,' Moss said.

'If it *were* the case, how might Blay have found out?'

The pride and shine had gone from Moss's face. 'Are you asking if he'd heard it from me?' he said.

'I'm wondering how he might have discovered,' Esther replied.

'Not from me,' Moss said.

'Understood,' Esther replied.

'You don't believe it? I was afraid of that. Grey areas can be grey and dubious even to people as experienced as you two. It's why I did some research on you, in case I had to try to hit back. Idiotic. I see that now.'

'Or suppose someone's having Tully's wife and wants him gone,' Esther replied. 'Jolliffe?' She spoke almost tenderly about Barry Jolliffe.'

'There might have been something, way back. She gets around. But this wouldn't be the motivation. He was hired, that's all.'

'Who turned him at the trial? You?' Sally asked.

'He decided it himself. I think Jolliffe wanted to give some tiny, too-late compensation to Pam,' Moss replied.

'Like you did – do,' Esther said.

'Perhaps I should have looked after Tully better. But he wasn't always sensible. I couldn't persuade him to live somewhere less resonant,' Moss said.

'Ah, the avenue. The trees. The porch pillars,' Esther replied.

'I'd used his ambition for the house and so on to get him listening in the first place, so later I couldn't go all out trying to discourage him. It would have seemed false. He'd be gradual and cagey in some things, but he wanted status for the family.'

'People do,' Esther said. 'I've no children, but I see it.'

'Grasses – they'll be *so* meticulous about how they run their work, but they also long to splash the cash,' Moss said. His voice had become a mixture of grief and hopelessness. 'They seem able to guard against one sort of danger, not the other. Or they don't want to. Tully was bright, only short-term bright, though. He thought he deserved Milton Avenue and he'd damn well have it. He thought Pamela deserved the clothes and jewellery and she'd damn well have them. He thought Walter deserved an education, to make sure he

194

wouldn't end up working with someone like Blay, and decided he'd damn well have it.'

'I know what Sally would like to ask is, who else worked for – with – Blay?' Esther replied.

'What's that mean?' Moss said.

'We'll need to look at all your bank statements, and Albert Chave's,' Esther said, with a grand, amiable smile, to continue that tenderness she'd promised. 'It's easier if you give permission. We'll do it, anyway. Chave's estate will have to show us everything, too.'

'I'd expect that,' Moss said. 'Also standard.'

'My view is, you would regard Chave's death as possibly – yes, *possibly* only – the pointless waste of a good man, and I know Sally would be glad to hear that you react so, whether he was tainted or not – glad you see it as the death of a man, rather than some slab of sign language in a park, previously a tip.'

'Father, husband, colleague, friend,' Moss replied. 'That's how he would wish to be remembered, and to date I don't know anything to deny him this.'

'Not all men could handle each of these roles with distinction,' Esther said.

'Mr Chave, yes,' Moss replied.

'When you say "friend", how would that differ from "colleague"?' Esther asked.

'As colleagues, we would, of course, be separated by rank,' Moss said. 'But now and then Mr Chave liked to dispense with that formality and we would be simply two people who understood each other and shared an equal devotion to our work.'

'When you say a friend, would you have expected Mr Chave to talk to you about it if he were contemplating suicide?' Sally asked.

'This came as an appalling shock,' Moss said.

'He never spoke to you about it?' Sally asked. 'Do you feel hurt?'

'We were up there when you arrived to look at the body,' Esther said. 'I don't think I've ever seen such authentic sadness in a park – previously a tip.'

195

'I'd be entitled to a lawyer for this kind of interview,' Moss replied. 'But I've waived that. I saw no need.'

'Chave did without, too,' Sally said. 'It's a remarkable similarity.'

'We both believed in openness,' Moss replied. 'Why not?'

'Many officers would view your decision to appear here alone as virtual proof you're hiding nothing,' Esther said, 'but Sally's the kind who hangs on to doubt. Because I'm marked about the face like an incompetent, back-alley knife fight, it doesn't signify I'm the hard one and she's all sugar.'

'What happens in an hotel room is private to the people in that room,' Moss said.

'Did you ask the hotel people to go through my stuff?' Esther replied.

'The fact that you've both got relationship troubles doesn't signify you're incapable of carrying out an investigation of this kind,' Moss replied. 'I accept that. Neither does the hotel fracas. But I think I was entitled to some curiosity about you, and therefore also entitled to start some research.'

'I know Sally will want to return and return to this word "friend" – as distinct from "colleague" – you used about Albert Chave,' Esther said. 'She'll stick at such things, often to the point of, in fact, the grossest tedium. She'll wonder whether such a friendship might mean you'd feel obliged to cover for him even if you knew him corrupt.'

'Thank God, I never had to make that sort of choice,' Moss replied.

'If, for instance, Chave had some kind of link with Percy Blay and could have mentioned Tully was producing good conclusive stuff about him which would soon be to CPS requirements for charges,' Esther said.

'This is why we're so keen to find any note Chave might have left,' Sally said. 'We feel that someone capable of that sort of gesture – the suicide, the placement of himself – someone who would do that was also someone who would wish to account accurately and in full for what he intended to do. You knew him as colleague and, more important, as friend, and perhaps you can tell us whether it's your opinion that he would feel intolerable shame at having betrayed

Justin Tully, and wish to describe that shame and its cause in explicit terms.'

'It's not in any way proved that he betrayed Tully. I agree that this death, as it stands, is an appalling conundrum,' Moss replied.

'Would he wish it to be that conundrum?' Sally asked.

Moss said: 'This is something I can't—'

Someone knocked at the door and opened it before any invitation. A short, square-made man of about thirty-six came in. He wore a hip-length, unbuttoned denim jacket, jeans and a black open-necked shirt and had fair, curly hair with a pigtail and Himmler glasses. His face was amiable, bright, confident, and plump. Sally did not consider his lips too bad, though thickish and hinting at ego. The open shirt showed chest hair, but no medallion or crucifix, and Sally thought the hair on its own all right, not deliberately frizzed up for a virility show. 'ACC Davidson?' he said. The voice might be educated West Country, laying it on a bit, Sally decided – the West Country, not the education. 'Matt Iperam? From the DPS? Directorate of Police Strategy? Home Office? You're expecting me?' The raised, querying tone used five times seemed meant to make him sound hesitant and tentative – a tactic Sally used herself occasionally. So did Blay. Matt Iperam was *not* hesitant and tentative. He closed the door behind him and took a few more steps into the room. He glanced around and mouthed silently: 'Mikes?'

'This is Detective Constable Bithron,' Esther said. 'We're interviewing Detective Sergeant Harvey Moss.'

'Grand – Moss the handler. I'll observe. Ignore me, do.' He surveyed the room again, more thoroughly this time, probably still searching for bugs. Didn't the Home Office know that listening apparatus these days was miniscule/invisible? Even the Home Office. 'I imagine this will be what might be termed a "winding down" session. I'm happy to have caught it. You're right to close the investigation properly, tidily.'

'We were trying to get at the significance of Blay in the Tully death and, possibly, in the Chave suicide,' Esther replied.

197

'Percy Blay, yes, indeed,' Iperam said. For a moment he sounded uncertain.

'He's not a big donor to the Labour Party, is he?' Esther asked. 'Are we on dicey ground?'

'My impression is that Blay will be pursued even more rigorously than before,' Iperam said. 'In that sense, the death of Chave has to be seen as a boon, as I'm sure you appreciate. I'm not going into all the formal blah about such a tragedy for a family man. This is someone who, via a skilled and considerate death, has told us where the corruption really lay in this force and has removed it – i.e., himself – for us.' No diffident queries affected his style now. He knew. He was a mandarin and knew like a mandarin. He did his eye tour for the bugs again and whispered, 'You see, I'm very aware that even in stating the post-Chave spruceness of this force, I'm disclosing that the department did, of course, have its doubts previously. Well, clearly, or your investigation would not have been ordered. I and the Directorate generally are embarrassed now at having harboured these suspicions. I don't mind apologizing head-on to Sergeant Moss, since he's here, but I'd rather not have such matters made explicit with the chief constable and Mr Notram. Put it down entirely to my lily-liveredness, if you wish – to bureaucratic footwork.'

'Sir Lawrence Matrinbanks sees things as you do – I mean, the Chave death,' Esther said. 'Its implications of closure.'

'There's hardly a choice, is there?' Iperam replied. He'd cut the whispering now. The vowels were big and assured and Somerset.

'You've discussed it?' Esther asked.

'We were hoping that, because of his closeness to Mr Chave, Sergeant Moss might be able to point us towards the chief inspector's thinking before his suicide, and possibly have some knowledge of a final letter,' Sally said.

'Entirely legitimate inquiry,' Iperam said, 'but my own impression, and the department's, is that exposition in words – either to Sergeant Moss confidentially, or in a letter – both, surely, would be not merely superfluous but at variance with the graphic statement of his self-destruction in the place he chose.'

'These ravages to my face were not part of a celebratory party to mark Chave's death and the end of our investigation,' Esther replied.

'I heard about that,' Iperam said. 'I don't regard a masonry hammer as odd for you to keep handy, in the circumstances. But perhaps it will be a happy development for you and your husband, Gerald, if a longer stay here becomes unnecessary, although I know you and Detective Constable Bithron have unhelpful circumstances to meet at home.'

Sally said: 'So, DS Moss, do we have to accept that you cannot give any help on the question of a Chave letter?'

'I will always think of him as a good and principled man, in the absence of other information,' Moss said.

'Yes, well, that's bollocks, but excusable and comradely bollocks,' Iperam said. 'In a concluding interview of this kind, I can understand the wish not to malign a chum. Isn't there some Latin tag about not slagging off the dead? But it is not to malign someone to say he was malign if he was. Chave actually invites us to say this of him, *commands* us. To praise him is to betray him.'

'The shirt – blackest black,' Esther replied. 'You the regular mortician for investigations that all at once need burying?'

'The hotel manager tells me you contrived to talk him around by familiarity and bullshit, Mrs Davidson, but the point is that he *knows* he was talked around, resents it in retrospect, and is sure to be very severe if anything similar to the tumult of seventeen occurred again. The department would be understandably horrified were an investigation unit headed by one of our comparatively few role-model woman ACCs banished from an hotel for impropriety and appallingly abused sheets. What the department has to consider is that Gerald may intrude again, Mrs Davidson. And then there is Sally. Does she, also, have potential visitors? We understand she gets about. A club? Pal Joey's? The manager is relieved to hear your assignment has ended, and I feel that you will be relieved also, Mrs Davidson, DC Bithron, since you will no longer have to dread involuntary participation in social outrage at the hotel or elsewhere.'

'What Mrs Davidson and I wondered, you see, DS Moss,

199

is whether, if Chief Inspector Chave told you in detail, as a friend, what he intended, you could get out to Knoll early, and even, possibly, do an examination of the scene, clothing and contents, pre-anyone,' Sally said.

Iperam said: 'From what I've seen in dossiers, Chief Inspector Chave strikes me as an officer possessing a true streak of nobility, despite overall degenerateness. I don't feel he would burden a younger colleague with the terrible knowledge of his – Chave's – planned death. The department is prepared to meet the bill for any private cosmetic treatment to your face, Mrs Davidson, including surgery, up to seven thousand pounds, following the incidents in seventeen last night, as long as such treatment relates only to the one night and is not aggravated by further damage. The minister feels it is harmful to the service for an assistant chief to display such marks, especially a woman. The department could not go to the public purse, though, if it appeared that the injuries were willingly indulged in for kicks, and any repeat of the first night would give rise to such an assumption. This is one reason I suggested you'd be very content to quit the area now, despite the messed-up relationships you'll both be returning to.'

Solo this time, Sally drove behind Pam Grange and Walter again on the school run. In one way, this was as much a slice of silly theatricals as re-enactment games at Knoll. She had no gun, of course, and would be capable of next to nothing if professional people did attack Pam or the boy, or both. But Sally felt she had to be there, all the same. It seemed to her that evil could reimpose itself here now, full-scale. God, that sounded melodramatic, grandiose, didn't it? Evil? Huge, woolly, medieval word. She couldn't think of another more exact or manageable one, though.

The investigation would shut. It had not shut yet. Iperam lacked such solo power, even if he were first division and middling-to-high panjandrum at the Drugs Strategy Directorate. He would recommend closure, though. That became clear from his attitude in the meeting with Esther, Sally and Moss. And, since he had been sent here in a hurry to recommend closure, he would be listened to by those who sent him.

He had been sent, also, to get as much damaging scuttlebutt about Esther as he could, to make extra sure the investigation died. She could be briefed against. Downing Street tactics would be applied. And when the investigation died, what remained? What remained was things as they had been before Esther and Sally arrived. That is, some sort of conspiracy to conceal all the lead-up to Tully's end, and to pretend the court verdicts on Chamberlain and Jolliffe marked the absolute finale to a bad episode. This police force would be conducted as it had always been conducted. The investigation had failed to find out *how* it had been conducted. Perhaps Esther and Sally were moving towards that discovery, but now they would be officially stopped. *Status quo* had won, and the *status quo* was evil, wasn't it? What else could she call it?

Consequently, this compulsion to get with Pam and Walter and do a bit more short-term token protection – because she could come up with nothing better. Even that wouldn't be possible in a week or two, maybe less, because she and Esther were about to be returned to unit. Although the Home Office didn't always move fast, she thought it might on this.

No incidents on the school trip – not even an encounter with Harvey Moss. Had that previous one been an accident? He also had worried about them and just happened to be near the school? At Milton Avenue, Sally parked outside the house and walked up the drive. Pam and Walter waited near the BMW, the boy looking as surly as ever, Pam with a fine smile, an affability smile, a polite smile, a why-can't-you-fuck-off-for-keeps smile. All right, Sally *would* fuck-off-for-keeps, would be *made* to fuck off for keeps. That's why she was here, waiting to be asked in.

Pam said: 'Walter told me we had someone behind us. I might not have spotted you myself. These skills are a genes thing with him.' They went into the Gauguin and Renoir room. Walter disappeared upstairs. 'So, is this farewell?' Pam asked.

'We can't look after you and Walter any longer.'

'I heard. The buzz is around. Oh, well, at least you'll be

able to get back into some decent clothes and ditch that junkie hairstyle.'

'What buzz?'

'Your boss, trashing her hotel room and in some sort of scuffle with a pick-up.'

'Her husband.'

'She and her husband still have that kind of vim? *So* lucky! Brilliant! Actually, I guessed someone with a jawline like hers would have a personality. But the government people who sent you are pissed off with the scandal, are they? So, curtains.'

'How did you hear?'

'Yes, the buzz is out. I mean, a four-star hotel. The word's sure to spread.'

'Who told you?' Sally replied.

'Lad called Aix. Operates at the Inclination. You know Peaceable, don't you? Justin had dealings with him now and then, of course. We stay in touch. It was never very much, he and I, but we stay in touch.'

'What was never very much?'

'He gave me a call about the hotel. He has clients working there.'

Pam poured a couple of sherries. Sally gulped most of hers. She said: 'Look, I wish you'd take Walter and get out of this area altogether. There are understandings and arrangements we can't fathom, and won't be allowed to now.'

'Well, of course I know there are understandings and arrangements. How Justin died, isn't it?'

'Can't you leave?' Sally replied. 'At once, that is. Sell the house, but don't wait until it's done. You've got some funds, haven't you?'

She gazed at Sally, sipped her drink and did not answer.

'All I want to know is, could you afford to set yourself and Walter up in a new place immediately?' Sally said.

Pamela sipped and gazed some more.

Sally said: 'God, you don't think I've been co-opted into one of those understandings and arrangements, do you? I'm not here to find out how much of Justin's money you're still sitting on.'

out. Aix looked rough, as if he had only recently
⋯ed after a night's work at the Inclination. They
⋯to the room with French windows and the view
⋯ul garden and net-covered pond. 'I heard there
⋯,' Peaceable said.

⋯order. The sort we have here.'
⋯s made to take care o'raskills,"' Moss replied.
⋯cop be saying that, even if it's true?'
⋯ok – *The Mill On The Floss*.'
⋯ou used to be into books, didn't you – before
⋯olice.'
⋯for law and order?' Moss asked.
⋯on a visit – the one who came to see me at
⋯er boss both told to pack up.'

⋯always win through, won't it? That's the
⋯th testaments. "The ungodly shall perish." But
⋯enteen situation, though – I mean!'
⋯er boy might perish. Who'll see them right

⋯em,' Aix said. 'The regime and the regime's
⋯hey can do what they like, and what they like
⋯o good for Pam and Walter. I always wondered
⋯rt of the regime, as a matter of fact.'
⋯urse you did.'
⋯not. I see it now,' Aix said.
⋯ys wondered if you had something going with
⋯e for a while, despite your conversion and
⋯oss replied.
⋯e girl.'
⋯eard anything around the club that she might
⋯kid snatched?' Moss asked.
⋯ne who hate her – even hate the lad.'

⋯e's probably good at looking after herself,'

⋯er herself? How can she look after herself
⋯, for God's sake?' Moss replied.

206

'Bernie Aix said you were smart – could pass yourself off
as anything.'

'Can you and Walter get out then – now?' Sally asked,
her voice thin and urgent. She drank the rest of the sherry.
Pam refilled.

'Bernie says he'll keep an eye open in our interests. He
hears plenty at the club. And he'll get hold of something for
me.'

'Something?'

'But, God, should I tell you this?'

'Something?'

'Yes, you know, *something*. Something to help me look
after myself, and Walter.'

'Something you shouldn't be telling me about?'

'Yes, that kind of something. I know how to use one. Justin
and I both taught ourselves the basics. But I don't think
you're going to run off and inform – inform! – Notram or
the others. You're not like that. I might be wrong. You don't
trust them, anyway, do you?' Pam replied.

'Why can't you just go?'

'I like the spot. Justin liked the spot. And the school for
Wal. Everything.'

'There are other good spots – better spots. Even better
schools. Better meaning safer.'

'It's kind – honestly. But we'll be fine.'

'This something Peaceable Bernard Aix will get you –
you're sure you know how to—?'

'Justin always said we should be able to look after ourselves
and Walter. It didn't work for Justin, did it? But, yes, I know
how to.'

Sally looked around the room, at the furniture and prints.
'You could take all your stuff, eventually. This is just a
standard-issue biggish house in a standard-issue suburban
avenue, not somewhere ancestral with ties. The school's a
standard-issue private one with a fountain and crabby staff.
Very nice and out of most people's reach, but none of it's
unique.'

'Justin felt really, really happy about what we'd made
here.' Walter opened the lounge door. He had taken off his

203

school gear and wore hang-arse beige skateboard trousers and short-sleeved red T-shirt. He said he was going out to join friends. When he'd left, Pam said: 'He's accepted in the avenue. We both are. Twice you've seen how good it is for him in this spot.'

'That could be matched somewhere else. Nobody would know about you.'

'They *do* know about us here, and we're still accepted. This is worth something. Justin would consider it really worth something. He'd think it was good for Walter to stay and be strong, not do a flit.' She turned her face to the side, perhaps to hide a brim-up in her eyes: 'Naturally, I wish Justin had been able to do a flit himself.'

T[

Harvey Moss found hi
and her son now the
to fold. It signalled thing
been. And this meant the
ality that existed between
– the mutuality which er
and could leave rivals lil
behind in his wake. Which
this. Notram? Matrinba
Chave been part of it? The
body told him nothing, e:
– that Chave intended fi

Moss fixed another m
Dick Patterson, to see v
possible attack on Walte
Patterson had nothing fi
admit he had nothing,
turn out to be a quality

This did not help at
Peaceable Bernard Aix':
picked up a lot of talk. H
him at his sanctified fir
spot after that mistake
Moss knew, she did n
been after information
information only. He c
Bithron was merely a
except through Moss –
the sale. Or not.

This was a weekday

seemed to
got up from
went again
of the beau
was a big
'Who fo
'Law an
'"The la
'Should
'From a
'Ah, yes,
you picked
'What wi
'The ladi
the club an
'Probably
'Right w
message of
that room s
'Pam and
now?'
'It's a pro
friends think
might not be
if you were
'Well, of
'But mayb
'And I alw
Pamela Gran
appearance,'
'Pam's a f
'Have you
be hit and th
'There's so
'Yes.'
'I do hear
Aix said.
'Looking a
against that l

'Which lot?'
'Right.'

In the afternoon, Sally Bithron came to Moss's desk and asked if they could meet somewhere, and soon. He had the feeling this might not be much to do with the formal proceedings of their investigation, if their investigation still had any. He was not clear whether Esther Davidson knew about this approach to him from her assistant, but thought probably not. 'Off the premises?' he asked.

'It might be best.'

Now and then Moss liked to play philistine: 'I don't get to the Central Library in Pilson Street much, or any library. I won't be recognized there. The reference department. There's a silence rule, probably, but it'll be OK to mutter.'

And, so, when they were seated opposite each other at one of the long mahogany tables, he muttered: 'This can't be just a postscript to the interview, or why the secrecy?'

'Crucial, crucial, crucial we find out the full tale Chave wanted to tell by suicide. Even more so now the investigation's nearly sunk.'

He had a copy of Debrett's *People of Today* in front of him, and opened it to the page where he would have appeared if he were a person of today. He stared at it. 'I'm not here,' he said.

'Neither of us is here. You're right, it's one of those off-the-record meetings.'

He gave the page a flip with his fingers. 'If I'm not here, does it mean I'll be one of the *People of Tomorrow*?'

'We could do some work on it.'

He said: 'Some people who are *People of Yesterday* wouldn't be included, I imagine.'

'Are you old enough for that?'

She had *Chambers Biographical Dictionary* open in front of her at Bi. 'No Bithrons,' she said.

He could have said one Bithron featured in the Old Testament, a place, but thought this would show too much reading. Hadn't Aix told him books and police didn't mix? Moss said: 'No Bithrons in *Chambers* yet. You'll have a golden progress, won't you, once you get to the accelerated-promotion course?'

'Are *you* getting a golden progress? You've done the course.'

'There are snags,' he said.

'Esther and me?'

Moss decided to give her a few seconds of that gaze he could do – the one people said seemed to see beyond whatever was actually there: 'Someone's been talking to you?' he asked.

'About what?'

'Has someone told you I can help with the full tale on Chave? You've had a whisper?'

'How would I?' she said.

'Why do you call a meeting if not? Time's short for you and Davidson now. Would you waste it on me? That's what I have to ask.'

'Ask whom?'

'Myself.'

'*Am* I wasting it?' she said.

'What?'

'My time.'

'When we were all talking – you, me, Davidson and then Iperam, I had the feeling you knew something extra.' He wanted to make sure she realized he had brainpower and insight and didn't get fooled. A presence, and with antennae. He wanted to make sure she regarded him as honest and straight, also, but, above all, that she realized he had brainpower and insight, the smooth, devious cow.

'*Is* there something extra?' she said.

He'd noticed she always wanted to turn things, get the initiative. 'Something I sensed,' he replied.

'I'm scared for Pam Grange and the boy.'

'*I'm* scared for Pam Grange and the boy,' he said.

'Why?'

'I don't know whom *I* can trust.'

'Who is it that makes you uncertain. Your chiefs?'

'All sorts.'

'*I* don't know whom *I* can trust,' she said.

'You don't trust *me*, do you?'

208

'I could.'

'But can't.'

'Yet,' she said.

'You think I'm holding back?'

'*Are* you holding back?'

'You think I got hold of Chave's last bit of writing, don't you?'

'Did you?'

'So, how do you know it?' he asked.

'Do I know it? *Know* it?'

'You want me to tell you something you already know, and then you'll trust me?' Moss said.

'Do I know it? *Know* it?'

'Has someone been talking to you?'

'Who?'

'I don't know who – but someone's been talking to you?' He reached into his breast pocket and brought out the folded piece of paper he'd taken from Chave at Knoll. He spread this over *Debrett's People of Today* and then pushed it across on to *Chambers Biographical Dictionary*, covering the spot where her name didn't appear. She looked thrilled for a moment as she started to read it, but then the excitement faded, as he'd known it would.

'This is all?' she said.

'Anyone can ask for that kind of print-out. It's dates available to Chave for retirement, with pension and lump-sum amounts according to when he decided to go.'

She traced with one finger the lines of a large ink cross which had been scrawled over the whole page. 'Who did this?'

Moss said: 'Albert, I imagine. It means none of that's relevant. He knew he wouldn't be reaching even the earliest retirement date. Look at the date. He's had it for ages – when he really thought he'd go the full career distance.'

'More fucking useless sign language,' she replied.

'Who saw me at Knoll with the body?'

'Staple.'

'I didn't expect you to say.'

'I trust you,' she said.

'Why?'

'You've admitted you were there and took the paper,' she answered, 'even though it's useless.'

'Yes, but I only told you because I thought you knew.'

'That's good enough. This is not a search for moral perfection. It's police work. There has to be some latitude. We're of the world, worldly – people of today, even if we're not *People of Today.*'

'Does Staple think it's Chave's letter?' Moss said.

'Yes, I expect so.'

He considered that. 'We could use him.'

Their table was becoming crowded and some people had begun muttering about their muttering. They left the reference room and went downstairs and out into the street. They stood in a shop doorway, fairly close, like a couple of secretive lovers before the age of the car backseat, about to have a quick one. He didn't think he'd like to get into that kind of nearness, though. She had too many complications back home. 'Yes, we could use him,' he said. 'We get him to go over to Percy Blay and give him the story of how he saw me frisk Chave. If anyone's going to hurt Pam or the boy, it's Blay – or Blay's people, the same as it was a couple of people commissioned by Blay who did Justin. He will think we've got dangerous information from Chave's letter about how things work between Blay and the police hierarchy, stuff that would send every bugger in this conspiracy to jail for ever.'

'Which conspiracy?'

'The one you were sent up here to investigate. The one they'd like to shut down now because it could go further than the Home Office ever imagined, and because Albert Chave dead provides a convenient general exit.'

It was a novelty shop's doorway. She turned from him and looked through the window at soft toys, posters, more plastic pistols. 'So, it's like this, is it?' she asked. She spoke as if to someone behind the glass. 'You recruited Tully to grass because you needed an informant who'd speak words in secret about Percy Blay. But you didn't know, and neither did Tully, that Blay has a business arrangement with someone much more powerful than you at headquarters. Chave? Above Chave? Way above Chave? You and Tully supply the information and pass it upwards. But it's never acted on – supposedly because a case is being built against Blay and there's not enough to do him in full royal style yet. Eventually, though, so much information exists, but remains unimplemented, that Chave, or above Chave, or way above Chave, start to fear that Tully and you will suspect Blay has big-rank police protection. Tully might talk. *You* might talk. And therefore Tully has to be taken out. Someone gives the word to Blay. Blay instructs Chamberlain and Jolliffe. If Chave helped bring about the death, it might have sickened him so much he finally had to get back to Knoll and make a sacrifice. Perhaps he felt too ashamed to write it down. He'd leave it to gestures.'

Scenarios must be her thing. Moss could see how she would have excelled in the mock-up situation tests for fast-track selection. She'd sight read them. How did such a gifted girl get her sex life so shambolic, apparently? But sex could be like that, couldn't it? Not much to do with grey matter.

Moss said: 'Once Blay is nice and scared, we go to see him and promise we'll do nothing with Chave's letter – supposed letter – as long as he guarantees not to harm Pam and/or the boy. That is, we'll do nothing except keep it secure in a bank deposit box.'

'Staple won't cooperate.'

'Why not? There's no risk to him. He's bringing Blay information, that's all.'

'Well, yes, he does do that, I know. But then when we roll up, it looks like a two-stage operation, with Staple as pathfinder. He'd see the hazards,' Sally replied.

'I think he'll help us.'

She was still studying the shop items but turned back to him now. 'You can do some arm twisting?'

'Staple lifted a wad of money from Justin Tully's corpse. The boys who killed him left it in his pockets. Of course they did. They removed any papers but wanted to make clear to the world he'd been killed for taking payment from the police. More fucking sign language. The money was all traceables given to Tully by Albert Chave from the grassing fund. Staple's still sitting on the find, afraid to spend it.'

211

'You *know* this? How?'

'He gave the court a beautiful show,' Moss replied.

'But?'

'A totter's a totter.'

'Oh, of course, research – like you did on Esther and me. You believe in dossiers, records, unchangeable natures, eternally constant profiles.'

'I've talked to him about it.'

'And talked to him,' she said.

'He could be made to believe I'll really start digging, unless he helps.'

'Pretty.'

'As a matter of fact, he knows *I* think he took from Tully. Plus, I can tell him I've come across someone lately who would launder his cash.'

'Have you? How do you happen to meet someone like that?'

'And so, if Tully does a favour for us, we do one or two for him,' Moss replied. 'He'll appreciate the point. Staple has sensitivity.'

'Definitely. Didn't it take him back to Knoll the morning you found Chave?'

'It's still possible Albert Chave was a good man,' he said.

'Yes?'

This smart, university-of-life bitch could make him sound naïve.

'Where are you pointing then?' she asked. 'How high?'

'Yes, Albert might have been almost all right.'

Early next morning they went out together to Springfield Heights tip and found Stanley Basil Staple bringing away quite a decent black, rearing-horse ornament with good flared nostrils. Although short of half a front right leg and the hoof, it was probably placeable on a window sill so the furled back curtain concealed this defect while leaving the rest very effectively displayed. Moss saw he was troubled, even before they put the proposal. Staple would guess that if Moss and Sally Bithron had begun acting together, he must have told her he thought cash had been stolen from Tully's body at Knoll.

When they mentioned the proposed Blay mission and his

role in it, Staple grew more agitated and at first refused, as Bithron had forecast. She said: 'This way, you could help the Tully family. I know you'd want that. You'd like to give back something as recompense for the loot you took, which really should have gone to them.'

That argument did not seem to reach Staple, though. He bent to pick up the ruins of a towel from the ground and wrapped his horse in it. 'I know Mr Blay, yes, and now and then I will call in and speak a word. But I wouldn't ever talk to him about that letter from Mr Chave and seeing you get it. Such talk – it's dangerous. It could make Mr Blay nervous, and when he's nervous he could do anything. Anything.' Staple turned away. 'I ought to be leaving now, Mr Moss,' he said. 'Cleansing staff will turn up soon.'

Moss told him about the laundering project. 'I'm not interested in anything for myself, Stanley,' he said. 'And only eight per cent to the contact as handling charge.'

'I don't want to be involved, Mr Moss,' Staple replied. 'Not with someone like Blay.'

'Heavy money hidden in your house – it could disappear, you know, Stan. I certainly haven't told anyone you robbed the body, and I'm sure Constable Bithron wouldn't either, but hints of a stash could leak.'

'How leak?' Staple said.

'Yes, leak,' Moss said.

'You?' Staple said.

'There are people who wouldn't care that it's traceables,' Moss replied. 'They haven't got your wisdom. To people like that, a pot of money is a pot of money. They might come for it.'

Bithron said: 'When we get Blay to promise no bother for Pamela or her son, we could include you.'

'No, now please. No,' he said. 'If you tell him I mustn't be hurt, it means there's something I *should* be hurt for, don't it? And that's not clever.'

'You'd impress him, Stan,' Moss said. 'You'd be giving him a true, first-hand account of what you saw.'

'He's going to ask what I was doing at Knoll, when it's not a tip no longer,' Staple replied. 'Going up there, like a grief thing – Percy's not going to be very happy about that, is he? He's going to say, what am I grieving about a bit of shit like Tully for? He's going to say, do I think he was wrong to wipe out Tully? I've told you, Blay can be edgy. He got a temperament. Someone with that kind of riches, they usually got temperaments.'

'Or he'll think you've created a lovely information system, Stan,' Moss said. 'It told you Chave would be dead there, and that I'd be up there, too. You'll sound brilliant, especially since you found Tully as well. There'll be true respect.'

'I got to be careful, Mr Moss,' Staple said. 'Three kids to raise. This is not a great job, you know.' He lifted the towel package for them to look at. The rear hoofs stuck out from the wrapping, both beautifully intact. 'All right, I find this horse. But this is not a horse that can be sold, on account of damage. This is only a horse for my own house. It's not, like, *income*.'

'That's what I mean about getting good, safe, spendable notes from the launderer for your Tully pile,' Moss said. It was dirty pressure, yes, but for a sound cause, surely. Surely. He remembered university discussions about ends justifying means – or about *not* justifying – but only barely remembered. This was a dump, not a humanities tutorial room. 'It's a duty to your family, I'd have thought. Think of the deprivation if those funds get burgled.'

'Eight per cent handling?' Staple replied. 'That's steep. Can't you get it down to five – six at tops?'

They drove over to Blay's place, Staple ahead in an old Cavalier, Moss and Sally Bithron far back in the unmarked Peugeot. Staple turned into the grounds. Moss stopped a few hundred yards away, up the country road, so they could watch. He'd thought about forging a last statement from Albert Chave to show Blay. It would detail how things worked – or how Moss guessed they worked – with Blay given clear, lavish, incriminating treatment. But then he'd decided that, suppose he really did have a final letter from Chave, he would not let Blay see it. The mystery of what it contained would be a more effective threat than knowledge. He had the retirement and pension statement with him to flash, if necessary, but folded with the blank side out, so it would look like a letter.

After about ten minutes, the Cavalier reappeared and, as agreed, turned in the opposite direction from Moss and Sally. They followed and rendezvoused with him in a lay-by about three miles on. He stayed in his car. Moss and Sally walked to the Cavalier and stood at the open driver's window. Staple looked bad. 'All right?' Moss asked.

'Percy and his wife are dead on a lawn in front of the house,' Staple said. 'Shot. Like a lawn for a game. Hoops.'

'Croquet?' Sally said.

'He wouldn't do security – thought it wasn't needed because he had protection. It looked like they'd come out for a little go at it, like with long wooden mallets for hitting the ball. There's trees. Someone might of lurked, easy. Gates wide open.'

'You didn't tot them, did you?' Moss asked.

'I told you, I didn't want nothing to do with it. I never touched them,' Staple replied.

'That's so sensible,' Sally said.

'You didn't tot them, did you?' Moss asked.

Staple had not switched off the Cavalier's engine and now put the car in gear and drew away. Moss saw the horse in its towel on the rear seat. 'Report nothing,' he called out. Staple stopped, obviously unable to hear. Moss went nearer. 'Report nothing. And we won't.'

Staple looked up at him dead-faced for a good ten seconds, as if it were lunatic to think he might announce anywhere what he had found. 'I heard Peaceable Bernard Aix most likely supplied Pam Grange with something,' he said. 'Did she get scared now everything's going back to like before? The street word says the investigation been given a dose of collapse.'

'You hear so much, Stan,' Moss replied. 'It's good. You hear a lot because you don't talk and can listen instead.'

Staple started to move off again. 'You going to try to get it down to six per cent handling for me?' he asked.

Fourteen

Pete arrived and, as ever, Sally thought he looked great. He had on a terrific dark suit. He knew suits. Owing to his good, relaxed confidence, nobody would think he wore this suit only to impress people here. If the suit *did* impress people here, it would be because it seemed so natural to him, not just on account of obvious quality in the wool and cut. This suit certainly made his leanness tellingly apparent, without emphasizing it in a tight, show-off mode. His hair was just right for style – managerial, yes, elderly no – and his eyes gleamed with curiosity and poise. He would definitely always be the sort of man she could respond to up to a point, and the kind of man who would always provide grand help and warmth to those he approved of, such as herself, for some reason.

Her hope was he'd be able to advise Esther and Sally now on ways to handle most of their difficulties, but especially the Home Office plan to end the probe. In his job, Pete dealt quite a bit with higher civil servants and might know how to affect decisions – even know how to reverse decisions already made. Once or twice she had met work colleagues of Pete's, and could tell they esteemed him as an executive. So far, she hadn't told Esther he was coming. It could be a little tricky suggesting to an ACC that she needed guidance from a DC's boyfriend, and Sally wondered how best to introduce him. But she felt sure – almost sure – that Esther would accept any aid Pete offered. Esther had wildness, but Esther had sense.

Pete said he needed to get a feel of the setting, fix the shape and contours in his head, and so they took a town tour on an open-topped bus, ignoring the commentary for most of the time. Pete often told Sally he was of a type who liked to deal in the concrete, rather than abstractions. The trip seemed right, not just as an introduction to the place for him, but a probable farewell for her. Near the far western edge of the town, Sally did listen to the courier as he pointed along a country road towards the Blay home and spoke about discovery of the two bodies on their croquet lawn. This would not be part of the usual rigmarole, obviously, but guides liked drama.

Pete said: 'Is that part of it all, the deaths?'

'Someone did half our job for us.'

'Revenge?'

'They were stupidly careless about security.'

'Who?'

'The Blays.'

'No, I meant who did it?' Pete said.

'He had enemies. That's why I say careless.'

The bus passed the base of Knoll and Sally gave attention again to the commentary – death of Justin Tully, death of Albert Chave. Yes, the newsy, the dramatic. Probably the guide's bosses wouldn't have liked these freelance additions to the standard script. They gave tourists a dark idea of the town. Accurate, though. People in Westminster should also get a dark idea of the town. Would it stay dark now, darker, all the dodgy questions permanently shelved? For example, *did* someone, someone official, let Stan Staple keep the Tully cash as a swap for possibly disastrous Tully jottings about his trade – too much information? But the first theory – that the boys who killed him had taken anything dangerous from his pockets – must be right, mustn't it? Mustn't it? Nobody would be asking these crucial teasers now. Blackout.

Or, then again, perhaps, after all, somebody would. Sally's mobile called her. Esther said: 'We're reinstated. Active. The investigation is reborn.'

'Because of the Blays?'

'Fuckwit. Of course. Even Iperam and his crafty, gibbering lords realize they can't shut us down after that. Imagine the publicity – the accusations of censorship and whitewash, worse than over the Hutton and Butler Reports on government two-timing pre the Iraq war. Now and then I'm lavishly in favour of a free press. Removal of Blay is only half the job.'

'I just said the same.'

'Who to?' Esther asked.

Pete's journey seemed suddenly unnecessary. And Sally glimpsed the mad contradictoriness of it, anyway. He'd come because he wanted to see her. But *she* hoped he'd help save the investigation – so she could keep the distance between them for at least a while longer. Crazy. Even cruel. 'And Pam and the boy should be all right, shouldn't they?' she asked Esther. 'There'll be such a spotlight here for ages now that nobody will risk touching them, school run or anywhere else.'

'Pam knocked over the Blays? Did I hear a whisper she'd picked up a piece from some one-time lover?'

'What about the other half of the job?' Sally replied.

'The vital half? The in-house half? Our dear colleagues? It can be done. Just possible. I'll get them. *We'll* get them, Sally.'

'Yes?'

'I'll snare the buggers,' Esther replied. '*We'll* snare the buggers.'

'Yes? How so certain? The emergency drill probably worked again, and Mr Notram has been out making sure nothing points to himself, and above.'

'They probably won't want to nail Pamela. Too much could come out in any trial. But I . . . *we'll* nail *them*, in due course,' Esther replied.

'Are you after Matrinbanks' job, ma'am?'

When the bus tour ended, Pete again suggested a different hotel, but Sally refused. She wanted him in sixteen. That seemed vital, too. It would be a smuggling matter, some quick moving when reception was distracted. Sally felt she owed Esther this nearness. They constituted a team, a unit, even if Esther, in that big-brass way, occasionally forgot it. Sally knew she must identify with her, as she had tried to identify with Tully and Chave – though, thank God, Esther

218

stayed alive. And so, Sally decided she should invite the same late-night disgrace as the ACC had brought on herself – get the hotel staff just as offended and gossipy. This would be the most vivid, resonant way of proving she and the ACC functioned as one, Siamese-twinned by coarse behaviour. They still had that half a job to do, the hard half, the official, stable-cleansing half. Their solidarity, their resolute sameness, their allegiance to each other, were crucial and should be made plain – noisily, outrageously, memorably plain. They'd need it to smash the solidarity, the resolute sameness, the allegiance to one another they encountered here among the crew under scrutiny.

The prospects had abruptly changed. No call for a housebreak and search now, since she knew Moss held the letter, which, in any case, had turned out to be no letter. Pete could help, but in a different style from what she'd meant originally. They didn't need to neutralize Iperam, because Iperam and those running him had caved in. As Esther said, in these new circumstances the Home Office dare not act as if everything had been nicely resolved, thank you. Slaughter of the Blays stopped that. So, still in the odd spirit of contradictions, Pete would be used instead to help Sally proclaim her glorious closeness to Esther, and the determination to stay insular and defiant and effective with her – yes, effective, effective, effective – in this murky, mucky domain. Nail them. It would happen.

Pete and Sally made it to her room all right, after a long dinner at an Indian restaurant. Number seventeen seemed quiet. Perhaps Esther wanted an early night. Around two a.m., as part of her lovely scheme to display unfading comradeship with the ACC, Sally began to punch and elbow Pete and to yell fiercely. Yes, the staff would be alarmed and ratty again, ready to spread the disgraceful, brilliantly binding tale about her now, not Esther. Luckily, Pete amounted to more than fine suits and always took up well on anything sexual. He gave back some violence, whooping occasionally, bawling curses. They swapped clever biting. Sally howled in blissful pain. She craved ostentatious face wounds.

Someone rapped on the door. Sally felt triumphant. It had

219

worked. And yet this was more than a rap, wasn't it – more than knuckles? Did she detect thumps from something metal and weighty on the wood? Sally wondered about a masonry hammer. 'Is that fucking bassoonist in there with you, Bithron?' Esther called.

04   06